IVORY
AND
BONE

IVORY
AND
BONE

JULIE
ESHBAUGH

HARPER TEEN
An Imprint of HarperCollinsPublishers

HarperTeen is an imprint of HarperCollins Publishers.

Ivory and Bone

Text copyright © 2016 by Julie Eshbaugh

Library of Congress Control Number: 2015958594
ISBN 978-0-06-239925-0

Typography by Erin Fitzsimmons
16 17 18 19 20   PC/RRDH   10 9 8 7 6 5 4 3 2 1
❖
First Edition

For my parents, George and Louise Krikorian
Thank you for teaching me to dream big dreams,
and to never stop believing in them.

The darkness in this cave is so complete I can no longer see you, but I can smell your blood.

"I think your wound has opened up again."

"No, it's fine." Your words echo against the close walls. Even so, your voice sounds small. "I ran my fingers over it. It's dry."

We need light and heat. I pat the ground, feeling for the remnants of the fire we made in here before.

"The wound is under your hair, Mya, and your hair is drenched."

"My hair is *cold*—wet with rain and ice. It would be warm if it were wet with blood." Injured, bleeding, freezing—yet still stubborn.

"I'm going to try to get a fire going," I say.

My hands search the floor, fumbling across silt and cinders, until they land on a chunk of splintered wood that flakes at the ends as if it's been burned. A short distance away the ground drops down into a shallow hole—the fire pit.

I crawl farther into the dark, one hand extended out in front of me, my knees grinding against knots of broken wood and nubs of rock. At last, my hand lands on what I remember as a deliberate, orderly stack of firewood piled against the far wall.

It's unnerving to be in a place so dark. It's even more unnerving to be here with you.

As I turn pieces of wood in my hands, my eyes begin to adjust to what little light filters in from outside. Black yields to gray as shadows become objects. I separate kindling and tinder. On a flat rock beside the wood I discover the starter kit—a long whittled stick and fireboard. "Give me just a little longer and I'll get you warmed up, all right?"

I wait, but you don't answer.

"Mya?"

"Go ahead and make a fire. I think I'll just sleep a bit."

"No—*no* sleeping. I need you to stay awake. I need company. Someone to talk to."

"What are we going to talk about?"

Rolling the firestick between my fingers, I hesitate. "What do you think we should talk about?"

Maybe I shouldn't have asked this question. There are countless things that could be said between us, and probably countless more that should be left unsaid.

I grasp the firestick between my palms, one end buried in a notch cut in the fireboard, surrounded by fistfuls of dry grass like clumps of human hair. Rubbing my hands back and forth, I twirl the stick like a drill. My hands pass down the entire length of the stick once, twice, three times.

Friction builds, and at last a ribbon of smoke curls around the board.

Distracted by my task, I almost forget the question I asked you. I'm not sure how long you've been silent. "Mya?"

"Fine," you say, the word scratching in your throat like you've swallowed bits of gravel. "I'll try to stay awake, but you need to give me something to stay awake for."

"Meaning?"

"Why don't you tell me a story?"

"I don't know any stories."

An ember catches. An orange glow blooms in the kindling. I lie on my side and blow a steady stream of breath into the grass, coaxing out garlands of smoke.

"Everyone who's ever lived has a story to tell, Kol."

As the fire spreads I sit up, turning your words in my mind. What could I possibly tell you? All my stories have become entwined with yours. "What do you want to hear?" I ask.

"Tell me something *wonderful*—a story that's startling and marvelous." Despite your grogginess, there's a lilt of expectation in your voice. "Tell me about the most startling and marvelous day of your life. . . ."

ONE

I lie in the grass with my eyes closed, listening for the whir of honeybee wings, but it's too early in the season for bees and I know it. I needed an excuse, I guess, something to say to get out of camp for a while, and the bees will be back soon, anyway. Before the next full moon comes, these wildflowers will be covered in bees and I'll be hunting for their hives. I'm just a little ahead of them.

"Kol!"

I sit up at the sound of Pek's voice, calling from the southern edge of the meadow. It's a wonder I hear him at all, with such a stiff wind pushing down over the Great Ice that forms the far northern boundary of our hunting range. He waves his spear over his head, and a brief flash of sunlight reflects off the polished-stone point—a momentary burst of light, like a wink of the Divine's eye. Pek calls out again, and it sounds like "a boat," though that can't be right. From so far away, into the wind, he could be saying anything.

Pek is a swift runner, and he reaches me before I have time to worry about what he has to say to me that couldn't wait until I returned to camp. The skin of his face glows pink and tears run down his face from the sting of the wind.

"A boat," he says. He sets his hands on his knees and bends, sucking air.

"Did you run the whole way from camp?"

"Yes," he says, tipping his head to let the wind blow his hair from his eyes so he can look at me. Sweat glistens on his forehead. "A boat is on the beach. A beautiful long canoe dug out from the trunk of a single tree—you wouldn't believe how beautiful."

I run my eyes over Pek's face, still somewhat soft and boyish at sixteen. He favors our mother—he has her easy smile and eyes that glow with the light of a secret scheme. "Is this a game? Are you playing a trick on me—"

"Why would I bother to run all the way out here—"

"I'm not sure, but I know that there's no such thing as a boat made of the trunk of a single tree—"

"Fine. Believe what you want to believe."

Pek rolls his spear in his right hand and peers off into the empty space in front of us, as if he can see into the past, or maybe the future. Without warning, he takes a few skipping steps across the grass and, with a loud exhale of breath, hurls his spear—a shaft of mammoth bone tipped with an obsidian point—at an invisible target. He had the wind at his back to help him, but I can't deny it's a strong throw. "Beat that," he says, picking up my own spear from where I'd discarded it on the grass earlier.

My spear is identical to my brother's—a shaft of mammoth bone—but instead of obsidian, I prefer a point of ivory. It's harder to shape, but ivory is stronger. I grip the spear, tensing and relaxing my hand until the weight of it feels just right. I take three sliding steps and roll my arm forward, hand over shoulder, releasing the spear at the optimal moment. It is a perfectly executed throw.

Still, it lands about two paces short of Pek's. I may be his older brother, but everyone jokes that Pek was born with a spear in his hand. He has always been able to out-throw me.

"Not bad," he says. "That should be good enough to impress the girls."

"I'll try to remember that," I say, forcing a laugh. There are no girls our age in our clan, something Pek and I try to joke about to hide the worry it causes us. But it's not a joke, and no one knows that better than Pek and I do.

Without girls, there will be no wives for my brothers and me. Our clan could dwindle, even end.

"You won't have to remember for long." Pek's gaze rests on something past my shoulder as an odd smile climbs from his lips to his eyes. Suddenly, this doesn't feel like a joke anymore. My stomach tightens, and I spin around.

At the southern edge of the meadow, at the precise spot where Pek had appeared just moments ago, two girls come into view, flanked by our father, our mother, and a man I don't recognize. "What—"

"Do you believe me now about the boat?"

I have no reply. I stand still as ice, unsure how to move without risking falling down. It's been so long—over two years—since I've seen a girl my own age.

My eyes fix on these two as they approach, a certain authority in their movements. They practically saunter toward us, each carrying a spear at her side. One, dressed in finely tailored hides, walks slightly ahead of the group. Her parka's hood obscures her hair and her face is half-hidden in shadow, but there's no question that she's a girl—the swing in her shoulders and the movement in her hips give her away.

The second girl is you.

From this distance I can't quite see your face, so I notice your clothing first. Your parka and pants must have been borrowed from a brother—they're far less fitted than those of the first girl—yet there is femininity in the smaller things, like the curved lines of your long, bare neck, and the golden glow of your tan skin in the sunlight. Your hood is back and your head is uncovered, letting your black hair, loose and unbraided, roll like a river on the wind behind you.

You come closer, and I'm struck by the beauty in the

balance of your features. I notice the strong lines of your eyebrows and cheekbones tilting up and away from the softer lines of your mouth. Your eyes—dark and wide set— scan the meadow, and I'm startled by the way my heart pounds as I wait for them to fall on me.

This may be the most startling and marvelous day of my life.

As the group advances, however, I notice you drop back. The closer you come, the more certain I am that you are miserable. Your expression—tense jaw, pursed lips—makes your annoyance plain. I imagine you've been dragged along on this journey. Your head pivots, your eyes sweep from side to side, taking in what must appear to you to be no more than a wind-beaten wasteland. To me, the meadow is like the sea, life teeming below the surface. But to most people—to you, clearly—it's just empty grassland.

My mind clogs with questions, but before I can ask Pek a single one, the five of you stop in front of us.

"Son," my father starts. There's tension in his voice. A stranger might not notice, but I can tell. "This day has brought us good fortune. These are our neighbors from the south, from the clan of Olen. They visited us once several years ago, when they were traveling from their former home north and west of here, to the place they now call home."

I remember this, of course. Our clan has such infrequent contact with outsiders that when a group passes through, I don't forget. It was five years ago; I was twelve. I remember young girls of about my age. I realize, standing here now, that I remember you.

You were traveling by boat, a small clan moving south in kayaks made of sealskin stretched over a frame of mammoth bones, just like the kayaks my own clan uses to fish and gather kelp and mollusks.

I think of the boat Pek described—a canoe dug out of the trunk of a single tree. I've never even seen a canoe, though I've heard stories of them—open boats made of wood instead of hide and bone like our kayaks, long enough to carry several people at once. My own father tells of wooden canoes he saw with his own eyes, on a scouting trip he made south of the mountains, long before I was born.

But I've never heard of a canoe made of the trunk of a single tree. I've never even imagined a tree that big.

Not until today.

There has already been talk of the need for our clan to attempt a move farther south. Our herds have been steadily dwindling—some have completely stopped returning from the south in the spring. Others, like the mammoths, have moved north, following the Great Ice as it slides away from the sea.

Yet there has been one insurmountable obstacle to any plan for a southerly move. When your clan departed our shores five years ago, you did not leave as friends, but as enemies.

Even now, with the years stretching out between that day and this one, I can remember the bitterness of your clan's departure. I remember the murmurs of a possible war. The fears that kept me awake as a twelve-year-old boy—fears that my father could head south to fight and never return. As I stand here today, with the intervening years to dim the memories, bitterness still takes its place like an eighth figure in this circle of seven.

Still, whether you brought the bitterness with you or it joined us, uninvited, the three of you are here, and that suggests new prospects. Could our two clans—enemies for five years—become friends, even allies? My mother must believe so. Nothing else would explain her presence out here in the meadow, since she so rarely hikes this far outside camp anymore. It would also explain the smile on my mother's face.

She knows opportunity when it lands on her shore.

"Father invited our guests to hunt with us," Pek says, raising his eyebrows while giving me a small nod—two things I think are supposed to hold some kind of veiled meaning. All I can guess is that he's warning me to keep calm and not try to back off from my role as a leader in the hunt.

Pek knows that I hate to hunt mammoths. Not because they are so dangerously immense, or because they are so difficult to bring down. Each kind of prey presents its own difficulties and dangers. No, I hate to hunt mammoths because their intelligence is impossible to ignore. They have more than a sense of fear; they have an understanding of death. They don't run just because they are being chased; they run to avoid being killed.

They know that I am trying to kill them.

I didn't always feel this way. Just a year ago, when I was Pek's age, I begged our father before every hunt to let me take the lead. Finally, he let me try. I went ahead of the rest of the hunting party. I gave the command when it was time to swarm the herd. And I threw the first strike that landed deep in the animal's side.

It was a clean strike, and as the mammoth ran, blood poured from his wound, leaving a bright red trail in the frost under our feet. That moment is forever fixed in my mind—as the blood dripped down, I believed I could feel the energy running out of the animal and flowing into me. I felt invincible. Pek landed a strike in the animal's throat, just below his jaw. That weakened him quickly. Blood flowed from both wounds as he staggered and fell to four knees. I ran up alongside him, ready to celebrate the success of the kill.

But when I came up beside the wounded mammoth, he wasn't ready to give in, wasn't ready to let go of the Spirit that dwelled within him. He struggled to raise himself once more, planting his left front foot and trying to stand.

The effort took the last of his strength. His huge frame

shuddered, and he dropped heavily to the ground, his head falling right at my feet.

I couldn't avoid looking into the mammoth's huge dark eye. Though his head lay half in snow and half in mud, he stared right into me. The dark iris was like a hole I'd fallen into. There was knowledge in that eye. Knowledge that he was about to die and that I was the one who had caused it. But there was no condemnation. Only defeat.

A sudden gust of wind comes down hard from the north, shoving me out of my memories and back to the present. The same gust hits you in the face and you grimace. It was warm lying in the grass—almost warm enough to encourage a honeybee to fly—but standing in the raw wind makes the day feel cold. My mother clears her throat. I realize that no one's been introduced, and we've been standing staring at each other for a moment too long. I break the awkward silence by falling back on custom—I step forward and nod to the man in your group.

"I'm called Kol," I say. "I am the oldest son of Arem and Mala."

The man nods in reply, the irresistible current of custom pulling us along. "My name is Chev. I am High Elder of the Olen clan. This is my sister Seeri." He motions to the first girl, and I smile but I doubt she notices. Her eyes are fixed on Pek. "And my sister Mya," he says, motioning to you.

Unlike Seeri, you meet my gaze. Your eyes narrow and

I hope this is a response to the wind in your face, but some-how I don't think it is.

"This is our younger son, Pek," my mother says, her eyes sliding to Seeri's face as she steps forward to pat Pek on one of his huge shoulders, ensuring everyone notices Pek was built to hunt. She's seen the connection between Seeri and my brother and she intends to encourage it. "You are lucky to have him with you today. He's gifted with a spear, this boy. He's—"

My father clears his throat. Mother's eyes shift to me and I know what she had almost said—*He's the best hunter in the clan.* It's true, but since I'm the oldest, it's probably not something my father wants her to say in front of guests. Not that it would matter. If you're going to hunt with us, you're going to find out anyway.

My father raises his eyes, judging the progress of the sun. "We should start on our way. The Divine has brought us strong hunting partners, and I suspect she may be sending more good fortune our way. If I am right, we will have a kill before the sun is high in the sky."

My mother pulls at the collar of my father's parka. He is stubborn and insists upon leaving it open at his throat on all but the coldest days of winter. He pushes her hand away, but he can't stop his lips from curling at the corners. "Don't fuss with us, Mala; we need to get on our way," he says. "Besides, when we get back, you will have six hungry hunters to feed. You'll need time to get the kitchen going for the midday meal."

My mother used to join in on the hunts, but that was a long time ago. Now the clan kitchen has become her personal dominion. Knowing this, and knowing what your visit clearly means to my mother, I can only imagine the sort of meal we have to look forward to.

Mother gives nothing away. She simply shakes her head and turns to our guests. "Be safe," she says. Then she pulls up the hood of her parka and starts back the way you all came.

Father defers to me to lead the way to the herd. I've been out here in search of hives every day since we last stalked mammoths—unsuccessfully—seven days ago. I know where the herd is gathered, just beyond the ridge that rises to the east.

I may be leading the way, but my father stays close behind. He makes sure he stays close to Chev, too. As we walk, my father explains features of the landscape and points out places where saber-toothed cats have been found to hide. This spring, these cats have become more active rivals for our game, but my father does not mention this. Pek walks almost shoulder to shoulder with Seeri, off to our right. I cannot see or hear you at all—not even your footfalls on the grass. I assume you are following at a distance, but I don't dare turn my head to check.

Maybe the thought of hunting mammoths sickens you the way it does me. Maybe that's the cause of your sullen silence. I doubt this is true, but I try to convince myself that it might be. More likely, there is a boy waiting for you in your southern camp and your head and heart are with him instead of with us. Or maybe you are thinking about what took place five years ago, the events that almost led our two clans to war. Perhaps you are reluctant to follow an armed enemy onto unfamiliar ground.

If I let myself think about it hard enough, I'd probably be reluctant, too.

Once we cross the open grass, I lead the group to a path that rises through the rocky foothills of the mountains that form the eastern boundary of our hunting range. Within these hills are tucked hidden plains and alpine fields where this particular herd of mammoths often chooses to graze, out of the open. As we walk, the grass gives way to gravel, and the grade becomes steeper as we slowly climb. At intervals, the path narrows. Rough boulders encroach from either side. By necessity, our party is forced to travel in single file.

I look back once to make sure we are all together before we navigate the final set of turns. It's then that I see you, just a few paces behind me. I'm startled to find you there. My brother and your sister have dropped back, and I suppose you ended up in front by default. I'm certain my face gives away my surprise at finding you so close.

Your gaze is unflinching. It has weight. Part of me wants to shrug it off; part of me wants to hold very still so it doesn't slip away from me.

"What's wrong?" you ask.

"Nothing." Your eyes are heavy-lidded, but I know not to be fooled—you are not tiring. A spark glows in your dark eyes. They are at once impossibly dark and impossibly bright, alive with activity, as if a million thoughts churn behind them. I imagine a honeybee—the way it zips from bloom to bloom. That is how I imagine your thoughts moving behind those heavy-lidded eyes.

My own eyes move to the rocks at my feet. "We're almost there. I wanted to let you know. The path gets a bit rough here. You should watch your step."

Thankfully, we are indeed almost there, and as we navigate the final bend toward the south, the scene that opens up in front of us is enough to distract from the stiffness of the previous moment. The path widens and turns at the head of a broad mountain meadow blanketed by wildflowers and tall grass, irrigated by twin rivulets of meltwater that run down from the ice to the north and the snowcaps that crown the peaks farther east. The two streams merge about midway across the meadow, creating a deep, still pool. Around that pool stands a family of six mammoths, their light brown fur glowing almost red under the bright sun.

I stop and let everyone catch up. The herd is downwind from us, so I worry they will soon know we're here. I usher everyone to a space behind a large outcropping that acts as a natural windbreak.

My father steps up beside me, and it's clear that from here on, he is taking lead on this hunt. It doesn't wound my pride to yield to him. It's customary for the most experienced hunter to take the lead, and in our clan, that's always my father. He pats me on the shoulder, and I take my place a half step behind him on his right.

My father crouches, and we all follow his cue. Bent close to the ground, we move through the shadows that obscure the eastern edge of the meadow. The sun beats bright against the low rocky wall to the west, but while the sun rises, the brush that grows along the gravel track to the east is still covered in cool morning shade. Out in the open, gusts of breeze flatten the tall grass, but in the shelter of the ledges, the air hardly stirs.

We move in silence. The mammoths do not appear wary—perhaps the wind didn't carry our scent to them after all. When we have come up alongside them on the edge of the meadow, my father squats down, but he signals for us to continue on beyond the herd. An animal with the speed of a mammoth cannot be run down—it has to run to you. My father will get them moving. The rest of us will be ready to cut them off.

Now they are extremely close, maybe just fifty paces away. I can hear the water splash from their trunks and see it spray across their backs.

Stay in the present, I tell myself. *Let the past go.*

My father raises his spear, and we all turn our eyes toward him. Then he stands and his arm comes down swiftly, signaling that the hunt is on. He plunges forward, racing across the meadow as fast as his feet will move.

The herd sees him, and like one body, they turn and run toward the south, toward the wide edge of the meadow that descends into a river valley. Once they are in motion the rest of us emerge, cutting across the open to intercept them. Maybe it's because you and your brother and sister are here, maybe it's because I have something to prove to myself and to Pek, but I run faster than I've ever run. The wind is at my back. I imagine it sweeping away the memories that haunt me. I outrun your sister; I outrun Pek. Only your brother, Chev, is ahead of me. My legs pump, my heels dig, and finally, I am moving stride for stride with Chev. I exchange a glance with him before pulling ahead. Twenty paces more and I will intercept the mammoth at the front of the herd.

I close my mind, raise my arm, and ready my spear. I tune to the rhythm of the mammoth's steps. The ground shakes like the skin of a giant drum. *Boom . . . boom . . . boom . . .* I feel the percussion of his pace roll through me with each step. When I know I can run no closer without risking being trampled, I let the spear fly.

But my angle is too wide. The razor-sharp point of my spear grazes across a thick mat of hair on the animal's side and falls away.

I slow my steps—I need to retrieve my spear from where it fell. I turn, ready to dodge out of the way of the others in the hunting party, to yield my position to Pek or to your sister or brother, but instead I find that you have all dropped back far behind. You are running hard with your spears ready, but you are not chasing the mammoths.

You are chasing the thing that is chasing me.

TWO

I n the space between us, a saber-toothed cat runs hard, his huge claws tearing at the ground. His head is lowered, but I don't need to see his eyes to know he is coming for me.

Glancing right, I spot my spear in the tall grass. Retrieving it means running back a few paces in the direction of the cat, and my thoughts crash together as my feet crash over the ground. My hand grasps the spear; he is still a distance away but closing fast. I don't dare take the time to raise my eyes to see if any of you are close enough to take the shot.

Inwardly, I call on the Divine to help me. My thoughts go to my mother; I think of all the times she counseled me to ask the Divine for help in the hunt, and all the times I've ignored her counsel.

Yet even if all the power of the Divine were suddenly supporting my every move, I doubt that I could bring down this cat with one hurried shot. Only the perfect strike will stop him, and I know I will need stealth and surprise to make that strike. I am almost certainly doomed to miss from my current position, and he would be on me in moments.

I cannot stand my ground. My only choice is to run.

Before the thought has fully formed in my mind I am flying over the grass, back toward the shade of the ridge. As I reach the trail, I spot a narrow track up out of the valley into the foothills, and I head for it with all the speed the Divine will grant me.

Jagged rocks and sharply angled boulders form the floor of the path, but I move over them with surprising ease. Apparently fear reveals a grace and poise in my movements that have never manifested before. In just moments, I reach the top of a rise where the path turns right and heads more steeply up the rough wall of rock. I allow myself the luxury of one quick glance over my shoulder and gasp.

Nothing is behind me on the path—neither cat nor human.

The temptation to hesitate lasts no longer than a heartbeat. The crack of rock falling on rock comes from my left and I spin around, my spear ready, but still, I see no one . . . nothing.

Spooked, I turn slowly in place. My own feet send a few pebbles sliding downhill. Wind whistles past my ears. Otherwise, there is only silence.

Despite the urge to retrace my steps, to slide slowly down

the path the way I came in hopes that the cat chose not to pursue me, I know I need to keep climbing. Cats, after all, are not restricted to paths. He could be overhead, I realize, as I raise my spear again and rake my eyes over the rock ledges above me. I navigate a tight turn that takes me out of sight of the valley below and wait, listening.

The faint sound of a skittering pebble reaches my ears from a spot on the trail just below the place where I stand. Then another . . .

Then another.

Steady steps are advancing toward me.

I squat against the rock wall, planting my feet wide so I won't lose my balance. I roll the shaft of my spear in my hand until it feels just right—or at least as right as it could ever feel in my damp and shaking hand—and rest it lightly on my shoulder. Unblinking, I stare at the spot on the trail where the cat will appear as he rounds the turn.

One more moment . . . One more moment . . .

A shadow breaks across my line of sight, and I spring to my feet and raise my spear. Energy ripples from my shoulder to my fingers as my whole body flinches forward, every muscle tensed.

But it's not the cat.

It's you.

In the smallest fraction of time—less than the time it takes an echo to fade or a snowflake to melt—your hand is over your shoulder and your spear is flying over my head. I duck, though your throw is more than high enough and your aim is true to its target.

I spin around in time to see the cat crouched on a crag of rock directly above me, the spear buried deep in his chest. He opens his jaws in a final growl and his teeth flash, a row of perfect razors behind daggerlike incisors, but no sound comes. Instead, in one silent motion, he rolls onto his side and falls to the ground at my feet.

I drop to my knees. A thick red stream runs from the hole in the cat's chest down the path toward your feet. My eyes follow it to the spot where it skirts around the tips of your sealskin boots.

Along with the pelt, this spear will be your trophy for saving my life. Grabbing it with both hands, I pull it from the cat's body and a rush of blood and fluid pours from the wound. I straighten to my feet, but a sudden dizziness overwhelms me. Keeping my attention fixed to the ground, I try my best to stop my hands from shaking. After a few long moments, I feel composed enough to hold out the spear to you. "With my thanks," I say, my eyes still locked on your boots.

Moments pass, and yet you don't move. I stand with my arm extended, but you do not claim your spear. At last, the peace of the moment is broken by the sound of feet hurrying up the path below. I raise my head and meet your gaze.

What I see there is easy to understand, but difficult to accept. Though you saved me, I can see that it wasn't an act of graciousness toward a peer, like bending to lift a friend who has stumbled, but an act of benevolence toward a fool, like snatching up a reckless child who has tumbled into deep water.

Disdain, sharp and clear, flows from your eyes to mine.

And I know at that moment . . . I will never have your friendship. I will never have your respect. If there was ever a chance for friendship, for trust, that chance was forever lost the moment I raised my spear as if to strike you.

I know that I would never have let the spear go, would never have let it leave my hand until my target was in sight. I know this, but you don't. And though some would assume the best, you choose to assume the worst. You choose to condemn me for a flinch.

All this passes between us as I stand holding out your spear as if pleading with you to accept some exotic gift or enter into an agreement whose terms you find unfavorable. You stare me down, silently refusing to accept. Finally, voices rise from the path just beyond our view, calling our names.

"We're here," you say. You jerk the spear from my outstretched hand while simultaneously looking away, making clear that no gift is accepted, no terms agreed to.

Pek is the first to make the turn and take in the scene. Seeri comes up behind him quickly. They both run their eyes from the cat to the pool of blood to the spear, glistening red in your hands.

"Well done," says Pek, his voice a low whisper.

"Simple necessity," you say. "Kill or be killed." Our eyes meet, and I see that you intend to leave it at that. My shame is sufficient enough if you alone know the mistake I almost made.

Your lips press together and a momentary softness reaches your eyes, a hint of some past version of you who might have been able to forgive. But then you throw your arms around your sister and whisper something into her ear and I feel the gulf open between us again.

As you and your sister drift back down the trail, leaving Pek and me behind, anger drains from me and the void it leaves quickly fills with fatigue.

"Father, Chev, and Mya all pursued the cat, each taking a different path into the hills. Seeri and I stayed on the mammoths, and together we brought one down. Seeri landed the first strike." He pauses and licks his upper lip, as if the memory is something he can taste. "These girls . . ." The wind reddens Pek's cheeks and sends tears running down his face, but his smile does not dim. "These girls are going to change our lives."

I look away as he says these last words, as he declares this bold prediction. I don't want him to read the worry in my eyes—the fear I feel of how my life may have already changed.

THREE

The dead cat looks small, lying motionless at my feet. It's strange how living things seem to shrink when the life is drained from them. Still, it won't be easy to carry. It probably weighs as much as me and Pek combined, but together we manage to lift it. My hands wrap around its shoulders and I notice the bristly texture of the fur at the base of its neck and the thick cords of sinew under its skin. I notice the chill rapidly chasing away its warmth.

This is what fresh death feels like.

Once we've joined the rest of you in the valley, we sidestep the dead mammoth and drop the cat at your feet. Again, I thank you for what you did. The sight of the cat and the blood-soaked spear in your hand starts everyone talking. I can't blame them—it's stunning. Still, I listen carefully and note that you never acknowledge my thanks.

I volunteer to run back to camp to bring the butchers.

The rest of the hunting party stands guard at the kill, protecting our food from scavengers. Where there is one saber-toothed, there is likely a pack of dire wolves nearby, or maybe even another cat.

I decide against going the way we came, but instead head south into the valley below us, running for a while along the river before breaking west toward home. Along the way I keep my eyes open, but I never see the other five mammoths. Will they move north, as other mammoth herds have, staying close to the Great Ice as it draws away from the sea?

I run the whole way, my feet splashing in puddles that dot the ground where winter ice has melted, the early summer wind chilling my ears and my nose. When I reach camp, I head straight to the kitchen, a long tent at the western edge of our close circle of hide-covered huts. Inside I find my mother sitting on the ground, working alongside her siblings and cousins. My mother has always been thin—strong in the way vines are strong—while her face, in contrast, has stayed full and rounded like a young girl's. But today, in the speckled light of the kitchen, her usually soft-edged face appears gaunt.

"Kol!" She drops the fist-shaped stone she uses to grind greens and roots in a bowl made of the hollowed-out skull of a bison. A smooth, flat rock lies in the hearth surrounded by burning coals, the remnants of a fire. The kitchen assaults my senses: my nostrils fill with the oily scent of cooking fish, and the tips of my ears sting as they thaw in the sudden warmth. "What news do you have?" My mother studies my face. Hope is trying to creep into her eyes, but wariness crowds it out.

"The hunt is a success," I say, and her stiff lips twist into a smile.

The kitchen tent is crowded—all available hands have been called in to help prepare what is usually a simple midday meal cooked by two or three people. As soon as the words have left my lips a cheer ripples through the room. At the back of the tent a flap in the wall has been opened to allow a second hearth to vent. Two figures bolt to their feet when I mention the kill. Though they are mere silhouettes against the light pouring through the open vent, I recognize my younger brothers before they even move.

"We've brought down a mammoth. The butchers are needed. But they must come quick. A cat was also killed as it stalked the same prey. Only I left the kill to bring the news; all the others stayed to keep watch."

My mother regards me closely. I know the questions she wants to ask—*Who brought down the mammoth? Who slayed the cat?* But she doesn't dare ask here. If the answers do not give credit to her sons, she doesn't want the others of the clan to hear. At least not yet.

"You need butchers?" My youngest brother, twelve-year-old Roon, rough-hewn and awkward like an unfinished stone tool, moves toward the front of the kitchen, clambering over seated figures. Kesh, lean and lanky at fifteen, follows right behind. "We'll come—"

"We have butchers," my mother says, as Ness, Mol, and Svana climb stiffly to their feet from the dimly lit center of the tent. These three are all siblings—cousins of my father who are experienced and wise with regard to butchering a kill. Still, they don't move with the energy and speed of my brothers.

"Let them come along, Mother, please. They'll be needed to help load the meat and pull it back to camp."

So the six of us go, pulling three empty travoises—overland sleds made of poles of birch and mammoth bone. I lead the way, enduring my brothers' relentless questions about you and your sister. "You'll meet them soon enough," I say. I step up the pace a bit. I feel an urgency to return to the kill, and I need a break from questions about what happened on the hunt.

When we finally come to the head of the rocky trail, everything I've described stretches out before us—the dead mammoth, the cat, my father, and Pek in the company of three hunters who were all but strangers before today. Kesh and Roon drop the travois they've been pulling and race each other across the grass, leaving me and the butchers to bring the three sleds the rest of the way.

The butchers set immediately to work, moving with such

practiced precision they hardly need to speak. One uses an ax to divide the carcass into sections, separating the limbs from the torso. The other two employ sharp knives that remove meat from bone. The process is like a dance to the three of them—no one calls out the steps; experience has taught them to anticipate each other's moves. My brothers busy themselves with collecting the cut portions and securing them to the sleds with long cords made from the stalks of fireweed and stinging nettle, while you, Pek, and Seeri truss up the cat. My father and Chev stand off to the side, speaking in low tones like old friends, only looking up from time to time to call out some instructions.

With so many hands set to the task, I feel unneeded, superfluous. What could I possibly contribute? I would only get in the way. So I let myself wander, roaming to a spot just down the hill, a remote stretch of tall grass drenched in sunlight. I lie down and close my eyes, focus my ears, try to relax—try to catch that distinct whir of honeybee wings—but my thoughts thrum too loudly in my mind. Voices mix in—Roon's high buzz overlapping with Kesh's lower hum. I try to block them out, but it's useless—the longer they work, the louder they become.

After a while, I stop trying and sit up.

Before me, the valley the mammoths fled to opens at the bottom of a gentle slope, and from the angle where I sit the wide expanse of undulating meadow gives me the same odd sensation of movement I feel when I sit at the edge of the bay. The land rolls out from me unbroken, the wind rippling the sea of grass like waves upon the water.

It's then that I spot you—kneeling in the grass at the base of the hill, you and your sister Seeri. Are you gathering? Your heads are bent, your focus on the ground. I hurry over to ask if you will need help carrying what you've collected. As I approach, I catch the sound of your voices trailing off, words spoken in unison. Seeri gets to her feet, but you remain kneeling in the grass, your head bowed, your fingers tying a cord around your neck. There are no roots or greens to be gathered up.

When Seeri sees me she flinches briefly, then color blooms in her cheeks. Have I interrupted something private?

"I wanted to see if you needed help. . . . I'm sorry," I say. Seeri glances at you, but you keep your head bent away from the sound of my voice. The air stretches taut with tension, like the skin of a drum. I continue. "I thought you were gathering. . . ."

Seeri offers a dim, melancholy smile that doesn't reach her eyes. "What we left behind can't be seen; what we gathered can't be carried." She says this without looking directly at me, as if she's speaking to someone unseen who's just beyond my shoulder.

I'm not sure what to make of this—is it a quote of some

kind? A few words of a prayer or chant to the Divine? I think of the words I heard you speak in unison. . . . Before I can ask, Seeri strides away, leaving me alone with you.

I stand there, hovering over the place where you sit, for long enough that I begin to think I will either have to speak or walk away. Thankfully, just at the moment I feel I will need to decide between the two, you silently get to your feet. You shoot me the briefest of glances—not really a *look*, but rather a means of determining where you *don't* intend to look—before dropping your eyes to the grass and pinning them there. Your hands move to the pendant that hangs from the cord at your throat, tucking it into the collar of your parka as you step around me.

"Wait," I say. "I'd like to talk to you. There's something I need to say."

You keep moving until your shoulder comes alongside mine.

"Mya, wait. I owe you an apology."

You stop. You don't answer, but you don't walk away, either, so I take this as a sign that you're at least willing to listen. I pivot toward you but you won't even turn your face in my direction—*so stubborn*—so I'm forced to speak to your profile—your shoulder, your sleeve, the ear you've tucked your hair behind.

"I know that you're upset with me about what happened, but I never would have thrown at you—you were never in any danger. I wanted to tell you that, and I wanted to ask you to forgive me." It feels ridiculous to say these words to your left ear. I take a few steps until I'm standing right in front of you. Your head stays lowered, though, leaving me no choice but to speak to the straight line that parts your jet-black hair. "Mya?" The next words are not easy to say, as if each one is a heavy weight I have to push uphill to reach your ears. Still, I will be the next High Elder, and selflessness and peacemaking are the defining traits of a clan leader. I take a deep breath and continue. "Mya, will you please forgive me?"

You remain silent so long . . . I have the chance to imagine a myriad of possible responses, each one more full of condemnation than the last. Finally you raise your head. Your eyes sweep over my face as if you are seeing me for the first time. "You don't know, do you?"

Of all the replies I was anticipating, this question was not among them.

I take this unexpected question and combine it with the cryptic words of your sister—none of it makes sense. My eyes dart from your face to the spot where you and Seeri had knelt in the grass. My mind races to piece things together, to give shape to this formless confusion. In the end I can only be honest. "I don't understand."

You regard me suspiciously, as if you aren't quite sure that I'm someone you can trust with the truth. "Five years ago," you start, "our two clans nearly went to war—"

"Yes, I know. Of course I know—"

"But do you know why?"

Do I? I always thought that I knew the reason why. I was young when it happened, but as I've gotten older somebody must've told me. "There was a misunderstanding. . . ." I fumble through my memory. Could it be that I've never learned the reason? "Something happened that led to violence—"

"*Something* happened?"

Once again I find myself standing in front of you, grasping vainly for the right words to say. "I'm sorry. That's all I know."

Your eyes narrow; you are assessing me. And it's clear by your tight lips that the assessment is not favorable.

Maybe you're right to judge me harshly. Maybe I should know more about the history between our clans.

"Thank you for your apology."

You walk away, as if there is nothing more to say.

FOUR

What help I failed to lend during the hunt I try to make up for when it's time to drag the travoises back to camp laden with hides, ivory tusks, and enough meat to ensure the twenty-four members of our clan will not fear hunger for at least a little while. The loads are heavy, but we have a saying that bringing food back to camp is never a burden. My mother meets us on the trail just outside camp. She beams. "Fish for midday, but mammoth for the evening meal."

Everyone sits in the square at the center of camp, and Urar, our clan's healer, offers a chant of thanksgiving for the Spirit of the mammoth who gave up life so our clan might eat and endure. People crowd around to meet you— the slayer of the cat—and to feast on fish, clams, and greens, but Pek and I take our meals and offer our apologies. Our father has requested that we work through the meal to erect a hut for our guests.

"A hut?" I ask. "They'll be staying long, then?"

"They may be frequent visitors. They may not. In any event, we will treat them like members of this clan. They will sleep in their own hut."

And so you will.

Not long ago, our clan was far more mobile than it is now. When I was a boy, maybe six or seven years ago, we followed the bison from place to place, ranging between the northwestern hills in the summer to the mountains in the southeast in the winter. The bison were plentiful then, and our huts were more like tents, easy to put up and take down and light to carry.

But one winter, the bison crossed through the mountains to the east and headed south in the direction of your current home. This was the first winter after you had visited us, and our two clans were not on good terms. The elders decided that we could winter without the bison herd, since the mammoths didn't migrate nearly as far and stayed within our hunting range all winter. We all trusted the elders—a council of ten men and women chosen by my father, the High Elder, for their wisdom and selfless contributions to the clan. So our tents became heavier huts, beams of mammoth bone anchored to the ground near the shore to give us easy access to the sea, at least until we were iced in for the hardest part of the season. We had always used kayaks to fish, but my mother's sister and her family became adept at hunting seals.

When most of the bison failed to return from the south two springs later, few people worried. We had become settled in this camp, remaining here nearly year-round. Mammoths were still plentiful, and following the bison herds no longer seemed practical. Instead, we made seasonal trips to hunt and gather, always returning home to this place. Our huts were sturdy and covered with thick hides. They were warm and comfortable, lit by seal oil we burned in lamps of concave stone.

Despite our new comforts, putting up a hut for you and your siblings now makes me yearn for the days of light and portable tents. Our father has instructed us to build you a hut of generous proportions. This one will be wide enough to separate into two rooms by draping hides from the ceiling, like the one my own family lives in.

Pek holds a post made of the chiseled thighbone of a mammoth as I dig a furrow to place it in. The post is thick and the cold ground is stubborn. I hack at the earth with the sharpened edge of a heavy flint stone lashed to a handle I cut from a poplar branch. The handle is rough and the skin of my palms splits from the effort.

"Let me take a turn," Pek says.

I wave him off. "You brought down the kill; I'll put up the hut." Still, bloody hands are slippery hands, and my progress slows. Pek leaves me struggling and returns with a second ax, borrowed from the butchers. Eventually, we force the ground to yield and dig out a trough wide enough for the support beam. We dig a second, then a third. The process becomes routine and my mind drifts to you.

"Pek, do you know what happened between our clan and the Olen clan five years ago?"

"I know someone from their clan killed someone from ours—"

"Killed someone? Who—"

"Tram's father."

Tram's father. I remember his death, of course. "He died during a hunt." As a child, I'd been fascinated by the burial—the spear laid in the grave, the bison horn in the dead man's hand. A hunter's burial.

We've just wedged the upright beams into place when the next question forms in my mind—why would a hunting accident almost lead to war? Before I can ask, Kesh and Roon join us, carrying hides for the covering.

"If this is for the girls, we want to help," says Roon. He is the adventurer among us, always talking about traveling out onto the sea in a boat and what he might find if he did. When the rest of us would complain or worry about the lack of girls in our clan, Roon would develop elaborate plans for trips down the coast or west across the hills. Often he would sneak out of camp early in the morning or late at night, hoping to spot smoke rising from another clan's fire.

He never did, but he never gave up.

"This is for the girls as well as their brother," Pek says. "And neither of these girls is young enough for you."

"Maybe not, but there are other girls in their clan."

"How would you know?" I shake out a coarse bearskin and drape it over the frame of the hut. A musky scent fills my nostrils. The fissures in my palms have stopped bleeding, so I'm able to grip the edge of the hide tight while Kesh binds it to the support beam using a cord made of mammoth sinew. We stretch it taut from beam to beam, creating the bottom layer of the new hut's roof.

"I asked them."

Leave it to Roon to be direct. Why wonder if you can just ask?

"I hope our parents didn't hear you," I say. Our mother would think a question like that was too forward. Still, I'm pleased to know that my baby brother took the initiative. I doubt he would have had a moment of sleep tonight if he'd been forced to go to bed wondering. Something about knowing that there are other girls in your clan drains a bit of tension from me, as well. Between Seeri's clear interest in Pek and your even more obvious disdain for me, I had already given up hope of finding someone from within your clan.

Of course, if all the girls in your clan are as arrogant and rude as you are, I would rather be alone forever.

When the hut is finished, our mother comes to fill it from wall to wall with fur pelts—bison, bear, elk, and mammoth for the floor; saber-toothed cat, caribou, and sealskin for blankets. You will sleep warmly tonight.

The sun is already moving into the western sky as we tie the final knots. "Go clean yourselves," our mother says. "And put on clothing reserved for feasts. When we sit down to eat the evening meal with our guests, I hope you will no longer smell like the game we are dining on." She smiles at me. "And be sure you speak to Mya," she whispers as my brothers shuffle toward our family hut. "The other clearly has eyes for your brother, but Mya, like you, is the oldest. Her eyes are like yours—as dark as the night sky—but there is a sharpness to her gaze that complements the warmth in yours. You two would make a strong match, I think."

The smile of impending success on my mother's lips is so endearing, I can't tell her how wrong she is. She sighs and I hear a note of contentment in her voice I haven't heard in a long time. No, I can't take that from her, not just yet. I simply nod and let her walk away.

FIVE

The sun has burned into the shade of gold it reserves for evenings in early summer, when it hangs low in the sky, refusing to set, stretching out hours of pale yellow light, painting long deep shadows on the ground. This is when the drums begin to send their rhythm through the ring of huts.

My brother Kesh is one of the musicians, and I catch the tone of his flute as it pierces the evening air, dancing above the beating of the drums. Not the oldest or the youngest, not the most gifted with a spear, Kesh found himself in music. He was offered a place among the musicians four years ago, when he was only eleven years old and causing constant mischief. He hid handfuls of snails, earthworms, and finally a dead vole in the music leader's bed, until she offered him a flute in exchange for a promise to stop. She had a flute of her own that he envied, and she meticulously copied it, carving the thighbone of a wolf to just the right length and carefully drilling each hole. The day he received it was like the day he was born, and that flute has been the focus of his life ever since.

Pek and Roon left the hut long before the shadow of the kitchen tent stretched to our door, but I wait it out as long as possible. I lie down, but I can't relax. My mother borrowed pelts from each of our beds to make up yours. The difference is slight—my bed is almost as thick and lush as it was before—but even this small change in our home unsettles me. I think of Pek's prediction that you and Seeri will change our lives.

Maybe I'm not ready for change.

The music grows louder, and I can't stay behind any longer. I head out to the open-air gathering place in the center of camp where our clan shares all its meals.

I spot you almost as soon as I step through the door of our hut. I wish I could ignore you, but it's impossible—my eyes are drawn to you the way they are drawn to a flash of light. You've changed into a tunic made of supple hides cut in a much more feminine style than your shapeless hunting parka. The hair around your face is wound into three thin braids that are gathered at the crown of your head, but otherwise your hair is down like it was this morning. You stand beside your brother, Chev, who is speaking to my father. I take just one step in your direction before you look up at me, almost as if you've been waiting for me to show, though I know better. As soon as you see me approaching you turn your head, and I change my mind about joining the three of you. I turn toward my brother Kesh, instead, and congratulate him on the solo he played during the gathering music. Lil, the music leader, interrupts. "A circle! A circle, everyone!"

The first song of the evening is about to be sung.

I move to a place near my brother Pek, and I notice Seeri beside him, smiling but clearly confused. It occurs to me for the first time that your clan might not follow all the same customs that we do. Do you not sing the same songs? Taking her by the elbow, Pek guides her to a place within the circle right between the two of us. She gives me a weak smile and shrugs.

"Follow along—it's easy," I say, just as the first line is sung by the whole clan as if by one voice.

Manu was a hunter lost in a storm, wandering far from home. . . .

Like all songs, this one is sung to the Divine. It tells the story of our clan's founding ancestor, Manu—my favorite story since I was a small boy. When I was ill or could not sleep, my mother would lie beside me and whisper it in my ear.

"There was a hunter named Manu who became lost in a storm, separated from home and clan," she would say, and I would shiver at the thought. "After wandering long and far, he lost hope of finding his way back. He was so lonely that he befriended a mammoth, but despite his hunger he would not kill it. *The Spirit of a mammoth is too precious to give its life to feed just one man*, Manu told the mammoth. In thanks, the mammoth gave Manu one of his tusks, and Manu carved a woman out of the ivory. The Divine saw Manu's selflessness, and said to herself, *I must reward him.* So she sent a little piece of herself to dwell in the carving, bringing her to life and giving Manu a wise wife. Together, Manu and his wife had many children, and their offspring became our clan."

This story always comforts me. Even now, singing Manu's song with my clan, I know that I am home.

The song has many verses, but the steps are simple—one foot over the other, one foot behind—as the circle moves over well-worn earth, slowly to the left. Seeri joins in at the refrain, which repeats the word *wandering . . . wandering.* She makes mistakes at first but she gets it by the second time through.

I glance over at you, but I can't meet your eyes. You have stepped back from the circle and you are turned away, your attention focused on the ground, as if you're searching for something no one else can see. Are you embarrassed because you do not know this dance? Even your brother is not afraid to try—he stands beside my father, who coaches him through the changes in the song.

As the music of the first song fades, ending on a ribbon of

melody that rises from my brother's flute, everyone stomps their feet in approval and readies for the second song. Everyone except you. I notice you speak briefly into your brother's ear and then disappear in the direction of your hut. My eyes follow you, but I cannot will my feet to do the same.

Turning my attention back to Seeri, I watch her as the clan sings the first words of the second song. This song is more subdued than the first—a reverent song of thanks—and her eyes are wide as she takes in the circle of my extended family. Though she apparently does not know the words to this song, either, her head swings in time with the tune.

As the third song is sung, the circle melts into a line that leads past the kitchen. My mother stands in the open doorway, the rich scent of roasted meat rolling out around her, as she hands each person a mat made of stiff, tightly woven stalks piled high with chunks of mammoth meat and cooked greens. Chev takes a mat from my mother, and though he is a few places ahead of me, I can hear him comment on the size of the portions. My mother nods and smiles, but as soon as he passes, her eyes dart over the remainder of the line. She looks at me, Seeri, Pek, then her eyes slide back to Chev and my father.

She is looking for you.

"Where is she?" She hasn't even placed my mat in my hands before she asks.

"She went back to their hut at the start of the second song."

"Why?"

"How should I know, Mother? Maybe she's ill. Maybe she's exhausted—"

"Take this to her."

I consider objecting to the idea, then realize that my mother is right. If you are sick or simply tired, as gracious hosts we should check on you and offer you something to eat. If you are being rude and unsociable, that doesn't excuse us from similar behavior.

As I approach the door to your hut, I notice music. After a moment's hesitation, I realize it's you, humming to yourself inside the hut. I don't recognize the exact tune, but it's similar to a lullaby my mother used to sing to me.

Could this be a song your mother sang to you? Since your brother is your clan's High Elder, I assume your parents must be dead. No one has spoken of either one of them.

"Excuse me," I say. The humming instantly stops, but you don't respond. "Excuse me, Mya? My mother sent food. . . ."

A few slow moments pass before your hand peeks out from between the draped hides and sweeps them back enough to reveal part of your face, lit by the thin rays of sunlight that filter through the huts so late in the evening.

"I intended to come back," you say. "I'm just tired."

"Of course."

Another long moment passes before you take the mat of food from my hands. Your eyes hold a message—not the hard disdain I saw earlier, but something just as dark. Loneliness? Your gaze moves away before I can be sure. "Thank you." And then the drape falls shut again and I find myself standing outside your hut, alone.

The meal is delicious and spirits are high, just as they always are when a kill is brought in. Several songs break out spontaneously and my father even brings out skins of mead made from honey and berries gathered last summer. Sacred and precious, our clan consumes mead only at the holiest ceremonies and most significant celebrations. Sharing it with your clan today is not without meaning.

As everyone drinks, the singing grows louder. Still, I can't quite shake the thought of that dark look in your eyes. It doesn't matter, though. Everyone is happy. No one even notices my mood.

No one except my mother.

"What did she say?"

"She said she was tired, Mother. Everyone gets tired sometimes. Let her rest."

But my mother is agitated. I can see it. She busies herself with gathering empty mats and collects many compliments on the meal as she does. It won't matter; I know her—she won't be appeased. The mystery of your absence is working her nerves. After a while, I feel her nervousness has jumped to me. As soon as she is occupied with some task in the kitchen, I take advantage of the opportunity to talk to her alone.

"What happened five years ago?" I ask.

My mother looks up at me. A strand of hair has come loose from the braid at the top of her head, and she tugs at it, tucking it back into place with restless fingers. "The Olen clan visited us. . . . They were moving south—"

"I know all that. I want to know what really happened. What happened between our two clans?"

She retrieves a large waterskin that hangs from a notch in a mammoth tusk that serves as a support beam, takes a long drink through the hollowed-out piece of bone attached as a spout, and offers it to me. "It's only water. Your father has all the mead outside." I take a drink. The water runs cool and soothing down my tense, dry throat. "Five years ago, on a joint hunt . . ." My mother hesitates. She does not want to say these words. The dread in her voice sends a tremor along my spine, and my mouth goes dry again. I offer my mother the waterskin, but she shakes her head. I take another drink, and as I do, she blurts out the rest of her story. "On a joint hunt, one of our men killed one of their women."

I try to swallow, but water pools as if it's caught in a knot in my throat. I hack and cough before I can speak again.

"What—"

"It was an accident, but that didn't matter." My mother is tired, her voice a hoarse whisper. "One of their hunters responded by killing the man who threw the spear."

The back of my hand runs across my lips, wiping away drips of water and salty sweat. I stare at my mother's unflinching face as if willing her to change this story, to tell me it isn't true. But of course it's true. It makes perfect sense. "The man who threw the spear was Tram's father," I say.

"Yes. How—"

"Pek and I were talking earlier. We remember the burial."

This is all I say before handing her the waterskin and pushing out through the door and back into the gathering place. In the center of a broad rock, seal oil burns in a shallow soapstone lamp—Urar is preparing to read the flame to interpret the will of the Divine. I navigate through the crowd, careful not to step on people seated together in clusters of two and three, sipping mead and telling tales, as I make my way back to my family's hut. As I walk, one thought crowds out every other—a man from my clan killed a woman from your clan, and he did it on a hunt. He did it when he threw a spear in error. Just as you feared I would throw my spear at you today.

Once in our empty hut, things are only worse. The thought follows me like a shadow, and I know it won't let me rest until I speak with you again. From a hook beside my bed I take a small pouch that was once used as a water-skin and head out to your hut.

Standing outside your door, I realize I am about to disturb you for the second time this evening. Your hut is both dark and quiet. Are you sleeping? Didn't you say you were tired? I know I've made a mistake when you suddenly pull back the draped hides and look out.

If you are tired, it doesn't show on your face. Even in the reluctant light of sunset, your eyes still shine. If anything, they flash with impatience rather than fatigue. "Yes?"

"I'm sorry. I didn't mean to disturb you. Did I wake you?"

"I heard footsteps stop outside the door. . . . Do you want something?"

My eyes shift, unable to withstand the pressure of your gaze. They slide to your hand, gripping the hide in the doorway. Your fingers curl tightly around the edge of the bearskin, and I think of how I just hung this door today—I remember how I'd begrudgingly allowed the image of your face to invade my thoughts as I built this hut, imagining its walls protecting you as you slept.

"I know why." These words come out in a hurried rush, as I'm suddenly overwhelmed by the need to retreat from this situation but also painfully aware that I can't walk away until I've said what I came to say. "I know why our two clans almost went to war."

"And?"

"And now I understand. A woman from your clan was killed. A careless throw by a man from my clan took her life."

"Yes. That's what happened."

"And it makes sense to me now. Today, you thought it might all happen again. I hope you'll forgive me for scaring you like that."

"There's nothing to forgive." You lean out of the hut a bit and look past my shoulder, back toward the place where everyone is still gathered. They are taking turns singing solos now, and I recognize my brother Pek's voice singing a love song. It's a song to the Divine, of course, but Pek isn't a fool. He knows how the words can be interpreted.

You glance at the ground between us. It's clear I've overstayed my welcome, if I was ever welcome at all.

Then I remember the small pouch I brought with me. "Take this," I say, placing it into your hand. You hold it awkwardly, pursing your lips. Your eyes flit from the pouch to my face. "It's honey. I gathered it last summer from several hives I was able to find—"

"No, thank you." You hold it out for me to take it back, but I hesitate.

"It's a gift," I say. I feel my face flush, but I'm not sure if it's from embarrassment or anger.

So much labor went into collecting this small pouch of

honey. Every day last summer I got out of bed early, chanted prayers to the Divine and the Spirit of bees, and went in search of hives. The first I found easily—it was closest to the meadow—but the process of extracting the honey can be difficult and dangerous. Once the hive is found, the bees need to be sedated with smoke. That first hive was in a cluster of half-dead dwarf birch, surrounded by dry brush. I had to haul green kindling from young growth closer to camp. It took hours of effort, and yielded only small amounts of honey. That process had to be repeated over and over again.

"We have honey at home. Here in the north, honey must be extremely scarce. You should keep what you have for yourselves."

I swallow and take a deep breath before I reply, striving to keep the anger from my voice. "I know our ways may be unfamiliar to you," I say, thinking of the way you'd withdrawn at the start of the singing before the meal. "But I assure you, we don't live in a barren wasteland. This may not be the lush south, but there's plenty of honey on this side of the mountains. Finding it just demands a bit more patience."

Behind me I hear laughter. I turn to find your brother, sister, and Pek just a few paces away. I take the honey from your hand and hold it behind my back, hoping that the others won't notice it.

I've suffered enough humiliation for one day.

I know I should stand in the doorway and exchange pleasantries with your brother and sister, but in this instant, my sense of social custom is no match for my pride. I nod and say a hasty good night.

Still, I can't quite drag myself away, and I duck into the shadows between two huts as your brother and Pek wish each other a restful night. I hear your sister offer a brief but sweet word of thanks to Pek for a lovely day. Then Pek walks right past me, under such a spell he doesn't even notice I am here.

Once Pek is gone, I can't help but notice the voice of your brother, Chev. His words are muffled, but if I didn't know better I would think he was scolding Seeri, but that can't be right. I assume he must be chastising you for staying away from the meal. After a murmured response, I hear a question quite clearly. It's your sister's voice, and she asks what you and I were talking about just now.

I know better than to listen in on other people's conversations, and the answer you give your sister is the punishment I deserve for doing something I know is wrong.

"He came to offer me a gift—a pouch of honey he'd collected."

"That's so generous—" Seeri starts, her voice lilting and light. I can tell she's happy for you. But you cut her off.

"I refused it. At home I can gather my own honey. I won't let some stranger think he can buy me with his."

I stalk back to our hut, each breath laboring against a heavy knot of anger that presses down on my chest, your mocking words thrumming in my head. To push the sound of your voice from my mind, I hum the tune to the love song I just heard my brother Pek sing.

I know my parents are hoping this visit leads to a new friendship between our two clans. Silently, I thank the Divine for Pek and Seeri.

SIX

I wake in the dark to Pek shaking my shoulders. I had been dreaming, and though the dream fades quickly, a haze of dread colors my thoughts—it must have been a nightmare.

"Come on," Pek says, clearly irritated. With Pek, a bad mood is unusual, but after yesterday, it's all but impossible. What could have happened? Behind Pek I notice Kesh is already dressed and pulling on his boots. A gust of wind rattles in the vent overhead, and the shrill sound, like the laugh of an angry Spirit, chills me. "This is the second time I've tried to wake you. Mother wants us all down in the kitchen to help this morning."

"She needs all of us to help with the morning meal?" I sit up and notice the pouch of honey where I'd dropped it on the floor last night. I push it out of sight, not wanting to be reminded of what I'd heard you say.

The last thing I feel like doing right now is getting up

and preparing food for you.

"They're leaving. Chev got up early and went down to put their things into their boat. Aunt Ama was at the shore checking her nets and spoke with him. Mother was already in the kitchen and she came straight to the hut and woke Father and me."

I let this story sink in. No one had ever told me how long you and your siblings were staying, but there was a definite sense you would be with us for a while, certainly more than a night. We'd put up a hut. We'd butchered a mammoth. This couldn't have been part of your plans yesterday. Something changed.

Could this all be your doing? Could it be that you've convinced your brother that there is nothing here worth staying for?

"Mother wants us all in the kitchen. She's determined to send them home with at least half of the mammoth meat, so it needs to be divided and wrapped."

"Fine."

Good riddance to you and your haughty disdain, I think, but any satisfaction I get from your early departure dissolves once I see my mother's face. The light that glowed in her eyes as she handed out mats piled high with her cooking last night is all but gone today. She sits on the floor in the center of the kitchen, a circle of tools and ingredients spread around her. She reaches for a sharp stone blade made from obsidian brought back from an expedition to the far north—her favorite cutting tool by far—but then sets it down again distractedly. Her hand moves to a bowl made of woven stalks of slough sedge, filled to the brim with bits of crab meat mixed with lupine roots gathered from the meadow. On a flat stone she's been cutting wild carrots dug from a tidal marsh a half day's walk from here. This was meant to be a meal that would rival the one she'd served last night.

Instead, she slides all these things aside and calls on Roon to help her move a large flat stone—a slab of rock split from an outcropping that broke into smooth, even layers when it was dug out from the hill. I remember my father presenting this stone to her—he had carried it on his own shoulders from the hill where it was quarried, knowing that she would find it perfect for cooking and cutting. An arm's length wide and two arm's lengths long, it holds most of the mammoth meat that was butchered last night. It's not all of it, of course—only about a third of the mammoth has been cut from the bone—but my mother is determined to send half of what we have with you.

She gets to her feet and hands out large, supple sheets of tightly stitched walrus gut. "I'll divide the meat into evenly sized portions. Each of you take a piece, wrap it tight, and tie it with a length of cord. I don't want it to dry out before they get it home."

Father's voice comes from outside the door, followed by

Chev's. If my father feels insulted by your sudden departure, he's much better at disguising it than my mother is. "Of course; we insist," he says.

Chev ducks his head to step through the doorway into the dim tent. His eyes sweep over the scene, stopping on the piles of mammoth meat on the cutting stone. "You are being far too generous. There's no need to send us with any provisions. By boat, it won't take much more than half the day to reach our own shores."

"The three of you helped bring in this food; you will take your fair portion. I will not risk angering the Spirit of the mammoth that died so that we could all eat." This comes out as a proclamation rather than a comment. My mother's tone has the definitive note she usually reserves for my brothers and me.

I drop my head and try to appear too caught up in my task of wrapping meat to notice what is being said. But then the door flips open and shut, light from outside splashing momentarily across the kitchen floor. Before I look up I know it's you—I already recognize the unique cadence of your steps.

You stand with your sister, just inside the doorway. Seeri's hair is tied up in a braid that wraps around her head, a style my mother and most of the women of my clan wear almost every day. I notice that your hair, as it was yesterday, is loose, falling over your shoulders and down your back.

You are both dressed in the clothes you wore on the hunt.

"We know you do not need our help to successfully bring down game." These words come from Seeri. "Thank you for the privilege of accompanying you yesterday. We all learned so much." Her eyes are fixed on Pek, and for the first time, her clear intentions toward him ruffle my nerves. Suddenly, I can't stomach the sight of the tender expression on her face. My eyes move to yours. You stare at the ground, falsely occupied in making a mental inventory of my mother's kitchen supplies. I guess it's what I should expect of you. You wouldn't accept my gift last night. Why should you even look me in the eye to say a proper good-bye?

"We can all learn from a hunt with Pek, that's certain," my father says. "He's one of the best with a spear that I have ever seen."

I'm stunned. I wouldn't expect my father to make such a blatant play to impress the three of you. Then again, I'm not intimately involved in managing and governing the clan, as he is. My parents are both elders of this clan, and there have been frequent meetings of the council lately. They would have a far better understanding of our situation—of the need to move south and the ways cooperation with your clan could reduce the risks involved with such a move. The ways a betrothal could encourage such a friendship.

I would rather our clan face extinction than reduce

myself to playing for your affections, but my father, I see now, is feeling the pressure.

"There used to be a girl in this clan called Shava," my father says. "She was so impressed by Pek's hunting that she wanted to marry him. She cooked every kill he brought in for the entire clan. She tried to make herself the ideal partner for him, I suppose."

Father's eyes cloud over and I can see in his smile that he is thinking back on Shava and perhaps wondering why we were ever so careless as to let her slip away.

"Pek wasn't interested in that girl, though, no matter how many mats she piled high with grilled bison or mammoth," I interject. The eyes of every person in the room snap to my face. It's quite bold to interrupt your own father as he relates a tale, especially if your father is Arem the High Elder, but I feel I need to put a stop to this one. "Apparently, being a great cook for a great hunter doesn't necessarily win his heart. Her cooking wasn't enough to buy his affection," I say, turning to look directly into your face.

You swallow. "Where is she now? I notice there are no young women in this clan."

Pek jumps in to answer. "We met up with another clan about two years ago—it turned out to be the clan of her mother's family. Her mother had left them years before to marry into our clan, but her husband had died, and when we crossed paths with them again, she was reunited with her family. Shava and her mother returned to the west with her mother's native people, to their territory beyond the northwest hills."

This simple story by my brother touches some nerve in you. Your head whips around in his direction. "What clan? A clan to the northwest? What clan is that?"

"Mya." The voice of your brother interrupts you sharply. I notice a very small shake of his head, a message to you. "Do not pester our hosts with such questions."

There are secrets here, I realize. Clearly, there is something your brother does not wish to discuss. But whatever secrets your brother wishes to keep, they do not interest me. "Excuse me. I'll carry the first load to your boat," I say, filling up my arms with packages of meat. I move toward the door, careful to keep my eyes on the floor as I pass by you.

To my surprise, you follow me out into the cold morning light.

"Kol." I stop, acutely aware that this is the first time you've ever addressed me by name. I'm not sure how I feel about the sound of it. Your voice is halting, less confident than usual. "If cooking isn't the best way to attract the interest of a hunter, what would you say is better?"

I turn to study you. This is a trick question, I'm sure, but I can't imagine what the trick is meant to accomplish. It doesn't matter. Last night you were quite direct with me. I won't hesitate to be just as direct. "Perhaps something more personal," I say, "like accepting small gifts that are offered without assuming they are meant to buy you. Even if you *could* gather all that you wanted at home."

Your lips part and your focus slides from my face; for a moment, you stare into the air, trying to piece together how I came to know the words you used last night. The softness of confusion fades and your features sharpen as you arrive at the only plausible explanation—that I heard you through the walls. As your eyes return to mine they narrow and draw together until a crease appears between your eyebrows.

"You shouldn't listen at doors."

"I couldn't help but hear," I lie. Still, what difference does it make now? After I raised my spear at you, your opinion of me is clearly unsalvageable.

"You misunderstood my refusal of that gift," you say. "Maybe my words were too strong, but what I meant was, you can't purchase a person's affections. They have to be won naturally."

Behind me, I hear the clan waking up. People stir inside their huts. I feel the need to end this awkward conversation before there are witnesses to it.

"Well, we have Pek and Seeri as an example, don't we? They have certainly come to share a mutual affection naturally. Clearly ties between our clans will be forged by those two."

You drop your eyes and take a step backward toward the kitchen. "I don't think that will happen." Your voice, like your eyes, has dropped. You speak so low I can hardly hear you. "They are an impossibility—Pek and Seeri—she is promised to a boy in our clan—one of Chev's closest friends."

Your words confuse me, though their plain meaning is clear. Still, it can't be true. If Seeri is betrothed to a boy in your clan, why would she lead my brother on the way she has?

And why would Seeri be betrothed before you, since she is younger? Certainly your family wouldn't have looked for a match for Seeri before you were betrothed.

Or could it be that you are already promised, too?

I'm sure it's obvious how your words have stunned me. I shift the packages in my arms and steady myself on my feet when, without warning, someone knocks into me from behind.

I spin around to find my brother Roon, his face flushed. Though he's younger and smaller than me, he's strong and sturdy, and when he grabs hold of my shoulders he upsets my balance and sends three packs of meat tumbling from my arms to the ground.

"Roon! Watch what you're doing!"

I bend to pick up the dropped packages, which, thankfully, did not unwrap and spill into the dirt. You retrieve one that landed at your feet, and my brother takes it from you and hands it back to me.

"I'm sorry; I just ran all the way from shore. I got up early this morning—very early. I'm not sure that I ever really went to sleep last night. It was as if I could hear someone creeping outside the huts, wandering through the dark. Anyway, when I got up I found nothing, but I could *feel* something there; you know? It was like the Divine was calling to me. I found myself all the way down on the western shore before the sun came up, and I kept walking until well after it rose. And *what* do you think I found?"

"Don't make me guess, Roon. Just tell—"

"Another clan! There is another clan, Kol, camping on the western shore of the bay. Two of them—a brother and sister—were out gathering kelp and they spoke to me. They said they come from land to the north and west."

"A brother and sister?" Your voice is urgent and unexpected, like a crack of thunder out of a clear sky.

"Yes—"

"From what clan? What name are they known by?"

"I don't know—I didn't ask them."

The color drains from your face, but I can't begin to guess why news of this clan should affect you so.

"Girls . . . ," Roon whispers. I know he's excited to talk to me, but I find myself watching you as your attention turns inward. You gaze into the air as if looking at something, but your eyes stay unfocused. "The brother and sister who spoke to me told me there are several girls in their clan. . . ."

Dragging my eyes from your face to Roon's is difficult, but when I finally turn my attention to my brother I see the triumph in his expression. He has explored over the grassland and along the coast, searching for some indication of another clan—any clan—but especially a clan with girls of marrying age.

I want to tell Roon how proud I am that he finally accomplished the goal that's been driving him for so long, but I'm interrupted by the sight of your brother coming through the door of the kitchen, followed closely by Pek and Seeri. Pek carries another three packs, identical to the ones in my arms. Chev sweeps his eyes over me, and I become acutely aware that I left the kitchen quite a while ago, claiming to be heading to your boat. His eyes move from me to you. "I'm sorry to take you away, Mya," he says, "but it's time for us to leave."

"We'll walk you down to the shore," my mother says. "Pek, why don't you carry Seeri's pack—"

"That's quite all right." Chev's voice is stern and his tone fills in some answers to questions that have been swirling in my mind. Now I understand this unexpected early departure. Chev is anxious to separate Seeri and Pek, to return her to his friend at home.

If Seeri is promised to another boy, this trip wasn't meant

to find someone for her. Perhaps Chev came here to find a wife for himself? I always assumed your brother had a wife, though I'm not sure anyone has actually said so. But if he were searching for a wife, why would he bring his two sisters along? No, this trip could have been for only one purpose—to find someone for you.

Chev's eyes meet mine and he holds my gaze for a moment before turning his attention to you. "We have appreciated your hospitality greatly. Isn't that right, Mya?"

"Yes," you say without looking at me, and I know that I have discerned things correctly. Chev had wanted to find a match for you, and we have disappointed him.

I wonder how differently things would have gone if Chev had left your sister at home. But then, even if you'd come alone, you would've found all the same reasons to reject me. Perhaps it would be you swooning over Pek—the born hunter—rather than Seeri.

Maybe that's what Chev regrets the most.

At the boat, your brother moves quickly. Roon chatters the whole time about the clan he met on the western shore. As you set your pack into your brother's hands, you whisper a message into his ear.

"This clan from the west," Chev says to Roon. "You told my sister earlier you thought someone was creeping through the camp last night—maybe someone from that clan? Maybe even a spy?"

Roon twitches and a smile flits across his lips, but then he wipes it away with his hand. "I thought I heard something, but when I walked outside, no one was there. It could've been a spy, I guess. Just as likely it was a Spirit, sent by the Divine to draw me to the shore."

"A Spirit . . . Perhaps. Or perhaps a ghost . . ." Chev's eyes move to your face and I wonder if we are all thinking of the same thing—the woman who lost her life five years ago on the hunt. Could her ghost have paced our camp last night? Could it be that the violence that took her life ties her Spirit here, preventing it from climbing to the Land Above the Sky?

Without another word, Chev moves quickly to prepare the canoe. His haste removes any opportunity for ceremony or formality as we part. Pek wades into the water, his seal-skin pants and boots protecting him from the icy cold, and holds the canoe steady as you and Seeri step in.

"Such an incredible boat," Pek says, and the sincerity in his voice almost breaks my heart. "The skill of your clans-people is truly impressive. I hope to pay a visit to you and meet the people of your clan soon."

I'm surprised Pek would say something so bold. Could our parents have put him up to it?

"We will look forward to meeting you all again . . . someday," Chev says. His noncommittal response is as good as a "no" to my brother's proposition. He gives a small nod to my parents. "Arem and Mala, we thank you and all the Manu for your hospitality."

Then the three of you push out. Three paddles stab hard at the water, drawing you quickly away from our shore.

As you round the point to the south where, even in summer, ice runs down from the eastern mountains like a frozen river to the sea, I catch a glimpse of a lone kayak far out on the horizon. The sun shines bright and the outline of a paddler is illuminated, long, loose hair whipping in the wind.

My heart pounds a drumbeat in my chest that rolls outward like an echo, vibrating along my skin. I turn and clutch Roon by the arm. "There!" I shout, pointing to the shape on the sea.

But just as I do, a cloud slides in front of the sun. Gray mist shrouds the water in shadow.

Ghost, spy, or just a trick of my imagination, the lone kayaker I'd seen so distinctly just a moment before is gone.

SEVEN

S eeri loved the sealskin blankets. This is the one true thing my mother and Pek have fixated on since your boat disappeared around our bay's southern point.

By afternoon, Pek and I are out on the water, hunting seals.

We each paddle a kayak custom-built by our aunt Ama from sealskin stretched over a frame of mammoth bone. Even our paddles are works of careful craftsmanship—their shafts carved from well-chosen spruce limbs, perfectly fitted to pairs of blades shaped from finely worked driftwood, capped at both ends with ivory. These kayaks are not just boats we sit in, like the canoe you and your siblings use, but they are almost like clothing we wear, tied at the waist and braced with straps over our shoulders to keep water out. "It will keep you comfortable. . . . Comfortable and safe," Aunt Ama said the first time I climbed into it, my legs sliding into the dry cavity under the deck. And she was right—I am both comfortable and safe. But still, I am miserable.

Grasping the paddle balanced across my lap, I'm reminded of yesterday's hut-building efforts and the deep fissures left in my palms. By last night the cuts were healing, sealed with a crisscrossing pattern of dark purple scabs. But scabs are no defense against seawater, and out here today, my palms sting and burn.

If only this were just a simple fishing expedition, one where Pek and I could float in a quiet cove with the sun on our backs, enjoying the warm air of early summer as we drop a net into the still-frigid waters to see what fish we might bring up. I could use a chance to rest and sift through all the things that have been done and said since you arrived yesterday. I feel out of balance—my thoughts have been stuffed to overflowing while my hopes have been drained dry. I know some time spent thinking—alone in the meadow maybe—would fix it, but my family has other plans for me. Instead of lying in a meadow, I find myself paddling out toward a cluster of rocky offshore islands, armed with a harpoon of walrus bone tipped with walrus ivory, tied to a long rope of tightly knotted kelp.

With his paddle, Pek points into the distance. Dark shapes stand out against the sun-bleached rocks—the seals are out. Our chances of success seem strong. I thank the Divine for this small blessing. I don't think I could take another failure today.

Before we reach the small islands where we will hunt, I pull my boat up next to my brother's and slow my paddling. He looks over to me, squinting into the sun. "You all right?" he calls.

"She didn't leave you willingly," I say. I feel like I need to tell Pek this, to undo any sense he may have of rejection. "Her brother, Chev—he took her from you. Mya told me. Seeri is promised to Chev's close friend. He took her from here because he could see how she felt about you, how you felt about each other."

Pek doesn't answer. Instead he drops his head, digs his paddle into the water, and makes a wide turn around me. Perhaps I've said the wrong thing. Perhaps it would have been better to leave him wondering if she'd rejected him. After all, Mya had called Pek and Seeri an *impossibility.*

Pek circles around the front of my kayak and pulls alongside me so we're facing each other. His head is lowered, but when he raises it and meets my eyes, he flashes a wry smile. "I already know," he says.

"You know? How do you know?"

"Seeri told me."

"But then why are we out here hunting seals? Why do you persist in planning a trip to their camp—"

"She's not married yet, is she? So there's still a chance. Things could change."

Where does Pek find this kind of faith? Is he being foolish

or wise? Distracted by these questions, my focus wanders from the surface to the sky, until Pek dips his paddle into the sea and flips icy water in my face. Startled, I wipe my eyes with the backs of my hands just in time to catch a fleeting glimpse of his laughing face before he ducks his head and paddles hard for the rocks. Seals sunbathe on at least ten ledges above the spray. I stab at the water in pursuit of Pek, but as we draw close we both slow our pace. Now, closing in, stealth overrides speed. Diverting our course around a smaller island that blocks us from view, we slide across the surface as soundlessly as possible.

Hidden by the southern edge of the island—little more than a rock, really—Pek halts his kayak. I stop alongside him and take stock of our position. We are well within range.

Something about Pek's resilience bolsters my mood. I feel emboldened by his refusal to be beaten. Good omens are all around: sunlight shimmers on the surface and the Spirits in the sea sing to me in the beat of the waves. I load my harpoon into an atlatl to ensure I get as much power into the throw as possible, and after making sure that Pek is out of my way and I have a clear and open shot, I let the harpoon fly.

It is a perfect strike. The spike lands in the thick flesh of the seal's side and he leaps into the water.

He struggles, and as he does the water colors red with his

blood. I hold on with my cracked and bleeding hands, as he dives and surfaces, dives and surfaces. Thankfully, his fight doesn't outlast the strength of my rope. His body goes still, sinking a bit before settling in shallow water at the edge of the rocks.

Now comes the trickiest part—bringing him in without breaking the harpoon or snapping the rope. I paddle as close to the rocks as possible, careful not to scrape the bottom of the kayak and risk tearing a gash in the hull.

The carcass lies on a jutting shelf just below the surface. With the blade of my paddle, I manage to leverage his weight enough to lift him up and pull him in. The seal drops heavily onto the deck of my kayak, one wet flipper sliding against my cheek as he falls. I almost avert my gaze—I remember the mammoth hunt and the way the mammoth's eye had opened like a pit—but the seal's head drapes over the side. I silently thank the Spirit of this seal for not looking me in the eye.

As I coil the rope, Pek paddles up alongside me. "Nicely done," he says.

My ivory-tipped harpoon is buried deep in the seal's side under the ribs. Despite the fight put up by the seal, the spike made only a small entry wound in the pelt. The rest of the coat is intact—a smooth, uninterrupted gradient of color, fading from golden brown near the head to a pale buff near the tail. Almost all the icy water has already shed from the fur and a breeze ripples across it, showing off its sheen. After a brief study of the wound, I decide to wait until I'm back on land to remove the harpoon. The unsteady sea makes unsteady hands, and I would hate to see even a scrap of this pelt wasted.

Though all the seals near my kill fled into the water, they sought safety by staying together and swimming toward shore. A second group still basks on a broad, flat island farther out to sea, calmly unaware and unalarmed. "I want to try something," says Pek, all the while keeping his attention on the distant seals. "I'll stay here and wait, out of sight. You paddle closer and make a noise, get them moving. The shortest path to shore is through these rocks. I'll take the shot as they swim past."

The dead seal makes a strange passenger as I paddle out, circling wide around the far side of the rocks. As I get closer I see that this group is much larger than the last. At least three dozen seals crowd against each other in the sun.

Out here, my back to the land, the sea grows calm and quiet. For a moment, I close my eyes and let my thoughts go quiet too. It lasts only a moment. Then my mind's eye snaps open and I see the cat you killed, crouching in the sky, all but hidden by the clouds. He stays low, but his eyes are on me. All at once he bounds forward, his immense claws tearing the clouds to wisps, closing in on the place I sit, helpless in this tiny boat.

My eyes fly open. Beyond the tip of my kayak there is nothing but unbroken sea. Spooked, I dip a blade into the water and turn toward shore again.

I watch the seals, completely vulnerable, as unaware of my presence as I was of the cat's. Then I let out a whoop and strike the surface with my paddle. Just as Pek planned, the seals leap into the water, diving in the direction of shore.

I paddle closer, moving in toward Pek, who waits beneath a low, overhanging ledge. He loads his harpoon into an atlatl and readies his throw.

The first seals reach the rocks across from him and surface, heads and necks rising above water as they look back to see if they are safe. As more heads appear, Pek takes aim. He lets the harpoon fly.

His aim is perfect, but his target dives just before the spike reaches him. The harpoon slashes into the sea but the rope stays slack—there is no strike. Hurrying, hoping to get another opportunity before the last seal dives, Pek pulls back on the rope to reel it in, but it catches and pulls fast. The harpoon must be caught in a cleft beneath the surface.

Watching him, I think through the process he will follow next—paddle closer, flick a wave along the rope to loosen the spike.

But Pek is impatient. He knows this is his last chance for a kill today. He doesn't paddle closer. Instead, he tries to loosen his harpoon by pulling sharply on the rope.

In an instant, his kayak flips.

One moment he is there, the next he is gone.

Pek has grown up paddling on the sea. This is what I tell myself as I watch and wait. This is Pek, who learned to paddle when he was still a child. Pek, who taught Roon how to right an inverted kayak.

"Roll," I whisper to myself. "Come on, Pek, roll."

A moment later I strip off my parka and untie the belt that holds me in place. With my knife in my hand I dive into the sea.

Under the surface, Pek's hair fans out around his head, floating up and over his face so I cannot see his features. It doesn't matter. I only have to see the way his hands claw at the belt holding him in, trying to loosen it so he can escape. Immediately I know why he hasn't rolled—while on the hunt, he knotted the kayak belt to his rope and wound it around his waist, a risky trick to prevent a stuck seal from getting away, taking his harpoon and rope with him. But Pek's harpoon isn't stuck in a seal—it's stuck in a crevice, the taut rope anchoring his flipped kayak to the rocks. Rings of rope swirl in tangled spirals around him.

His hands grasp at the water between us. He's running out of time.

Above water the knife in my hand could cut three of these cords in one stroke. Underwater, each cord bloated and slick, it takes two strokes to break just one.

Time changes, each passing moment slowing and widening, like a ripple of the one before. I cut through one . . . then two . . . then three strands. Curls of rope float open and outward. A fourth strand . . . a fifth. Finally, Pek slides from the kayak, swimming through the loops as they unravel around him.

We break the surface at the same time, and I notice how gray his skin is—almost white. His eyes stand out against this icy background like two round stones, the whites having turned a dull, bluish gray. Before I can ask if he's all right, he turns and grabs the hull of his boat, flipping it upright. Within moments, both of us are out of the water and back on our kayaks.

Still, we're in danger—the water is frigid. Wet clothes leech heat from my skin. My ears and nose burn with cold. My heart pounds.

"We need to go back," I call to him.

"Not a chance," he answers.

"That wasn't a question." Resilience is one thing; recklessness is another. "What would you hunt with? You have no harpoon. You have no rope. And you will have no brother alongside you."

"I'll dive back in and get the rope—"

"Not right now you won't. You've lost too much body heat. You need to get warm. We both do."

Pek's soaked hair drips into his lap as he sits, slumped

forward, on top of his kayak. He doesn't bother to slide back under the deck. It would be pointless. The boat is drenched inside and would not warm him.

"Pek," I say, but he doesn't lift his head. I have never seen my brother more defeated. I pull his paddle from the spot where it bobs on the surface between us. When he won't take it from me, I slide it across his lap. "You'll lose your strength if you sit out here. Come in and get warm. Then we'll try again."

I turn and start to paddle in without him. "You need to stay strong if you're going to win her," I call over my shoulder.

I don't need to glance back. I don't need to tune my ears to the sound of his paddle breaking the surface behind me. I know he will follow me in. Whether by faith or foolishness, Pek will follow Seeri wherever she leads.

Once we're on shore, Pek insists on helping bring in the fresh kill, though shuddering waves of cold rack his body.

I watch him, stubbornly struggling to grip the carcass with hands streaked red with blood and cold, and I remember his words—*These girls are going to change our lives.*

Those words have proven true a thousand times over in just two days.

I can't help but worry what changes are still to come.

EIGHT

On the third morning after your departure, Pek and I are up while it's still dark, standing on the beach as the sun gradually fills in shadows and reveals the edges of things. Together, we're loading one of the long, two-man fishing kayaks for Pek's trip to visit your clan. In three days we've collected seven seal pelts, and some of the meat of those kills has been butchered and wrapped as a gift to your clan, as well. Pek and I pack everything into the hull, filling the space where a second paddler would sit.

All this preparation has been overseen by our father. Though this visit may appear to be the work of one lovesick boy, it is actually part of our father's larger plan to befriend the Olen. A betrothal between Pek and Seeri would help create a bond between our clans, enabling us to move south.

"Here, put this with the sealskins, away from the meat," I say, handing Pek the pelt of the saber-toothed cat you killed, tightly wrapped to stay dry. Since you left, Pek has watched me work a special tanning solution mixed by Urar into this hide every night, and stretch and pull it every morning—even early on this morning—so it would be ready in time. I explained to Urar that I feared the Spirit of the cat had not climbed to the Land Above the Sky, but remained among the living as a ghost. Urar then combined ingredients that would give the hide strength while setting the Spirit of the cat free.

The results were worth the effort; the pelt is more soft and supple than any other pelt I've ever tanned. I can only hope the Spirit is gone now that the hide is done.

As Pek takes the pelt from my hand, he hesitates. "Hey, don't worry about her, all right?"

Why would he say this, I wonder? Do I *appear* to be worried about you?

"You don't need an ill-tempered girl like Mya, Kol. You're ill-tempered enough on your own."

"Thanks," I say, pushing the pelt into his hands. "Just take care of this until you get it to her. It's not what you think. I'm not trying to impress her or earn her affections. I just think she deserves this."

"Of course," Pek says. "But while I'm gone, you should take Kesh and Roon and visit the clan camping on the western shore. Maybe among the girls there, you'll find someone sensible enough to appreciate a gift of honey."

Why did I tell him that story? Was it to soothe his own feelings of rejection and failure? Whatever my reason, I regret it now. That should have stayed private between you and me.

"Just try to stay above water, all right? I'd like the pelt to be dry when it reaches her."

"Nothing to worry about there." If I meant that last comment as a bit of a dig to Pek's ego, it has no effect. He smiles broadly. He's feeling confident, maybe even a bit cocky, this morning. "That pelt will enjoy a comfortable tour down the coast. It will be clean and pristine when I lay it in Mya's unappreciative hands myself."

And that's it—the last I will speak of you to Pek or anyone else, I think. At least I hope it is the last.

My mother and father come down to the water with more gifts to be loaded into the boat, a few more than I might have expected, but the number and quality of gifts are clearly intended to improve Pek's chances of receiving Chev's welcome. My father puts in several tools to give to Chev—three flint points he flaked himself from a single core just yesterday, another core flaked along one edge to make a fine, fist-sized scraper, and two ivory shafts carved from a tusk of the mammoth your family helped us bring down. My father's brother, Reeth, our clan's best carver, has worked on these shafts since you left our camp. My mother hands in three large cooking bowls of woven slough sedge.

"Enough," I say. "If you overload the kayak, he won't be able to maneuver it. Do you want all your gifts in the sea?"

"Don't speak of that. Don't wish bad luck on your brother," my mother says.

Pek climbs into the kayak and ties the sash at his waist. I wade in, coming close enough to speak into his ear. "The Divine has always shown you favor," I say, as I grab hold of the kayak's tail. "She will keep you safe." Before Pek can give me a reply, I push him out into deep water.

With Pek gone, life in the clan becomes an exercise in waiting. Roon paddles out into the bay at least twice, out to a spot where he can see people fishing on the beach of the western shore. He comes home saying he thinks he glimpsed a few girls, but a glimpse is all he gets for now. Since he is really just a child, my parents forbid him from making any formal introductions to the clan. That is my father's role, and while Pek is gone, he refuses. Perhaps he is hoping Pek will return with good news before he has to make that effort. Roon whines and begs him to go, but Father argues that he would not want his sons marrying into different clans, which I can only agree with—it might mean never seeing one of them again.

The chance is small, of course—a bride generally joins her husband's clan—unless she is the oldest child of the High Elder. Then she would be presumed to be the next

High Elder herself, and her husband would go to her and her family.

As long as Pek is pursuing Seeri—as long as the Manu are pursuing an alliance with the Olen clan—Roon will have to wait. My father will not take the chance that one of his sons might meet the daughter of another High Elder while he still has hope of moving our clan south.

I head to the meadow every morning to search for honeybees, but I have little patience to lie still and listen for the sounds of their wings. Lying in the grass, my mind always turns to you and your clan and my brother Pek, and I end up on my feet, pacing. On the seventh day without news from Pek, I reach the meadow and find I don't need to hunt for bees anymore; they are everywhere. They crawl on every flower. Before the sun is high in the sky, I have located the first hive.

That afternoon, I return to camp and find my mother standing on the shore, watching the water. Her eyes are rimmed in red and she chews on the inside of her cheek. "I'm worried, too," I say. "In the morning, I'll set off to find him."

"You can't go on foot," my mother says.

I squat on the ground outside the door to the kitchen, prepping my pack for the journey by the dim glow that comes just before sunrise, though at this time of year, as the days grow longer and warmer, the night sky never goes completely black. Instead it darkens to a deep blue—as blue as the sea that reaches up to meet it at the horizon.

I went in early last night, hoping to store up on sound sleep, but my night was punctuated by bad dreams. I saw the Spirit cat, running hard toward me, its bloodstained claws tearing the grass, leaving a bright red trail. It flew at me, its curved teeth coming so close I felt the cat's breath, as hot as flame, against my throat. Other times my dreams were visited by Pek, his body inverted, his hands clutching wildly but unable to reach me, his face hidden by his floating hair.

Morning couldn't come soon enough.

"I'm not taking that kayak, Mother." My personal boat is too small and volatile for the open sea, and our clan has only one other large kayak. They'll need it to fish while I'm gone.

"It won't be an easy trip overland."

We both jump at the sound of my father's voice. Neither of us had heard him approach—we'd thought we were completely alone. My mother's head whips around at his words.

"What are you doing sneaking up like that?"

"But it won't be as difficult as it might have been before we learned where the Olen clan camp," my father says, without acknowledging my mother's question. He hasn't come as close as I'd thought—he stands just a few paces beyond the door of our hut—but even speaking low, his voice carries. At this hour, the air of the meeting place is still and silent. "We know it's a day's walk from here—"

"A day from first light to last," my mother interjects, "which in summer is a very long day. He will tire—"

"The sky is clear," my father continues. "You shouldn't encounter any storms." He hesitates, knowing that he will anger his wife if he lets me reject the kayak, but also knowing how much the clan may depend on that kayak for food with both Pek and me gone. Since the kill we had with your family, we've seen no sign of the rest of the mammoth herd.

"Let him go, and let him leave us the kayak. The Divine will watch over him as she makes her slow trek across the summer sky, helping him arrive before last light. When he gets to Chev's clan, he can return with Pek in the kayak he left in."

There is an extended silence, and I know that my mother and father are thinking of Pek and hoping that I find him well when I arrive in your camp. I never told them what happened on that first seal hunt. It doesn't matter. They both know how dangerous the sea can be.

We all know.

When I leave, loaded down with weapons to the same extent that Pek was loaded down with gifts, my brothers and my parents each give me a kiss on the cheek. We did not do this with Pek, and I know that we all wish we had.

In my pack I carry provisions for several days, since I know the general direction and the approximate distance, but there's no way to be certain I won't become lost. If I don't find your camp within two days, I'll have no choice but to turn around and come back.

I leave with an assortment of dried foods—berries and roots and some dried meat, all chosen for their lightness. Among the dried rations, I also carry my pouch of honey. A small amount will give me the strength to keep going when I have eaten all my allotted food for the day. I also carry a healing salve of oils and medicinal plants mixed by Urar and stored in a bull kelp bulb. If I become injured, the oils will soothe the pain and the herbs will return strength to the wound.

Besides my fire starter, I carry a bit of dry kindling in case I walk into bad weather and everything gets soaked. Still, there are no dark clouds, and if I'm fortunate enough to cover the distance and find your camp's fires by nightfall, I won't need to make one of my own. This is the prayer I chant to the Divine, creating a rhythm for my steps as I start on my journey.

I carry my spear in my hand, but slung by a strap across my back I carry another, just in case the first gets lost or broken. I also packed a trio of darts I carved from a shin-bone of the mammoth killed on the hunt with your family. I began working the bone when Pek left, and I packed them in hopes the Spirit of that mammoth might protect me. To throw the darts, I brought my atlatl. Lastly, I carry a light-weight flint ax with a wolf-bone handle that I've learned to throw with fairly good accuracy. Only Pek throws better, something he never tired of showing off. I think of all the times I wished he would stop, and how happy I'll be the next time he shows up one of my throws.

In my belt I carry my favorite knife, the same one that cut the ropes that held Pek underwater. This knife knows my secrets, and just having it at my waist makes me feel less alone.

As the sun rises slowly and reluctantly into the sky, I hike through rolling waves of purple and white flowers that cover huge swaths of the meadow. By the time I climb into the eastern mountains, following the pass that the bison took until they ceased to return, thirst burns in my throat. Still, even in the promising cool shadows of the rocky slopes, I won't let myself take a drink. I force myself to wait until I hear the music of running water before I slide my waterskin from my shoulder. Perhaps I'm being overly cautious—I feel fairly certain that I'll always find water in the hills—but this route is new to me. I've never traveled to the other side of these mountains, and though I've heard stories, I don't know what conditions I will find.

I follow the alpine trail, widened and worn under the

hooves of so many bison, as it winds to my right, turning south, hugging the base of a steep slope of sharply angled rock. High peaks soar overhead, their ice-covered summits casting a deep blue shade across the ground.

Water trickles along gaps in the rock. In the few places touched by sunlight, scrubby shrubs spring from crevices. The highest peaks are still to the south, and wind from the north gusts behind me.

Ahead of me are rows of ridges still to climb.

Eventually, the path widens, and I find myself standing on a high ledge. The valley below is broader than those I've passed through so far. A frozen river—a finger of the Great Ice—fills the eastern end of the valley, silvery blue in the sunlight. West of the ice lies a broad, meltwater lake, hemmed in by tall grass. As I descend, the north wind swoops over the frozen summit behind me, pushing hard against my back and prompting me to cover my head with my hood. But as I drop down farther between the ridge walls, the wind calms. Grasses grow across the gravelly slope, joined by scattered shrubs at the base of the hill.

As long as I travel along the valley floor, far below the high walls to the north and south, the air is calm and warm. But once I reach the southern slope and the trail rises toward the next rocky peak, the wind picks up. Shrubs thin to grasses and then yield to barren gravel again as I climb.

My ears sting with cold. Looking back toward the north from the crest, gusts of wind stir up swirls of sand and dust at my feet.

From here, the trail turns sharply downhill. A lower, grass-covered ridge blocks my view to the south until the trail bends right and heads lower still, down through a wide gap between squat, rolling hills.

These are the foothills of the southern slopes. The eastern mountains are finally at my back.

I'm amazed by the change in the landscape, as my eyes sweep over slopes protected from the harsh north winds. My father has told me the story of his own trip south many times, but until now, that's all it was—just a story.

My father has told me how the broad shoulders of the eastern mountains hold back the north wind. He has described how the high peaks shelter the land south of the mountains from the harsh cold carried down from the Great Ice. Still, it never felt real to me until now—now that I stand here at the foot of the southernmost slopes and see the green land that rolls out in front of me. Protected from the north wind's punishing cold, exposed to the sun's warmth, the land that opens south of the mountains is remarkably different from the land to their north. All around me, shrubs and thickets blanket the ground. As I descend lower into the valley, trees spring up, growing as high as my shoulder, their trunks as wide as my waist. The sun heats my face with a strength I've never felt before.

The farther I walk, the taller the trees around me grow, some rising high above my head. The trail narrows abruptly, cool shade replaces the heat of the sun, and it becomes harder to stay on the path. I notice scents I've never smelled before—a surprising mix of growth and decay. Brush encroaches on the path from both sides, and I'm forced to pull my ax from my pack in order to clear a way through. As I go, I catch the sound of waves crashing against the base of a cliff. I know the ground must fall off to the sea to my right, though I cannot see the ledge through the dense trees.

I try to relax, try to remind myself of everything that is going well. The sound tells me I'm not far from shore. Though the tall trees block out the sun, I can determine its place in the sky based on the shadows cast on the ground.

Long fingers of shade stretch toward the east. It's late in the day. The sun is dipping toward the sea.

Hunger gnaws at me, so I allow myself to pause long enough to rest and to have something to eat. I sit in a clump of soft, thick moss that seems to thrive in the cool shade, covering the ground under the tallest of trees. I've never been surrounded by trees so tall they could block the sun, and the strangeness of this place makes me uneasy. I can't sit long before I'm on my way again.

I don't travel far before the trail widens and the trees thin. The whispered roar of rushing water announces that

I'm approaching another waterway.

When I reach it, I find that it is broad but shallow. Still, the current is swift and I don't know the riverbed at all—I know better than to try to cross it here. I follow the bank west, hoping to come to the mouth where it empties into the sea. But the sound of the waves has faded; the coastline must have changed.

After following the twists of the stream for a while, the ground becomes damp and marshy, and the forest fades to brush. The sun reaches the top of my head. I stop and squat down a moment to rest and listen.

That's when I hear it for the first time.

The grass moves as seemingly every living thing around me scatters—rabbits and squirrels race by and birds take flight. Ducking lower, I pick up the murmured rustle of a breeze moving through the brush. But unlike the breeze, it is constant and measured. Without turning around to look, I know I am being stalked.

Still sitting on my heels, I open my pack, draw out a dart tipped with an obsidian point, and load it into the atlatl. I can launch a dart, unlike my spear, without having to stand to my full height. I sink down as low to the wet ground as possible, crouching behind shoots of tall grass. My eyes scan the riverbank. Something moves in the corner of my vision, and I pivot my head.

That's when I see him. A cat nearly identical to the one you shot on the mammoth hunt. My heart pounds in my temples at the memory of that cat's claws, digging at the ground as it pursued me. I whisper a prayer and cock my arm back at the elbow. Rising up on one knee to gain a clearer view, I let the dart fly.

It flies true and finds its target, plunging into the cat's shoulder. But this is one dart, and he is a large cat. I'd hoped the dart would slow him, but instead he lets out a horrifying sound—part growl, part groan—and leaps in my direction.

I know I don't have time to load a second dart. I spring to my feet, sling my pack onto my back, and crash into the river. The water chills my feet and legs right through the fur and hides of my pants and boots, but I cannot slow my pace. Pressing my weight into each step to hold myself against the fierce force of the current, I stride, stride, stride. Each new step threatens to throw me off balance and pull me under, yet each new step puts more distance between me and the cat. Finally—drenched, coated up to my knees in muck, every bone in my body rattling with cold—I reach the far bank. Exhausted from the effort, I drag myself up, clawing at the sand and gravel bank and crawling on my belly until I reach the tall grass and take cover.

My spear still tight in my fist, I allow myself to lift my head. Just ten paces downstream I spot him, immune to the swift current, moving above the water. He walks on a broken tree limb, wedged between jutting rocks on one side and red clay on the other, forming a crude bridge.

In my panic, I'd failed to notice it. But the cat did not.

Now, just one leap away, the cat is coming for me.

NINE

I am out of options. He will be on me before I can make the shot with my spear. In hopes of reaching thicker cover and disappearing from sight, I turn and race toward a line of scrubby brush and stunted trees that rises from the grass just twenty paces away. My heart pounds in my chest like a drum—like the rapid drumbeat used by Urar to denote the heartbeat of the Divine.

Let this be my prayer. . . . Let my pounding, racing heartbeat be my prayer.

I hear him, his feet trampling the same grass as mine, just a moment behind. I watch my own shadow running at my feet, until it is overcome, swallowed up by a larger shadow. Something heavy falls against my back and knocks me to the ground.

I fall . . . roll . . . land on my back in time to see the eyes of the cat as he prepares to pounce. He coils back, thick bands of muscle in his legs twitching with power.

My spear slides in my sweat-drenched hand.

Just as he springs, I pull my spear in front of my chest. As the cat lunges—mouth open, curved teeth aimed at my throat—the spear plunges into his belly. Before the whole of his weight can pin me down, I roll to the side and he falls, bleeding, beside me.

I scramble to my feet and grab the knife from my belt. Remembering the chilling look in the eye of the mammoth I'd killed last year, I lean over and slit the cat's throat with the blade to bring him a quick death.

A horrid sound—a gurgle of fear and loss—rises from the cat's open mouth. The sound echoes in my ears and I wonder if I, too, let out a cry. I can't be sure. I drop to the ground, the blood-covered blade in my blood-covered hand.

As my own fear drains away, pain takes its place. My back throbs in stinging waves as each beat of my heart echoes in the gashes torn open by the cat's claws.

Fighting to sit up, I shrug off my parka and see that the back is shredded and bloody. I strip out of my wet pants and boots, and I wade back into the creek, staying close to the bank, and ease my wounds into the water. The chill quickly numbs the pain but also brings a rapid ache to my limbs. I can't stay in the cold water long, so I climb out again, crawling up over silt and sand.

I want to lie down and rest, let my clothes dry, maybe eat something—but I know I have to keep moving. That cat may not be alone. Scavengers, even other predators, are likely nearby. Too weak to get to my feet, I drag my pack and my clothes to the cover of the tree line. I allow myself the time it takes to change into dry pants and boots and do the best I can to apply salve to my wounds. I reach my hand around to my back and try to rub the grease across my cuts, but blood washes it from my fingers and my hand comes away wet and sticky. Still, I have other cuts and scrapes on my arms and chin from my fall, and as I work the salve in, these calm and cool and some of the pain eases. Finally, I pour a few drops of honey onto my tongue before I force myself onto my feet.

I decide against pulling on a clean parka. The cuts across my back still throb with pain, and the thought of a hide pressing against them sends a wave of nausea through me. Instead I stay stripped to the waist, my tattered parka tied above my pants. I sling my pack and the extra spear over my arm to leave the wounds on my back exposed to the warm, dry air.

Standing in the murky shade, I notice for the first time how long the shadows have grown since I first became aware of the cat on the other side of the water. The sun is already low in the sky, its rays fading to pale light.

No wonder I'm hungry. At home, my clan has finished

eating the evening meal by now. Seal, most likely. Seal served with arrow grass and nettle gathered in the meadow. Right about now Roon is collecting empty mats and Kesh is playing his flute.

I let my eyes fall closed for just a moment, searching my memory for the sound of that flute. A songbird in the tree above me sends out a tune, startling me out of my reverie.

I climb up out of the valley using the blood-soaked spear as a walking stick. The terrain on this side of the river has turned rocky. The ground rises to a broad ridge, and at the crest I overlook a long stretch of rolling land, dotted with clumps of tall trees of all colors—varieties of trees I've never seen before. Some have branches that hang down like the fronds of ferns, glowing pale green in the sharply angled light of evening. Others have leaves shaped like open hands.

My eyes sweep over the sprawling view, taking in tree-covered low hills to the east, and to the west, the sea. Near the sea, from a clearing surrounded by trees tall and thick enough that a canoe could be dug out of a single trunk, a wisp of blue smoke rises into the air, before being scattered by the breeze.

I have reached your camp.

I trudge back to the spot where I'd left the dead cat at the side of the river. I realize I can't leave the carcass here; it's too close to your camp to risk attracting other predators.

Instead, I search the area for fallen limbs, long and light enough to fashion into a makeshift travois.

After collecting two long poles and a shorter one, I set to lashing them together with the cordage I carry in my pack. Lifting the cat is impossible, so I slide the limbs under him and secure him to the poles. The cat's blood, thick and slippery, soaks my hands, and I'm forced to return to the river to wash them before I can get on my way.

Before leaving the woods, I drape my tattered parka over my shoulders, tying the sleeves around my neck so I can strap the front ends of the travois poles around my waist. In this fashion—my pack over one shoulder, the cat dragging behind me, my back exposed to the air under the shredded remnants of my coat—I start downhill, my eyes locked on the rising smoke, my mind locked on the warm hearth at its source.

About halfway down the slope the clearing ends and the woods begin again, but at the edge of the trees I discover a worn trail. It's not wide, but wide enough for me to drag the cat behind me. The closer I come to the bottom of the hill the denser the forest becomes, and everywhere I look I spot another unfamiliar plant—crawling vines, broad-leafed ferns, thornbushes covered in tiny white blooms that smell as sweet as honey. The closeness of the trees creates a pocket of silence—the wind dies and a shiver of dread creeps along my spine. I keep my eyes open, but I see nothing but a few squirrels chasing each other from tree to tree. I listen, but I hear nothing but a distant gurgling—somewhere ahead there's a brook.

Then, not loud but clear, a sound comes from behind me—the snap of a twig. I stop and spin as well as I can in my makeshift harness, but I see no one. Still, nothing but a foot on the ground could've made that sound. My eyes search for any movement, but there's nothing, just the ripple of sunlight on the path, as the wind finally stirs the leaves and changes the shapes of the shadows.

Whoever is back there doesn't want to be seen.

My hand on the blade in my belt, I turn and take a few more steps forward. Nothing responds. I return to the pace I'd set before, when the unmistakable sound of feet running toward me comes from behind. I turn, the blade in my hand, when my eyes fall on a familiar form. He is still at least fifty paces away, but I would recognize him from twice the distance.

He lets out a shout, and it's obvious he recognizes me, too. "Kol!"

Pek hurries down the path until he comes close enough to get a clear view of what I drag behind me. He slows. His eyes rake over the hastily made sled, the dead cat, and my tattered parka. "Kol," he repeats, but instead of a shout, this time my name is more like a murmured prayer.

Pek approaches me with soft steps, as if pieces of me are

spread out on the ground and stepping on one might break me. He eases himself around the beams of the travois, pushing into the brush that edges the path, his eyes fixed on the cat. When at last he comes up beside me, he wraps both arms around my shoulders and pulls me into an awkward embrace, careful not to touch my back. "Wait until Chev sees what you've done. This cat . . . we've all been hunting it. You can't imagine how this cat has threatened this clan."

"Has it?" I start, but Pek dashes ahead of me.

"You wait," he says, "and I'll bring others to pull the load the rest of the way."

I stand still for a few moments after he disappears, but the woods are too lonely and strange now that I've seen my brother. There's no reason for me not to pull the cat the rest of the way. I've brought it this far, and seeing Pek, alive and well, has taken weight from the load.

About a hundred paces farther down the path, light stirs in the underbrush to my right—a pattern of gold dancing across a sea of green. Something is moving, bending the branches that filter the sun. I stand staring, my attention held captive by the mystery, when all at once from out of the dense growth that borders the path an elk leaps, landing directly in front of me. He stands still for just a moment— nostrils flaring, hide quivering with tension—before he leaps as high as my shoulder and disappears into the trees to my left.

His place on the path is empty only a moment before it is filled by the hunter pursuing him—a girl with a spear raised in her outstretched arm, a girl who moves with a grace that rivals the elk's.

You.

You see me, and your arm drops to your side. You stumble back as if I've struck you, though I don't dare move. Confusion swims in your wide eyes—a moment ago your thoughts were focused on nothing but the elk. Now, finding me standing here completely unexpected, you seem to have forgotten everything else.

Countless questions tangle my thoughts—*Did Pek deliver the pelt of the cat you killed? Were you pleased with the quality of the hide? Are you haunted, as I am, by the Spirit of that cat? Have you seen it stalking you in your dreams?*

I want to tell you what happened with this cat—*It didn't give chase, like the one you killed, but instead stalked me from under the cover of tall grass. I heard it just in time to react, but not in time to escape its attack without harm.*

I thought of you when I feared the cat might kill me. I wondered if my body would be found, and if you would learn of how I'd died.

When the silence between us stretches to an unbearable tension, I'm forced to speak. "I came for Pek," I say.

"Yes."

And that's all. We stand still, looking at each other in much the same way we did at that first meeting in the meadow. Just as bitterness joined that circle, it seemingly has followed us here.

A large shadow passes between us—a buzzard is circling. Another joins it. "They were quick to find your kill," you say.

At last you acknowledge it. I was beginning to wonder how long you could ignore the dead cat strapped to a sled behind me.

Your gaze fixes on a spot just below my left eye. Taking one slow step toward me, you lift your hand to touch my cheek. "You have blood on your face," you say. Your voice is soft, as soft as light falling on leaves. I think you touch my face, but if you do your touch is just as soft, so soft I can't be sure.

"The cat's blood, I think. Not mine. He got me across the back, mostly."

You move another half step closer and peer around my side, gently lifting away the shredded pieces of my parka. You stifle a gasp. "You should thank the Divine you're alive. Your back . . . ," you say, but you don't finish. "I'll fetch the butchers."

"Thank you, but Pek already went. . . ." My voice trails off; you aren't listening.

Before I can get the words out you turn and run, disappearing into the shade that cloaks the path.

TEN

I'm brought to your camp, but I don't see you again. Instead, I see no one but Pek, Chev, and your clan's healers—Ela and her twin brother, Yano. They are young for healers—maybe just a few years older than I am. Both wear their hair pulled into a single long braid; both are dressed in plain tunics of black bearskin.

"You will stay in my sisters' hut," Chev says. "It is large, close to the healers, and close to me. You have done a great thing for this clan and I want to be sure you are comfortable while you heal." Despite the gnawing ache in my back, something in my chest stirs. My senses sharpen as I enter the place where you sleep each night, the place where you dream.

The hut is cool and well lit—a flap has been opened in the side wall facing west, letting in a shaft of sunlight. I'm struck by the rich array of pelts—not just forming the beds but also elaborate rugs and banners—furs and skins cut and sewn into ornate patterns, spread across the floor and hung from the walls. One design suggests the stars in the sky, another the sea.

The healers help me undress and lie facedown on one of the beds, arranged on the floor in just the right spot so the light will fall directly onto my back. A rich, musky scent floats in the air; some of these pelts are new. Ela and Yano stand on each side of me, helping me ease my aching body onto the bed. My hands reach out to brace my weight and I notice a blanket of sealskin. Despite my pain, inwardly I smile, knowing that you and your sister accepted Pek's gifts.

The healers begin their work of examining the gashes in my back. They clean each one with the edge of a sharp blade, picking out small flecks of dirt and debris. The process sends spikes of pain through me, but I force myself to stay alert. "Deep cuts," Ela says, either to Yano or herself— I can't be sure. She calls for a certain type of leaf, but the name of the plant is unknown to me.

The process drags on, each individual cut painstakingly opened, painstakingly cleaned. Sweat drips from my face and neck and pools in the small of my back. I struggle to stay silent and still, but I can't suppress every flinch or hold in every gasp. Now and then, pressure is applied to my back with a soft pelt that's been soaked in cold water, opening a brief window of relief. Chants are offered by Ela and Yano, sometimes in turns, sometimes in unison.

Pain thrums a drumbeat in my temples, mixing with a roar in my ears, drowning out voices. I know that Chev is speaking, but his words fade to a hiss and I cannot distinguish what he says. All I catch is the tone of his voice, but even that is enough to startle me. His voice is gentle and warm, a tone reserved for a beloved child, or, more likely, a spouse. Could he be speaking to Ela? Could it be that she is Chev's wife?

I lose track of time. The light in the room grows dim as the healers methodically work at their task, until finally, I feel the even pressure of fingers smoothing cool strips of leaves across my skin. And then, at last, there is no pressure at all. The task is done.

Through the throbbing, through the roar, through the hiss and buzz that fill my ears, whispered words reach me. It's the voice of my brother Pek; I feel his breath on my cheek. "Chev has sent for our family," he says. "Rest well, knowing that our parents and brothers will be here soon."

With the music of these words pushing back the din of pain, I fall into a deep sleep.

When I wake, my back feels tight—scabs have formed beneath the protective layer of leaves. I open my eyes to see you—just you—sitting on the bed across from me.

"Look who's awake."

"Have I been sleeping long?"

"Not really. Maybe half the night has passed. The healers wanted to be called when you woke."

You stretch before you stand—your muscles are stiff. How long have you been sitting here? Have you been on watch the whole time I've slept? As you brush back the door, you call to me over your shoulder. "I'll be right back. I'm just going to let Chev know to bring Ela and Yano—"

"Wait. Before you go, I want to ask you . . . Is Ela Chev's wife?"

You stop and turn to face me. In the weak light thrown off by the sputtering flame of an oil lamp in the center of the floor, I think I see you smile. No—not smile . . . smirk.

"You're correct in guessing that one of the healers is Chev's mate, but Ela is not my brother's wife. Yano is Chev's spouse. He is the one my brother loves."

You pause a moment in the doorway, watching my face, smiling as bewilderment is replaced by clarity.

It makes sense now. Of course, I know that love is sometimes like that—some men love men, some women love women. But I hadn't put it together. Now I understand why I always perceived that Chev was a man with a mate, yet no one had mentioned his wife.

"I'll be right back," you say again. "I'll bring your brother, too."

And then you push back the door, and I feel a door in my

chest pushed back at the same time. You step out, leaving darkness and quiet and emptiness behind you.

A void opens up in this room—opens up in my chest—from the lack of you.

A short time later, Ela and Yano stand over me. The large leaves that had been draped across my skin are removed, but I feel nothing more than a slight pull when one occasionally tugs at a scab.

"Very nice," says Yano, admiring his own work with a smile and a nod. "You should sit up and drink now. And take some honey. Honey will give you strength."

Chev hands me a heavy skin full of water. "Mya, run to the kitchen for honey," he says.

As much as I enjoy the thought of you being sent to the kitchen to bring back the honey that you claimed was so plentiful here in the south—the honey that is apparently so superior to mine—I stop you before you can rise to your feet.

"I have some," I say. Pek rummages around in my pack until the pouch—the very same pouch I'd tried to give you—is found.

My own honey never tasted as good as it does at this moment. I gulp down a greedy portion of the water Chev offers and stretch out again. I'm just wondering where you and Seeri are staying while my brother and I occupy your hut when I drift off to sleep.

The following day I sleep until the sun is glowing gold against the wall that faces west, waking well after the midday meal.

Pek and Chev bring me a mat full of elk and caribou meat and sit with me to keep me occupied. "If you would like, your brother can sleep in here."

If I would like? "Where have you been sleeping, Pek?"

Chev answers before Pek has the chance. "We made room for him in the storage hut. We moved some firewood. But he can join you in here, if you wish."

The storage hut. I had wondered how well Pek had been received. If he's sleeping next to the supplies, I think I can guess the answer.

The healers stop in briefly to check my progress. They both seem pleased, but neither will relent when I request that I be allowed out of bed. "Not until the evening meal," Yano says. He tries to remain stern, but at the door he looks back and gives me a brief, sympathetic smile. "It won't be long," he adds, before ducking out behind his sister.

I learn that boats left at first light, heading for my camp. They are to bring back my parents and my brothers, "to help celebrate our triumph over the cat," Chev says. I had suspected my family had been sent for because my injuries were so grave, in case I had gotten worse instead of better. I have seen injured hunters fail quickly. I'm sure Chev has, too. But I don't say anything about that. Instead, I simply smile. "A celebration will be wonderful, but I'm not sure what you mean by 'our triumph over the cat.'"

Your brother sits forward. "This cat, it was a rebel," he says. I study his face. Chev is older than you and Seeri by maybe as many as six or seven years. Like the other Olen men, his hair is always pulled back tight in a braid. This differs from the style of the men in my clan—we generally cut our hair with sharp blades to keep it short and out of the way. Something about this style gives Chev a stern look, his features exposed and his eyes intense, as if he is constantly forming a plan. There is a sadness, too, that shows in the set of his mouth and the lines at the edges of his lips.

"This cat no longer had a taste for bison or elk." He raises his face and stares at the hides on the wall, but I know he is looking at something else—a memory. "It was not long after we returned from your camp. This cat killed a hunter who was stalking game. After that, this cat stalked all of us. No one could go outside of camp. I had to forbid it.

"But one did—a child. She tried to sneak off to the river in the valley beyond the hills. We found her that night. Her own mother could not recognize her face."

Chev goes silent as his eyes darken.

"That's the reason I stayed," says Pek. "I've been helping patrol the camp and hunt for the cat. I promised to stay until he was no longer a threat."

"The Spirit of this cat was a demon," Chev says. "We offered prayers and chants to the Divine, and now the demon has been slain." He gets to his feet and strides for the door. "My clanspeople are busy in the kitchen, preparing the evening meal for you and your family. This meal will allow us to express our thanks."

With that, Chev ducks quickly through the door and is gone.

"So he's happy?" I ask Pek, half joking. Chev is not a man who is open with his emotions.

"Maybe with you, but not with me."

Pek sits cross-legged on a pile of pelts that make up the bed across from me. His head is bowed, but he raises his face slowly and gives me a smile completely devoid of joy.

"Seeri?" I don't need to ask. Of course it's Seeri.

"He's quite serious about her betrothal to his friend. I believe that he sees me as unsuitable and unworthy."

"And you know this how?"

"His words, carried across the space between huts as he shouted at Seeri."

My brother—the one who was born with a spear in his hand, the one who could always out-throw me—seems beaten. The lowered head, the drooping shoulders—I've seen that only once before in him, on the first day we hunted seals so he could bring the pelts to your clan. Even that day, Pek had started out hopeful. It had taken defeat and a near drowning to weigh him down.

"I'd planned to win him over by killing the rogue cat, but you've solved that problem. I think there's little left that I could do to change his mind."

I lean forward and feel the scabs across my back tighten as I reach for Pek's shoulder. "Sorry for killing the cat before you could, but it really left me no choice—"

"I didn't mean—"

"I know," I say. "But don't give up. After all, aren't you the one who said there's still hope? She isn't married yet."

I turn and lie down again, my body suddenly heavy. I press my chest against the sealskin blanket, my wounds open to the air. My eyes close. I catch myself just as I drift into a dream and I shake myself awake, but Pek is already by the door.

"Sleep," he says. "Don't fight it."

"I've slept all day—"

"And you walked all of yesterday. And fought a cat. And dragged its body to camp. And now you're healing. So sleep."

I want to argue—my mind begins to form the words— but before my lips can give them shape I fade into a deep, dreamless sleep. I wake only when voices reach my ears, calling from shore.

I open my eyes. Light in the hut is fading, but judging by the sounds I hear, I woke just in time. The boats that were sent for my family must have finally returned.

I find myself alone for the first time, but the solitude of the hut has a texture all its own—rich and comforting. I climb to my feet and find a clean parka at the foot of the bed—one crafted from the pelt of a cat so soft it won't irritate my wounds.

I pick it up and hold it in the light, confused by the mystery of it. But then I notice the details—the way the light brown fur fades to pale tan at the edges, the swirled pattern in the grain of the hide in one corner, the slight blemish where a drop of blood dried into a permanent stain of red.

This was made from the pelt of the cat you killed, the one I tanned and sent to you.

ELEVEN

I follow the mix of voices to the beach, drawn along by the singsong tones of my mother's lilting laugh. Though I've rarely given any thought to the sound of my mother's laugh, at this moment, its familiarity quenches a thirst inside me I didn't even know was there.

I realize as I slow my steps that I haven't heard anyone laugh in so long. My mother could be laughing at anything—perhaps the boat rocked as they stepped out and someone was splashed—her laugh comes easily most of the time. Here in your camp, my injuries have been treated with such seriousness, and I'm grateful for it, but there's a warmth and affection in the music of my mother's voice that heals me from the inside out.

Yet as I approach and catch my first glimpse of them— not just my mother but my father and brothers, too—I know they are being told about my injuries for the first time. Chev is speaking to them, gesturing as he tells the story. His back is to me, his words carried away by the sea breeze, but I can read the tension in my father's shoulders, my mother's sudden silence. She reaches out for Pek and holds on to him as if she might fall if she let go.

Thankfully, Yano and Ela are there, too, and as Chev quiets, Ela steps up. My parents' eyes turn to her, and from my vantage point—close enough to see but far enough away that I haven't yet been noticed—I can tell that her words reassure them. My father steps forward. My mother nods.

I take a tentative step in their direction and my mother's attention shifts.

She spots me on the path, and when she speaks my name—just my name—it's as if an entire song has been sung.

She lets go of my brother and hurries to me. Her face glows red with windburn and her gait is uneven after a long trip on the sea. She falls against me and her arms encircle my back.

Over her shoulder my eyes are drawn to your face as you react to the pain you imagine I feel—your teeth dig deep into your bottom lip as she embraces me. But although her touch stings, it also brings relief to another kind of pain, and I won't pull away. Instead, I clench my jaw and lean into my mother's embrace. The pelt of the new parka presses against the cuts in my back, but the pain recedes to the edges of my mind as contentment crowds it out.

As we head back up the path together, I manage to get close enough to speak to you without others hearing. Standing so close, I notice a scent around you, the same scent I'd noticed in your hut—the warm fragrance of musk.

"Thank you for the parka," I say.

"Of course," you answer.

For the briefest of moments the world around me holds its breath—the breeze dies away; birds quiet their songs. The only sound is the crunch of gravel beneath our feet as we walk side by side.

But it doesn't last. It's only an illusion; one that fades as soon as you speak again. "I started it the day Pek gave me the pelt. I couldn't accept it—the cat was killed on your land. It belongs to your clan. I figured the parka was an efficient means of returning it to you."

Efficient?

"The pelt was meant as a *gift*—"

I stop myself mid-sentence. Hot, angry words rush to my lips but I bite them back. Why bother? What could I possibly say that might reach you? "Excuse me," I say instead, and hurry to catch up to my family.

We join the rest of your clan in a large meeting area at

the center of the circle of huts, strikingly similar to our meeting space at home, though there is one significant difference. Your clan has erected four large poles carved from the trunks of trees in the corners of the meeting place, and pulled tightly overhead is a roof of hides pieced together with cords of sinew. The sides are open to allow both the breeze and your clanspeople to easily pass in and out, but the covering overhead ensures that you will always be sheltered from sun or rain while gathered. At home, we simply huddle in the kitchen or eat our meals in our huts if the weather is foul. I remember a fleeting look that crossed your face when you first saw my clan gathered in the open air after the hunt. Now I suspect it was disappointment—or worse, disdain—at our lack of sophistication.

Just as there are differences in the space, there are also differences in custom. Unlike home, there is no music, no singing. A solitary drum calls people to the evening meal. Even conversation is muted. At home, some people in my clan—especially my mother's family, who tend to be big in size and big in voice—greet each other at the evening meal with an enthusiasm that suggests they haven't seen each other in days, when it's been only since morning, if that long. In contrast, the few bits of conversation I catch among your people are exchanged in hushed, polite voices—a comment on the hearty fragrance of cooking meat coming from the kitchen, a question about how a sprained ankle is healing.

At least the children are a bit noisy. I overhear a trio of boys chattering about the traps they set this morning. One boy brags that he has already caught a squirrel, and I smile, thinking of me and my brothers at that age. Pek was always the one bragging.

Once we are all collected under the roof, your brother Chev motions for us to be seated. Pelts have been scattered across the sandy soil, and I find myself sharing one with my mother and Roon. Kesh and my father sit beside us. Your clan is bigger than ours—maybe thirty to thirty-five people, counting babies and small children—where our clan is twenty-four in all. With so many people crowded together, I lose sight of you once we are seated, but I know you are somewhere at the opposite edge of the crowd where I'd noticed you standing with Seeri. Pek is not far from you, seated with strangers he must have befriended while he's been in your camp.

When everyone sits, I notice the towering lattice of firewood arranged in a large hearth between the edge of the canopy and the kitchen. At home such a large fire would be considered extravagant, even wasteful, an affront to the Spirits of the trees. But here, wood is much more plentiful, and the tree Spirits more generous.

Chev signals to the drummer, who resumes the slow, even beat that called us to the meal. From the kitchen, two figures emerge, each wearing a huge mask of carved wood—so huge they cover their bodies from head to waist. I've never seen a mask of wood before—Urar makes beautiful masks of bearskin and walrus hide painted with ocher—but these are so different, so fierce and intensely foreign, a shiver runs over my skin. The face depicted on each mask suggests a cat—a square nose dug out of the center, narrow eyes and sharp whiskers carved at opposing angles, slanting away from a wide mouth framed by long, curved teeth. Each of the masked figures carries a burning torch. As they circle the hearth, moving with exaggerated steps in time to the beat, they set their torches to the kindling at the base of the firewood.

"Spirit of the cat," the masked figures chant in unison, "climb this smoke to the Land Above the Sky." They chant in low, furtive whispers, but I recognize the voices of Ela and Yano. "Climb this smoke. . . . Climb this smoke. . . . Climb this smoke. . . ." They circle the hearth once as the flames catch and travel over the branches. The chanting stops, but the drumbeat quickens. They circle faster and faster, their steps becoming leaps, the flames climbing higher, billows of smoke rolling outward and under the roof. I pull in a deep breath of soot and a wave of nausea crashes over me. The beat of the drum grows louder, faster, louder still, my heart races and my head swims, until I slump against the bearskin on the ground. My eyes fall shut, but instead of darkness, the fire's glow presses against my eyelids, surrounding me in white light.

Then all at once, the drumming stops. My eyes open. Ela and Yano are gone, leaving only Chev beside the towering fire. I sit up groggily, as if waking from a dream.

"Friends," Chev says, raising his hands, "the Divine continues to make this a prosperous clan. We thank our visitors from the north, from the clan of the Manu, especially Kol, who with his skill and strength has slain the man-killing cat."

As these words echo in my head, my younger brothers, Kesh and Roon, pat me on the arms and make a scene of congratulating me. "Quit showing off," I say under my breath. "It's bad manners."

"Kol," Chev calls. "Come take your place at the head of the line."

I search the periphery of the crowd until I find my brother Pek. He looks back for a moment—I know he's seen me—but then he turns away.

All his life he's out-hunted me. Now when it really matters, I've come and shown him up.

As I try to shake off the feeling that I've let my brother down, a girl of about twelve comes up to me and takes me by the arm.

"Kol?" she says. "I'm Lees. Chev is my older brother. They wouldn't take me along when my siblings visited your clan, but I'm happy to meet you now."

Lees looks like a miniature version of Seeri—her face is

crowded with wide eyes and a broad smile. She rounds up my family—all except for Pek, who I see across the crowd has joined up with you and Seeri—and steers us into line ahead of everyone else.

After a short time under Lees's supervision we each have a mat containing bison meat, roasted water parsnips, and a small portion of the meat from the cat so that we may each take in a bit of its Spirit's strength. But making our way back to sit, we are stopped frequently by members of your clan who introduce themselves and wish me well. Everyone is friendly and polite, but I can't shake an eerie sense of disconnection that started when I first saw the masks—a disorienting sense of being outside myself, looking in. It's as if the Spirit of the cat still claws at me, as it makes its way to the Land Above the Sky. I cough, and the acrid taste of smoke fills my mouth.

At last, Lees leads us to a place to sit, right beside her brother Chev and her sisters—you and Seeri. Pek is beside Seeri, and although I attempt to take the place on the opposite side of him, Lees takes it herself and I find myself seated between your brother and my father.

Sitting beside Chev, I notice his demeanor is subtly changed. Maybe it's because we are in your camp. An aroma of sweetness wafts from his breath, and a skin lies on the ground beside him. Is he already drinking mead? A large knife made of a heavy point hafted to a bone handle rests to the right of the skin. Surveying the group seated around him, Chev lifts the knife and with it skewers a piece of bison and stuffs it into his mouth. He turns toward me and a hazy lack of focus clouds his eyes.

His cheeks flush red as he smiles at me.

"Let me introduce you, our visitors from the north, to one of my oldest friends, Morsk." He stands, and with the knife he points to a man of about his own age seated directly across our small circle from Seeri and Pek. "He is Seeri's betrothed."

My mother's eyes blink rapidly before her head spins toward Pek, who looks away. My father swallows hard and then coughs into his fist. Like the day we were all introduced in the meadow, a taut silence fills the space between us. And like that day, I am tempted to fill that silence with tradition.

I could get to my feet and move to Morsk's side. We exchange nods—the customary formal greeting. I could introduce my parents and my brothers Kesh and Roon. I could break the growing tension.

But is that best?

I have spent long stretches of time with my father, learning what the Divine expects of a leader, what qualities she will bless and honor. I know that I need to show patience in the face of anger. I know that harmony needs to come before my own pride.

Sometimes these qualities are easy to embody. But not today.

I hope that harmony is not what the Divine requires here, because I cannot bring myself to work for it. Not now. Looking at my parents' stunned expressions, I see that Chev has used the fact of Seeri's betrothal as a weapon. He has claimed control over this meeting between our two clans, but my father will not allow him to keep it.

"We were not aware that Seeri was betrothed," he says. If he's trying to conceal his shock at this news and his sense that Pek has been cheated or led on, he doesn't succeed. It's quite clear he is offended.

He turns in his seat and scans Seeri's face as well, though she has turned her attention to her food and seems to have no intention of ever looking up again. My father lets his eyes rest on her long enough that his glare comes across to all the rest of us as an accusation. "How long has this arrangement been in place?" he asks, his eyes never leaving the top of Seeri's head.

"For years," Chev says, stuffing another large piece of meat into his mouth with his fingers. "As a brother, I want the best sort of husband for my sisters, Seeri included."

"And what makes the best sort of husband?" my mother asks.

They are so bold. They are teetering on the edge of rudeness, but I can't blame them. Chev has set them up, and they are right to fight back.

"Well, in this case, I would say the best sort of husband is one who is familiar. Morsk has been my friend my whole life. We learned to fish sitting side by side in the same boat. I can trust him. There's no dark history between our families that has yet to be resolved."

I startle at this mention of history. Could Chev be using Seeri's betrothal to Morsk to provoke a discussion of the past? I turn my eyes to you, remembering what you said to me about the specter of distrust and resentment that will forever overshadow our two clans. Are you glad the past is being dragged out into the light?

It's impossible to tell. Your head is down. At least for now, you do not intend to join the conversation.

"Plus, Morsk is a skilled craftsman," says Lees, too innocent, perhaps, to understand the tone of the conversation she's joining. "He built this roof we're sitting under. He's excellent with wood. He can make a canoe out of the trunk of a single tree. He can build anything."

"So he can make things out of trees. So what?" says Roon. Pek's eyes leap to our youngest brother's face. Though he's the same age as Lees, Roon is not as naive. He gets the subtext of this discussion, and he intends to jump into the fray. "My brother Pek can hunt down a mammoth, skin it, butcher it, and make a boat from the pelt and bones.

Can your friend Morsk do that?"

Lees doesn't reply. Instead, she just stares at Roon as if she's just noticed him for the first time. But if she overlooked him before, she makes up for it now. In all the ways she resembles her sister Seeri, she looks at Roon in the same way Seeri looks at Pek—with a look of sudden recognition. It's as if she's always known him and is somehow surprised to find him here—right here, in front of her—right where she left him before time began. "I'm sorry, what was your name?" she asks. A miniature version of Seeri's smile blooms across her lips, and the trancelike expression I've seen on Pek falls over Roon's young face.

My eyes sweep from Roon to my mother, who sits beside him. Her lips press into a thin line, and her usually bright eyes are dim with hurt.

That's all I can stand. My mother's pained expression pushes me to speak.

"These are all strong traits to find in a man—familiarity, friendship, family ties, and as the children pointed out— talents and skills in craftsmanship are valuable, too. We are fortunate to have not just one man, but several like this in our midst."

"This is true," says Chev. "Several men seated here would make very worthy husbands."

These words of Chev's are ambiguous, of course. He

could mean Morsk and Pek, or he could mean only men of his own clan. But it is a bit of a concession, and my father seizes it.

"I agree," he says.

"Yes, several indeed," adds my mother.

I draw in a deep breath as the tension eases, if only a bit. Voices fall quiet as everyone eats.

But it doesn't last long. My second bite of bison is still in my mouth when you speak.

"What about women?" you ask. No one replies at first, and I wonder if maybe I imagined your voice. But then you continue. "We've talked about the traits that make a man a good choice for a mate. But I wonder what might the necessary female traits be?"

"Well," I say, without looking up. I shoot a quick glance at my brother Pek, hoping for help, but his eyes are averted.

Of course they are. Why should he help me? He probably blames me for all this—for coming here and killing the cat before he could.

Beside me, my father clears his throat. Could he possibly know about the friction between you and me?

I wedge my hands, palms down, under my legs, digging my fingers into the fur of the bearskin that covers the ground. The fur is coarse on the surface, but underneath, closer to the hide, it's soft. My mouth has gone dry, but I force myself to swallow before I speak again. "The traits that make a woman a good choice for a mate . . . That list could include many things: even-temperedness. Cooperation. Patience." I try to look at you—it would be rude to reply to your question while staring at my food—but I can't force my eyes to meet yours. Instead I study a pendant you wear, a carved white disk of bone or maybe ivory that lies against the base of your throat. It hangs on a simple cord strung with a few bright white beads. "Above all, a lack of a certain kind of arrogance that might cause her to assume that every offered word or gift—whether a simple pouch of honey or the pelt of a cat—is meant as a bribe."

I wonder if I've gone too far. My gaze finally flits up to meet yours. No discreetly dropped eyes—instead, you are watching me with a piercing stare. You are game for this exchange.

"That's truly a shame," you answer. Your eyes darken, but a fleeting twitch tugs at the corners of your mouth before you purse your lips, banishing any hint of a smile. "If those are the standards by which a woman is to be judged, then I will certainly never find a mate."

"I wouldn't say that. After all, every man is unique. Every man would have his own answer to your question."

"I can only hope to find that to be true," you say. The curl returns to the corners of your mouth—the most cryptic smile I've ever seen. Are you mocking me? Baiting me? My eyes drop back down to your necklace, lingering on the curved lines of your throat. My heart jumps around in my chest like a startled bird, its wings hammering against my rib cage.

Everyone continues eating, and I do the best I can to finish my food. Lees scrambles up from the ground and begins to collect empty mats. Roon and Kesh get to their feet to stretch, and Chev excuses himself to fetch another skin of mead. If his conversation during the meal was a bit inhospitable, he clearly intends to make up for it in the sharing of drink.

"I'd like to go down to the shore and take a look at the boats," says Roon.

My father weighs this request as he climbs to his feet, and I wonder if he thinks acknowledging their craftsmanship might give Morsk too much credit.

"Take Kesh with you," he says finally. "Even with that cat dead, we don't know this land. I don't want you wandering off alone."

As the meal ends and people get to their feet, several of your clan's elders greet me with the customary nod. They congratulate me and introduce themselves. Though I try to learn their names, my head buzzes like a hive. I return their nods and smile, hoping my distraction doesn't show.

Chev comes back from the kitchen, a bulging skin full of mead slung over his shoulder. You stand and announce you will bring cups from the kitchen for us to drink from.

Watching you stride away, I wonder what side you fall on in the matter of Pek and Seeri. Do you want to see them together and happy, or do you believe Seeri should follow through on her betrothal?

"I think you'll be impressed by this mead," Chev says, interrupting my thoughts of you. Had he seen me watch you walk away? "It's unlike any I've ever had in the north— it will fill you with the warmth of the Divine from the inside out. There is a berry here in the south that grows on a climbing vine—a bright red berry with a strong flavor. It makes all the difference."

You return with the cups. Like my mother's bison skull bowl, these cups are carved from the skulls of some smaller prey—small enough to fit perfectly in the palm of a hand, but large enough to hold a generous portion of drink. Your brother circulates, dispensing the mead, releasing the heady scent of honey. A cup is poured for my mother, my father, Pek, Morsk, and Seeri. Kesh pushes into the circle, a cup in his extended hand.

"Wait," I say, glancing around when I don't see Roon. "Where's your little brother?"

"Calm down. I didn't leave him alone. He went off with that girl. She followed us down to the beach with a water-skin of mead she snuck from the kitchen. Anyway, they seemed more interested in each other than in the boats, so I came back. They kept talking about going exploring."

Sometimes, I am jolted out of a sound sleep by the sensation that I am falling. It always happens the same—one moment I am on solid ground, and the next, everything beneath me disappears.

This is the feeling I have as I process what Kesh is saying.

He's left Roon and Lees alone in the murky twilight of a summer night, when the ghostly pale sky conceals the stars and the unbroken shadows make it impossible to judge direction. Roon—a boy whose favorite activity is to explore the coast alone. Home he would be safe, but here? And what do we know of Lees? By now she could be back in her hut, and Roon could be just realizing he's lost.

I glance from face to face. My father, my mother, Chev—everyone is distracted, chatting about the craftsmanship of the cups, the quality of the mead. Only you have a look of alarm on your face that matches the feeling in my gut.

"Let's go," you say.

You stride off, turning back only briefly to glare at me and Kesh and our empty hands. "Neither of you has a spear?"

"Who brings a spear to a meal—" Kesh starts.

"Who are *you* to speak to me like that? You—stupid enough to leave two children alone in the dark—"

"It's hardly dark—"

"Who knows what kind of predators are out there—"

"I left them on a *beach*. When was the last time you saw

a saber-toothed cat attack from the sea?"

"Do you think that cats are the only hunters out at night? Or that the only dangers are predators? They could climb the cliffs and fall from a ledge. They could take a boat out and get pulled away by the current—"

"All right, *all right*," Kesh says. "You talk like they're little babies. They're only a few years younger than I am—"

"See this?" You shove the left sleeve of your tunic up to your elbow, revealing a jagged scar on the underside of your arm. "I was Lees's age. My best friend became lost at night. It was late summer—the days were long like they are now—there was the same half-light sky. But half-light is also half-dark, and climbing over rocks searching for her, I fell.

"I was *the same age* as my sister—*the same age* as your brother. Do you think only babies can get hurt?"

"I never said—"

"Both of you, *stop*," I say. "Look . . ."

While the two of you argued, we had hiked all the way to the beach. And just as you predicted, a boat is out on the water. A long canoe, its silhouette standing out against the pale blue sky.

"Lees!" You call to her at the top of your voice, and a head pivots in our direction. While we stand on the sand and watch, powerless to stop her, she gets to her feet and waves her arms. The canoe rocks violently.

"What's happening? What's she doing?" Kesh gasps.

"She has no experience with canoes," you spit. "Only kayaks. She's only ever been in a kayak before. The canoes are only used for traveling great distances—long scouting trips or when we came to visit your clan. That trip was the only time I have ever been in a canoe, and I was amazed by how different it was from a kayak—how much more volatile on the water . . . how much more easily it could tip. She has no idea what she's doing."

Of course she doesn't. And neither does Roon.

The boat pitches hard and Roon reaches up, maybe to grab the hem of her parka. A short burst of sound flies from her—something between a squeal and a scream.

She wobbles, shudders, and for one long, hope-filled moment, she stretches her back, arching over the side, her arm extending toward Roon, her hand almost touching his.

Then she twists in the air, tumbles, and falls, splashing into the sea.

Living on the water, taking out kayaks to fish and gather kelp, I know the dangers. When the water is its coldest—in winter when ice thickens in the bay and eventually blocks the harbor—the cold of the water could end your life before you could swim into shore.

But this is early summer. Most of the big sheets of sea ice have melted. She should have a bit longer than that to save herself. Twice as long before her limbs begin to go numb, maybe? The bigger threat—that the sudden shock of the cold could knock her out and cause her to drown—is just as real a danger in the summer as in the winter.

I have to do something. I can't stand on the beach watching while the life is chilled out of your twelve-year-old sister. Two kayaks are stacked against the rocks about thirty paces away. Before I can think, I am pushing one out into the shallow waves and climbing in.

I hear splashing behind me. I don't need to look back to know that you have followed me with the other boat.

Everything seems to slow down as I paddle out—the strength of the current seems to push me back to shore and the water feels as thick as mud. The sky grows ever darker, but what I lack in sight, I make up for in hearing—Lees splashing, Roon yelling, you shouting.

Then I am almost next to them, just a few boat lengths away. The final, fading gold of the sky reflects off the surface, and everything glows.

Where's their paddle? Either they've lost it, or they left shore without it. The canoe is simply drifting, and the two of them are at the mercy of the waves.

Without a paddle to extend to her, Roon takes off his parka and holds it by the hood, leaning over the edge of the boat and casting it out to your sister like a net. I paddle closer, closer, closer as Lees grasps it by the hem and pulls herself alongside the canoe.

With Lees pulling down, Roon's weight suddenly shifts, and the side of the canoe tilts sharply toward the surface.

"Hold on!" Roon calls. "I've got you!"

But he doesn't have her.

A dark wave crashes over her head, pushing her down and hiding her from sight. Roon's arm reaches over the side. For a moment, his open hand dangles above the empty sea.

Then, all at once, Lees's hand reaches up, her head and shoulders reemerge from the wave, and their arms clasp. He pulls hard, braced against the side of the canoe. The boat tips, rocking wildly. I am certain that Roon will fall forward into the water.

But the canoe rocks back, and Roon rights himself. The breathless moments of struggle come to an end as a dripping, shivering child swings her legs up and climbs back into the canoe.

By the time I pull my kayak alongside their boat, Roon and Lees are huddling together in the hull, shivering and laughing like it's all a wonderful joke.

I take off my parka and toss it into the boat. It falls across a waterskin I assume contains the stolen mead. "Wrap yourselves in this," I say. "That ought to keep you warm."

I throw a quick look toward shore. You've already turned your kayak and have made it nearly halfway back to the beach.

Tying the tow rope around my waist, I dig hard with

the blades of my paddle, dragging the two most impulsive twelve-year-olds back to land.

You do not speak to me when they climb out of the canoe. You don't speak to Roon or to Kesh. Instead, you yank your little sister by the arm and whisper something into her ear. Then, without another word, you drag Lees up the path and out of sight.

My new parka lies discarded in the bottom of the canoe. It's wet and dirty, but still, I shrug it on and lead my brothers back to camp.

"I understand now," Kesh says, as we trudge up the path, out of the dunes and back into the eerie darkness under the trees.

I look at him, wondering what great mystery this dreadful evening has clarified for him.

"I couldn't make sense of why you were against Mya. I noticed that you didn't like her, but I couldn't understand why."

I catch myself. I was about to say that I do like you. I was about to say that if circumstances were different, I might actually like you very much.

Water sloshes in my boots as we reach the clearing—I wasn't dressed for wading. My pant legs are soaked through with ice water from the knees down.

We catch up with you in time to see you drag Lees into a hut, without a word of thanks or even a glance back.

I turn toward the hut where I've been sleeping—your hut—and I remember waking to find you there. I'd been naive enough to assume that you were worried about me—that you were there out of concern instead of duty.

But in so many ways, you've shown me your true feelings. The return of the pelt I'd sent you as a gift. Your ungracious behavior now that Roon and Lees are safe.

It couldn't be more obvious that you have no concern for me at all.

Which is fitting, since after today, I have none for you.

TWELVE

A terrible evening fades into a terrible night. Despite the softness of the pelts I lie on, enough salt water splashed on the cuts on my back to cause them to ache and throb. For a long time I toss restlessly, and just when I resign myself to lie awake all night I fall asleep and become lost in a nightmare.

In the dream I'm running up and down the bank of a river, pursued by a cat I never see, one that casts a shadow three times the size of the one I killed. I run and run, but I can't escape it—it's always right over my shoulder. Finally, I feel its hot breath on my neck and I turn and throw my spear with all my strength.

But as I turn, I find that the cat is not there. Instead, I've struck you with the spear; it juts out at me from a gaping wound just below your collarbone. Your eyes dim, and you crumple at my feet. I turn in place, calling for anyone to come help me try to save you. But when I bend to pull out the spear, it isn't you lying in a pool of blood. It's the mammoth, the one that haunts me, still staring at me with that look of defeat, still silently beckoning me to throw myself into the dark hole that opens up in its eye.

When I wake in the daylight, the back of my neck drenched in sweat, I thank the Divine that the final night in your camp is behind me.

My family emerges from our borrowed huts before the morning meal, but Chev meets us with a basket loaded with dried berries—many I've never seen before—as well as several parcels of salmon, cooked and wrapped to be eaten on the journey.

No one else greets us from your family. Only your brother and the oarsmen who will row us back to our own camp are outside, as the covered meeting space buzzes with quiet preparation. The rest of your camp is silent and still.

Pek carries my bag to spare my back as we head down the trail to the beach, and following this path this morning fills me with an echo of the fear I felt last night. Roon runs ahead of me. Even this morning he overflows with a sense of adventure. It's odd, I think, how the thing you love most in a person can also be the thing you sometimes wish you could change.

The path seems to have doubled in length while we slept. I don't remember passing under so many trees before reaching the water. The soil underfoot becomes sandy and the trees more scraggly. Just as we come to the spot where the trees give way to shrubs and grass, I hear a voice calling my name. I turn, but I see no one.

I hesitate. Last night's nightmare is still too clear in my mind, I think. My senses are tricking me. Scanning the trail just once, I turn again to follow my family, who have all gone ahead of me and are probably loading the boats, wondering where I am.

I emerge from the trees and suck in a breath; the strip of rocky beach looks so different in the daylight. Even low in the sky at our backs, the rising sun has burned away the horrors of mist and shadow that were so perfectly illuminated by the setting sun last night. The briny scent in the air is a welcome sign that we are heading home and I can leave the bad memories I've made in your camp behind.

I'm within just a few steps of the rocks when I hear it again—a voice calling my name.

I turn, and this time the source is clear. This is not a voice from my nightmare, but the voice of your youngest sister, Lees. She runs hard down the trail from camp, waving her arms to catch my attention.

When she reaches me, she stops and looks into my face with the expression I'd seen at last night's meal—the expression I'd mistaken for innocence. I know better now. It's far from innocence. It's more an expression of cunning.

"Did you run all the way here to say good-bye?" I ask.

"To say good-bye, yes, but also to say I'm sorry. I caused a lot of trouble last night—"

"You did—"

"But I didn't mean to. I'm sorry for everything."

Just then, Roon calls her name from the water, but when we both turn, we see Kesh grab him by the arm. They are already seated in a boat and I can see Kesh isn't risking any wild behavior from Roon. Maybe Lees and Roon had hoped for a more personal farewell—perhaps even an embrace—but they'll have to make do with a vigorous wave.

"Kol!" my mother calls. "Everyone's set to go."

"Good-bye, Lees. Try to stay out of trouble," I say. She smiles that cunning smile and I begin to turn away.

But before I can turn, she grabs me by the shoulder. I'm caught off guard, and I spin my head around to face her. As I do, she pushes up on her toes and presses a soft kiss against my cheek.

I step back. "Was that a thank-you for helping you last night?"

"No," she says. She lowers her voice, as if she is about to bestow upon me some rare secret. "That wasn't from me; it was from her." She turns and looks up the trail and right there—right at the place where the last trees cast a blanket of morning shade—you stand.

You raise your arm and wave. Such a small gesture, but

the simple movement of your hand fans a flame inside me that I've tried again and again to smother out.

Without thinking, I raise my hand and wave back. I want to jog up the trail and speak to you, but I'm not sure what I want to say.

"Kol!" Now it's the voice of my father. "What's wrong?"

"Be safe," your little sister says, "and come back soon."

I want to ask Lees if this message, like the kiss, was sent by you, but my father calls my name one more time, so I turn and hurry to the water's edge. Wading out to where the water reaches my knees and my feet ooze into the silt of low tide, I climb into the long canoe and we are off.

When I look back over the beach, Lees still stands waving, but you are gone.

As soon as we push into your bay, we head out beyond the pull of the tide to deeper, calmer water. From here, the coast is a long swath of green—an unbroken line of trees soaring above rocky gray cliffs. At places, the cliffs tower high over the sea and at others, they bend so close to meet it that they are no longer cliffs at all, but low bluffs that wrap around cozy inlets.

We move farther north, and the wind grows cooler as the trees grow thinner. Here, the rocky shore is interrupted by frozen waterfalls that plunge to the edge of the sea. These rivers of ice run down from the ice-covered peaks of the coastal mountains. They are as cold as they are beautiful, but still my heart warms as they come into sight. We've reached a boundary, a sort of gateway to the north. I'm reminded of the moment on my hike south on the inland trail when I realized the mountains were all at once behind me, holding back the north wind, protecting the south from the chill that blows constantly down over the Great Ice.

Out here on the water, I know those mountains aren't far. Soon, the north wind will blow hard against my face again. Soon, the trees on the shoreline will disappear. Already they've diminished to a broken line of scrubby, tangled patches where there is still sufficient shelter to the north. Just ahead the line of land bends west. When we reach that bend, the mountains, still white bumps against the sky that could pass as low clouds, will rise up to welcome us.

My mother sits in front of me. She turns and smiles. "You look hungry," she says, misreading only slightly the look of longing she sees on my face. She unwraps slabs of fish and passes them to me, my father, and the two oarsmen who wordlessly paddle this boat—one at the head and one at the rear.

Out on the water ahead of us, my brother Pek leads our group in the kayak he used to come to your camp, while another oarsman from your clan paddles from the rear seat. Pek had argued that he could handle the boat by himself, but considering the distance, it was decided the presence of an extra paddler made more sense than my prideful brother paddling alone with the second seat empty. Behind us, a second canoe similar to this one but a bit smaller in size—a boat I suspect may be the exact canoe Roon and Lees took out last night—carries Roon and Kesh as well as two more oarsmen from your clan. Roon is almost finished with his piece of fish—that boy is always hungry.

I pivot in my seat again, turning my back to the shore and facing west, allowing myself a long moment to look out at the horizon—ever constant despite the changing coast-line. I linger over a few deep breaths, reveling in the familiar scent of the sea and the whisper of the paddles as they cut the surface. So familiar . . . I let my eyes close and I almost feel that I'm home. I open them again and imagine that the sea beside me is the sea that stretches from our bay.

It's then that I notice them—distant shadows moving across the gray sea.

Boats.

Far away toward the line that separates surface from sky they glide along, hardly more distinct than the shadows of seabirds or the breaks in waves, but yet distinct enough. Three in all: I can make out the point at the front of each boat, cutting through the spray, and the rhythm of the strokes that propel them forward almost in time with us. Almost, but not quite in time. A beat or so slower, they gradually fall behind. I turn in my seat to watch them recede, wondering what clan might have boats out on these waters—halfway between your camp and mine. Could it be that Chev sent rowers to follow us to ensure our safety? It seems unlikely, considering five of his clansmen are escorting us home.

Could these be the spies Chev wondered about, on the morning Roon discovered the clan on our western shore? I remember your brother's speculation as you hurried to leave our camp.

By the time they disappear, I suspect, as Chev did, that these were not spies but something else—Spirits sent by the Divine—perhaps to aid or even impede us. Not knowing which, and not wanting to cause a stir, I keep my thoughts to myself and say nothing. Before long, my eyes tiring from the sight of water rolling out in every direction, I decide they were never there at all, but rode the waves only in my mind.

The sun slides west and the wind picks up. Other than these small signs, everything suggests that time has stopped. Surrounded by circles—the circle of the paddles, the circle of the waves—I wonder if the day itself has closed into a circle, an endless loop rather than a line leading to an end.

But then the coast turns westward and the trees that have lined the land for most of the day abruptly stop. The snow-capped peaks of the eastern mountains seem to spring from out of nowhere, and my father calls out and stretches his arms in front of him as if to embrace them.

We've made it home.

On the other side of those peaks are the meltwater streams, the wildflower fields, and the windswept grasses. The paddles quicken and we pick up speed, pulling closer and closer to shore. We round the point that juts out over the sea at the foot of the tallest peaks, and we are officially in our bay. Nothing—not fatigue, not my throbbing wounds, not the prickly memory of the Spirit paddlers I'd seen along the way—can diminish the joy I feel at the sight of our land.

Yet once the boats have landed—once I'm climbing out of the canoe, stretching the cramps out of my legs—I notice something feels off. At this time of day I would expect to find Aunt Ama's family fishing or gathering shellfish, but no one is out on the water or on the shore. It's still, far more still than it should be. Gulls circle overhead, their squawks calling attention to the otherwise complete quiet. I drag my heavy feet up the steep bank to dry land, following close behind Pek. I think he and I both spot it at the same time— something out of place on our familiar strip of rocks and sand—a kayak.

Of course, there's nothing strange about a kayak, but this boat is not one that I recognize. It lies on its side, displaying a hull that is longer and more narrow than the hulls of the boats my aunt's family constructs. The sides are deeper, the bottom flatter.

This boat was not built by anyone I know.

This boat brought strangers to our shore.

THIRTEEN

My mother does not appear to notice anything out of place—she's too distracted by her social obligations to the oarsmen.

"The midday meal has already been eaten, I'm sure," she says, stumbling out of the canoe, not willing to wait for someone to help her. She must be as anxious as I am to feel our own land under her feet again. "But come with me. I'll make sure that you are well fed and rested before you return home." My brothers and I drag the boats up and ground them on the rocks not far from the strange kayak. As we do, Roon lets out a yelp.

"This boat! I've seen this boat before!" Standing on our beach now, with the sun high in its arc overhead, Roon points to a thin wisp of smoke rising from the far western edge of our bay. Before I can ask him what he's thinking, he dashes up the trail and disappears from my view.

Pek throws me a glance full of caution and questions before hurrying after Roon.

Kesh shrugs. "And I thought the adventure was over."

As we climb the trail behind Roon and Pek, music reaches my ears. A drumbeat and a voice. "The song of friendship," says Kesh. I recognize the voice of the singer—my father's brother, Reeth, one of the elders of the clan.

We reach the circle of huts and there she is—the person who brought the boat. Sitting on the ground in the center of the gathering place, directly beside my uncle and his wife, is a girl with a long braid on either side of her face, her dark, deep-set eyes presiding over round cheeks and a wide smile. Hers is a face I know well—a face I grew up with.

This is Shava, the very same girl who once cooked every kill my brother Pek brought in.

She had wanted to be betrothed to my brother, but he had convinced our parents to decline. "There's nothing wrong with her," Pek had said when my parents had pressed him. "Can't I like her for a friend, but not for a wife?"

Two years ago, my parents agreed not to force the matter. I think they would have changed their minds by now, if she and her mother hadn't left the Manu. But when her mother's native clan—the Bosha—passed through our land two years ago, they rejoined them.

So the Bosha must be the clan camping on our western shore.

My eyes scan the group. Kesh and Roon stand at the edge of the meeting place with my parents and the oarsmen, listening to the song, but Pek is nowhere to be seen.

Though it was just a little over two years ago that I last saw Shava, it feels like a different lifetime. Back before fear about the lack of females in our clan really took root, when we still had intermittent contact with other clans. Back before the sight of smoke rising from camps to the west or north disappeared completely.

But even then, panic over the lack of prospective wives for me and my three younger brothers didn't develop overnight. Two years ago I was fifteen—old enough to marry but certainly not old enough to worry. The clans that crossed our path were more transient than we were, and my father and mother frequently mentioned that they suspected they had followed herds to the west or even inland, far to the east, along the southern edge of the Great Ice. Still, everyone spoke with confidence about the coming day when another clan—one with many young women—would camp nearby.

A clan would arrive in the summer, when the days got longer. That was my mother's constant refrain. When summer was half over without a sign of anyone, my father said that the fall would bring a wandering clan to our bay, where the fishing was easy. Fish helped feed a clan into the winter when hunting got more difficult and the game harder to find. Even once the harbor froze over, fishing was still possible, especially from a bay like ours, bordered by points that extended beyond the ice to the open sea. Of course a clan would come—maybe more than one.

Then fall came, then winter, then spring, then summer again. When a year had passed since we'd seen signs of another clan, worry began to grow. Like a vine, it sprang up and sent out shoots into every part of my clan. It sprouted in the thoughts of my mother and father, its tendrils binding all of us so that the more the worry grew the more it restricted us. We stopped talking about the other clans. We stopped planning for one to arrive. Only Roon, when he was just eleven years old, was bold enough to face down the fear. He would take off and search, wandering the shoreline, looking for any sign. After two years of no contact from outside, my clan hadn't given up all hope, but it was close.

As hope faded and fear grew, the prospect of a move south became the focus of our elders' plans. And then you arrived, and everyone believed we were saved. All our fears were banished when Chev came to shore with a beautiful boat and two beautiful sisters.

Your arrival was so captivating to all of us—so amazing and wonderful—that when another clan finally camped nearby, no one except Roon even cared.

But this afternoon, finding the strange kayak on the beach and Shava sitting in the center of my camp, knowing everything I've come to know about you and your clan and the impossibility that betrothals could ever take place—the arrival of another clan is very welcome indeed.

The friendship song comes to a halt as our clanspeople rush over to welcome us home. Shava springs to her feet as my extended family peppers me with questions about what I've been through. It seems the oarsmen who came to camp two days ago to bring my family south told the tale of the cat I had killed and—outside my family's hearing—shared a gruesome description of my injuries. Everyone wants me to take off my parka and show my wounds.

My mother asks for volunteers to help her prepare a mid-day meal for my family and the oarsmen, and Shava is quick to offer help. My mother thanks her and gives her a warm embrace.

Of course she does. Now that she knows of Seeri's betrothal, she could only believe the Divine herself sent Shava back to our shores.

As soon as Shava disappears through the door to the kitchen, Pek emerges from my family's hut. He must have been staying out of sight.

I turn to him and smirk. "Shava's helping in the kitchen. It's like she never left."

"That's not funny," he says.

"Maybe you should give her another chance. She likes you and she's available. Don't take that for granted. At least she isn't betrothed to her brother's best friend—"

I barely get the words out when Pek shoves me with both hands, sending me staggering backward.

"Calm down. I only meant that you shouldn't rule her out—"

"Shut up." Pek doesn't even bother to pick up the two packs he carried up from the boats. He leaves them at my feet, right where he must have dropped them the moment he saw Shava. He strides away, retreating back into our family's hut.

I consider following him, but decide against it. Instead, I head into the kitchen to help with the meal, hoping that keeping busy will make it easier to clear my head.

The atmosphere of the kitchen is calming, and I slowly get my thoughts ordered again. I feel less of the sting of Chev's rude behavior in your camp yesterday, and I begin to let go of the fury I've felt ever since you marched your little sister into your camp without a good night or even a glance in my direction. Focusing helps me let go, and as I chop fireweed stems and combine them with nettle leaves, even the chatter of Shava as she asks my mother an endless stream of questions about Pek doesn't bother me.

The only threat to my sense of peace is the constant interruption by my younger brothers. First they come in to tell me that Shava came to our camp in the strange kayak with another girl—apparently the same girl who Roon met while she gathered kelp in the bay with her brother. Then they come back to tell me a second kayak has landed on our beach, carrying the brother and another girl. They come back a third time to tell me this new girl, who introduced herself as the daughter of the Bosha's High Elder, is the prettiest girl they have ever seen.

"Next to Mya," Kesh says.

I glance up, to see if this comment was made only to provoke me. After all, Kesh expressed his dislike for you just last night. But I can see he's being sincere. Apparently, a bad temper and ungracious behavior have no impact on Kesh's assessment of a girl's beauty.

"Well, I've never seen a girl prettier than Mya's sister. Lees is the prettiest girl out of all of them."

I smile at the affection in Roon's words, remembering the kiss Lees gave me this morning . . . the last time I saw you, standing in the shadows farther up the trail . . .

"Kol, run and fetch me your honey," my mother says from the place where she sits behind me, spreading the steamed and chopped roots of clover on a mat. "I'm going to mix a bit in with this to add a little sweetness to the meal."

"Is Pek in your hut? Can I come with you?" Clearly, Shava hasn't gained any subtlety since she left our clan.

"No, thanks," I say, but she gets up anyway. "I can get it myself. My mother could surely use you more in here. . . ." These last words I let trail over my shoulder in Shava's direction as I push my way through the partly opened door out into the daylight.

As I do, my eyes fall on the face of a beautiful girl. The second most beautiful girl I've ever seen in my life.

It turns out Kesh was right.

FOURTEEN

I have to stop suddenly to keep myself from charging right into this girl. Her eyes widen and her hands fly up to protect herself, but then a broad smile breaks across her face. "Sorry for being in the way," she says.

"My fault," I answer. I try to think of something to say next, but I'm distracted by a landslide of small details—the windless warmth of the day, the sudden heat in my cheeks, the brightness of the sun reflecting off the girl's hair, so bright I need to squint. I become swept up in all the pieces of this girl—not necessarily all the things about her that make her attractive, but rather all the ways in which she is both similar and different from you.

I would guess you are the same age, though she might be slightly younger. Like you, she wears her hair down, but she's smaller and more narrow-shouldered than you are. She's almost birdlike—there's a tension, an energy, about her. As she stands blinking at me, I notice that her face is more rounded than yours—her eyes, her cheeks, even her chin has a roundness to it.

The image I hold in my mind of your face dissolves when this stranger speaks to me again. "I'm Lo," she says. "I'm from the Bosha clan, camping on the far shore of the bay. My father is the High Elder. I hope we're not disturbing you."

We . . . It's only this word that alerts me to the fact that this girl is standing with two other people—a boy and a girl.

"These are my friends Orn and Anki."

I nod to each of them while insisting that no one is intruding or disturbing us. "Your father is High Elder?" I ask. "Is he with you?" All at once I realize that perhaps my father should be called.

"No, we came on our own. Just a friendly visit, since Shava already knows you all." Lo smiles and gives a small shrug, as if she's embarrassed to have come uninvited and without official sanction. "Sorry if we're—"

"No, not at all. Don't say you're sorry. You're welcome to visit. We're glad you're here."

I excuse myself, and as I hurry off to retrieve the honey I make note of another difference between you and Lo. Her manners are much better than yours.

With the pouch of honey in hand, I head back to the kitchen. As I pass through the gathering place again, I see that Lo and her friends have sat down with a group of elders and children who are working flint into points. I nod and Lo smiles, and I tell myself how lucky I am that you wouldn't accept this honey when I offered it to you.

At my mother's insistence, Pek finally emerges when we gather to eat, though he hardly acknowledges Shava at all. Still, she won't be deterred, and she seats herself beside him. Kesh manages to claim a place beside Lo, but she slides over to make room for me on her other side.

My mother presents the honeyed roots last, after all the other parts of the meal have been consumed. Lo runs her tongue over her lips after the very first taste.

"I haven't had honey in so long," she says. "We've been traveling too frequently over the last two summers. We were never in one place long enough to hunt for a hive."

"Do you like to hunt for beehives?" my mother asks.

"I do," says Shava.

"Do you? Well, Shava, I'm sure you remember that my son Kol is an excellent bee hunter. The best." Her eyes stay on Lo. "Maybe he could take you and Lo—"

"I'd love to go," says Shava.

I cannot bring myself to raise my eyes. Waiting for Lo's answer, I feel the muscles in my jaw tighten, so that I can no longer chew. My mouth goes dry, and I consider offering to fetch water from the kitchen, but then Lo finally answers my mother's question.

"Of course, I'd love to go, as long as he doesn't mind taking us." She turns in my direction, and I notice the woven mat that lies in Lo's lap, piled high with a generous portion of honeyed roots. Her fingertips lift another taste to her lips, and I realize that my mother is the most cunning matchmaker in the land.

The next day I am standing on the beach just after first light, which is remarkably early. This is the time without darkness, the time of year when the sun comes up almost as soon as it's down. Pek stands reluctantly beside me. Our mother insisted he come along. It appears she is hoping to match me with Lo and Pek with Shava, despite his resistance.

"I'd rather you go home than ruin the day." His posture alone—all his weight on one foot, his shoulders slumped to one side as if he were leaning on a pillar built of his troubles—is enough to make anyone miserable. "Why don't you take this outing as an opportunity to test if your feelings for Shava could change?"

The breeze coming off the water makes me squint, but my eyes don't tear. We are in the short window of the season when the breeze is without its bite.

"I can't." Pek squats down on the rocky ground and runs his hand through the stones. He picks one out and holds it up to the light. I notice it's not a stone at all, but a broken shell worn down by the constant waves. "I can't give Shava a chance when I love another girl."

His words startle me. "Do you really think you love Seeri?" I ask.

"I don't *think* I do; I *know* I do."

You can't know that. You haven't known her long enough to know something like that. These are the things I want to say, but just at that moment, Pek straightens.

"There," he says, looking out toward a kayak only just becoming distinct from the foam on the waves. Lo and Shava, our guests for a day of hive hunting, are not far out from shore.

I grab our spears from where we propped them against the dune grass. I can only hope two will be enough since the girls climb out of the boat empty-handed—they haven't brought spears of their own.

Trusting, I think, noting another difference between you and Lo.

I lead the group out to the meadow by the path that skirts around the back of the camp. It's a fairly short hike, but it seems much longer when you have to walk it in awkward silence. I assume Lo is politely waiting for one of her hosts to start up a conversation. That doesn't really surprise me. Shava, however, confounds me with her silence. Last night she spoke almost ceaselessly, either to Pek directly, or—if he managed to separate himself from her for even a moment— she would speak to someone else *about* Pek. "Is Pek still the best hunter in the clan?" was definitely the rudest thing she managed to say to me over the course of the evening.

Still, as irritating as it could be to suffer through a conversation with her, it was somewhat sad to think how futile her efforts were and how even after having been away for almost two and a half years she still wasn't over him.

When we make it to the other side of camp and start up the section of the trail that rises through the last scrubby, twisted shrubs and slowly evens out as it opens on the plain, I begin to think that Lo has tutored Shava about how to handle herself on this outing. I would never have believed Shava was capable of going so long without speaking.

Though it's a nice change not to have to struggle to slide a word into the conversation, the quiet becomes more uncomfortable the longer we walk. I know Pek would probably gladly spend the morning without hearing her voice, but I can't take it much longer, and as we crest the hill and the wide meadow rolls out in front of us, I finally ask a question to break the silence.

"Are you experienced in hunting for honey?" I ask to no one in particular.

At first, neither girl replies, but I see Shava throw a glance at Lo that seems to be begging for permission to answer. Something about this strikes me as pitiable. It's touching, actually, the lengths Shava will go to try to attract my brother. It may annoy him, but he really shouldn't complain when two girls are showing such strong interest in him. Ten days ago, we didn't know where or when any of us would find potential wives. He may not want Shava and he may have a difficult battle ahead to win Seeri, but he has girls interested in him, and for that he should be grateful.

I know I would be.

I glance over at Lo, trying to move only my eyes instead of my whole head, in hopes she won't catch me looking at her. I think she may be interested in me, but she isn't very forward about it. I just wish I had a better understanding of her feelings. With Shava and Seeri, there's no doubt they adore Pek. With you, there's no doubt you consider me unworthy of you.

Finally, the silence is broken. "I used to search for hives a lot when I was younger," says Lo. "My father would take me."

"I've never had the chance," says Shava, the words flying out in a rush. "When I was growing up in this clan, I spent a lot of time helping in the kitchen, but it was always Kol or Urar who brought in the honey. But I've always wanted to try it." She waits a moment, perhaps to see if anyone else has anything to add. This must be a piece of advice Lo gave her. As the "new" Shava shows herself more and more, I begin to wonder if Lo came along only to enable Shava to be close to Pek. "What about you, Pek? Do you enjoy searching for beehives?"

At first Pek doesn't answer at all, and I think he's being intolerably rude. He doesn't have to flirt with Shava, but he *can't* be rude. I'm about to say something to him when he finally turns and looks back at us from his place ten paces farther up the trail. "If the right person were here, I would be happy no matter what we did."

Lo pauses on the path for a moment, tracing the toe of her left boot in the dirt. Shava stops behind her, but she isn't as subtle as Lo—her face is like a shattered shell, as broken as the one Pek held up on the beach.

"Is there a girl—" Shava starts.

"Yes. There is." Pek hesitates just a moment longer before turning and plodding on. There's nothing for us to do except follow him until we reach the southern edge of the meadow.

The last time I was here was the morning I met you.

Not much time has passed since that morning. We have seen only one full moon since that day. Still, the abundance of life in the grass is startling. As we walk, insects spring out in front of our feet—grasshoppers are everywhere. I head for a spot in the center of a cluster of blue flowers that spread out like frost covering the ground. When we get there, no bees are visible, but I know that doesn't mean they're not here.

"This is the best part," I say. "Or at least, the most challenging."

My gaze moves over first Pek's face, then Lo's, then Shava's. This is the first I see the tears in Shava's eyes in response to Pek's blunt confession of his feelings for Seeri. It's hard for me to understand her endless optimism, considering he rejected her so thoroughly a few years ago. Maybe my mother has given her the idea that there is hope.

Or maybe, she thinks she's really in love.

My attention moves from Shava's red-rimmed eyes to Lo's ambiguous expression. I try to decipher the tension in her lips, but I understand so little about girls. I look away. Pek stands brooding at the edge of our group, so far away from the rest of us he's beyond the patch of wildflowers. I can only study the back of his head; he stands with his hands on his hips, facing into the wind coming cold over the Great Ice.

I glance back at Shava. The hurt I see in her reminds me of the hurt I've seen too often in Pek. I can't stand it anymore.

"Let me show you the best way to track bees," I say. I lie down in the grass and gesture to the place next to me. "You need to lie down, close your eyes, and listen." Shava lies down on the grass and as she does, her hand brushes mine. I glance at her but she is just closing her eyes.

"Now what?"

I wait for Lo to lie down on the grass on my other side, but she shuffles out of sight, heading over to try to talk to my moody brother.

"Now we listen. You'll know it when you hear it—the whir of their wings. It comes and goes as they fly and land, fly and land."

I close my own eyes and tune my ears, but I can't distract myself from the murmured conversation between Lo and my brother. I try to make out their words, but they are too far away, their voices nothing but an intermittent buzz.

Hiking back to camp, I feel that the outing was at least partially successful—we tracked two bees that Shava spotted until they joined up with a larger group. Those bees led us to the shade in the foothills of the mountains. We discovered their hive in the middle of a stunted poplar, growing in a secluded grove protected by sharply rising cliffs at the edge of the meadow.

"We'll watch it, now that we've found it," I say. "Then later in the season, we'll smoke the bees to calm them and cut a piece of the hive away."

"This has been one of the best days of my life," Shava says. Every head turns toward her; this statement is so strong. Shava meets my eyes and her smile is somehow odd. "I've seen so many bees but never *really* seen them—never seen how they live. Thank you so much for teaching me."

Recognition washes over me. I realize Shava isn't acting odd—she's acting as she always has.

She is looking at me the way she has always looked at Pek.

FIFTEEN

It's just before the midday meal, and as the group of us hike back to camp, the crunch of gravel underfoot and birdsong overhead is joined by music rising from the gathering place. A strange melancholy grips me—I haven't been home for the midday meal for days, and the cold formality of your clan has made me long for the warmth of my own.

I'm homesick.

As we walk, I try to make out the song my clanspeople are singing, but the wind is at our backs and the sound moves out and away. Shava walks beside me, pummeling me with questions about bees and hives, so that what I can hear of the music is drowned out and incomplete.

It isn't until we are just outside the ring of huts that I recognize the tune. The melody is simple—the kind that makes you want to sing along. Vocals dance over a plain drumbeat . . . *Oh great Divine, you taught us to make rope of many cords. . . . Two cords are stronger than one. . . . This rope of many cords, wrapped and woven, will remain unbroken. . . .*

This is the song of friendship my people were singing when my family arrived back on our shore and found Shava here visiting. I can only assume that more of her clan has arrived from their camp across the bay.

The trail ends at a gap in the huts that reveals the gathering place. A girl stands outside the circle, long dark hair, straight and loose, flowing down her back—a girl wearing an ill-fitting parka that appears to be borrowed from a brother.

I know it is you long before I see your face. Standing beside you, her posture tense and taut, is your sister, Seeri. She strides toward us as soon as Pek steps into view.

I want to ask why you're here, who came with you, if your brother is also here, how long you will stay. But I realize that your rude treatment of me and my family wouldn't merit that type of greeting. Instead I smile and turn to the girls who walk beside me.

"Seeri, Mya . . . this is Shava and Lo, our neighbors from the Bosha clan. They are camping across the bay and have come to visit." I glance at Seeri's face, but she is looking past my shoulder. I turn to you and your eyes are on the ground.

Such flagrant arrogance.

"These are our *neighbors*," I repeat. "This is Shava, and this is Lo. We just came from an outing to the meadow. We went in search of honeybees."

"And we were very successful," Shava adds. A loud giggle escapes her, and my nerves jump along my spine.

I wait for your nods, for your acknowledgment of these strangers. My eyes shift from you to Seeri and back again. Both of you stare absently, ignoring the introductions being made.

Could it be rivalry that prevents you from greeting these girls civilly? Certainly not rivalry over me, but maybe Pek? I might expect disdain from you, but not Seeri, who has shown good manners under the worst of circumstances.

Until now.

"I'm sorry. I'm not feeling well. Please excuse me." That's all you say before you turn and walk straight to the door of the hut we built for you the last time you visited. You never even lift your eyes from the ground.

"I should go check on my sister," says Seeri. At least she meets Pek's gaze when she speaks. "But first I need to tell you both the reason we're here."

My eyes flick to my brother. He stands completely still, as if he fears he's dreaming that Seeri is here and if he moves he may wake and it would all be gone. "My brother Chev regrets his behavior the night you were all in our camp. After you left he realized that he had treated you rudely. Too much mead, he says."

Seeri attempts a laugh but no one else even so much as

smiles. Pek still stands motionless. I turn to Shava. Her eyebrows are drawn together in a scowl. She watches Lo, as if waiting for cues.

"Chev's heart is burdened with regret. He says he owes your clan a celebration in Kol's honor. My whole family has come, as well as our clan's council of elders. We've brought a feast to serve in your camp tonight."

"Your council of elders? Does that mean your brother has changed his mind about—"

"He says he values your clan's friendship very much. He's brought this feast as a show of good faith. Those were Chev's own words—*good faith*. He is sincere about building a bond with the Manu."

"So then there might really be a chance—"

"I have to go," Seeri says, and almost as quickly as you, she turns on her heels and disappears in the direction of your hut.

"He must have second thoughts, right?" Pek's face is a study in contrasts. His eyes are the eyes of a man who's been lost in a dark cave and who's finally found the tiniest glimmer of light through a thin crack in the stone—his eyes are alight with the possibility that he's finally found the way out.

But his mouth belongs to a different face. His mouth is a hard flat line—the mouth of a man who knows his hopes are false, a man preparing himself for the coming sting of disappointment.

"Is one of those girls her?" Shava asks.

Neither of us responds. "Is one of them the girl you spoke of earlier?" she asks Pek.

"It's none of your concern," he says, his words jumbling together as if he can't spit them out fast enough. He turns and heads back up the path in the direction we came.

For a long moment the three of us stand there in silence. Voices reach us from the huts—Chev and my father, laughing.

"I need to leave," says Lo. "I need to get back to my own camp."

"But there's a feast—" I start, but stop when I notice the intensity of my tone. I won't let myself sound desperate. I take a deep breath and start again. "Wouldn't you like to stay?"

"I'm not invited—"

"You're our guest. Of course you're invited—"

Lo turns her face up toward the sky to the west, and for a moment I think she is wavering, but when she speaks, it's clear her decision is firm. Perhaps she was just searching for words.

"I promised my father I'd help him with something after the midday meal. He's our High Elder. I couldn't break a promise to him." Lo smiles, but distance opens between us. "Ready, Shava?"

Shava flinches when Lo says her name. It's subtle, but

unmistakable. "I didn't make a promise to your father to return at a particular time." She speaks in the tenuous voice of a child who knows she's going to be in trouble.

"My father will be expecting both of us," Lo answers. Her tone carries meaning beyond her words. Is a threat implied? "And how would you get back? We came in the kayak together. I need you to paddle it back with me—"

"But this is my old clan. I want to stay for the feast."

"I have an idea," I offer. "There's a trail along the cliffs that circle the bay. It takes longer than crossing by kayak, but it leads to the other shore. I could show you the way. I'll walk you back to your camp right now, Lo, if you'll promise to come back later tonight for the feast." I allow myself the indulgent risk of touching Lo—a light, brief touch on the wrist. Her skin is warm. "You could bring your father with you. My father, I know, would welcome the chance to meet him."

Lo purses her lips. She shifts her weight from foot to foot as she thinks. "All right," she says finally. "If you'll walk me, I promise to return tonight. But Shava, may I speak to you briefly—alone—before I go?"

Shava looks from Lo to me and then back to Lo again. "Of course," she says.

"I'll go to the kitchen and get a waterskin for us to take," I say. As I walk away, I tell myself that Lo is most likely giving Shava advice about Pek. I will not let myself hope that she wants to say anything in private about me.

Lo and I take the trail that winds through the thin forest of birch trees that grow in the rocky soil near the shore. This swath is among the few patches of trees we have within our hunting range—these weathered, spindly trees that manage to dig their roots into the narrow strip of soil that forms a buffer between the sea and the wide stretches of grassland. The path is steep in spots, climbing up the cliffs to a summit that overlooks the bay before turning and heading back down to the western shore. In a few spots, the forest floor grows rocky, and it's dangerous if you don't watch your step. Still, it's mostly easy on our feet, carpeted by sedges and mosses that form a cushion under the soles of our boots. And it's secluded and private, so it's the path I choose. Lo doesn't seem to mind.

The day is bright, and the path is covered in broken splashes of sun and shade. Wind off the sea stirs the branches, creating a rushing sound that almost sounds like rain. I glance at Lo as she walks just an arm's length from my side. Her eyes are down, carefully watching her feet to avoid sticks and exposed roots. The light flits across her dark hair like stars in the night sky. Something inside me longs to reach out and touch her, and I find myself imagining her tripping, her toe getting stuck on the edge of a rock and her balance being lost just enough to justify a hand under her elbow or even better, an arm thrown hurriedly around her waist.

For some reason, this thought brings you to my mind. I remember the cold disdain in your voice as you made your excuses and ran away to your hut when I'd introduced you to Lo.

"Do you mind if I ask a question? If it's something you'd rather not answer, just say so."

Lo wobbles as her foot settles on a loose rock, and for a brief moment I think I will have to reach out to catch her after all, but she rights herself and regains her balance almost instantly.

"Ask me anything you want." Her tone is open and inviting, and I convince myself that the reason she doesn't look up is to ensure she doesn't land on another wobbly rock.

"Well," I start. I stop a moment and watch Lo's hair bounce against her back, and once again, I can't push the thought of you from my mind. Your hair is a bit longer and straighter than Lo's. Hers has the waves of hair that's been braided while wet.

"I wanted to ask you about the girls I introduced you to earlier. Seeri and Mya. Have you met them before?"

"Are you asking because they were so rude to me?"

A gust of breeze blows her hair, obscuring her face, but it doesn't matter. As soon as she answers I know she knows you. There's anger in her voice—a wound that hasn't healed. Or a debt left unsettled.

"It was impossible not to notice," I say.

"Of course it was. Those girls are worse than rude. They're selfish. The whole family, the sisters, their brother . . ."

We walk a bit farther in silence. My heart quickens, but I can't be sure if it's reacting to the climb or to what Lo said. The path turns away from the coast a bit and rises to a rocky slope. I let Lo go ahead of me, but that denies me the benefit of watching her face. I feel that if I could see her face as she spoke I might decipher some sort of mystery. Not just a mystery about the cold reunion I'd witnessed, but a mystery about *you*—about what experiences in your past have made you so rude and arrogant.

Not that it ultimately makes a difference to me. If you choose to be unfriendly and superior, I can only feel fortunate not to have been matched to you.

In this stretch of the trail, the ground is eroded to the rock bed below. Boulders stand out at angles, allowing us footholds, but the steepness makes my heart pound harder and my breath come quicker.

"So, when did you meet Mya and Seeri? Do you know them from before they moved south? Did they visit your clan as they passed through five years ago?"

"Five years ago . . ." Each word crackles from Lo's lips like new wood hissing in the flame. Finally, she stops and looks back at me. Even from a distance, her eyes are like fresh-cut obsidian, hard and dark, but with a glow deep inside. "They didn't pass through my clan." The whispering in the trees falls silent. "They *are* my clan."

SIXTEEN

My pulse quickens, drumming in my temples. I hurry to catch up to Lo, leaving the trail and scrambling over a steeper section of rock, so that I reach the crest at the same moment she does. I take in the hardened angles of her usually rounded face—the tight lines drawn around the edges of her mouth—before she hurries ahead again.

"They *are* your clan? How is that possible? You're from the Bosha clan. They call themselves the Olen. . . ."

She doesn't reply, doesn't speak at all. The thrumming in my head grows louder, making it hard for me to think.

Lo continues to climb, though she slows her pace. I stay as close as I can; I don't want to miss a whispered word of her answer. Finally, without looking at me, she speaks. "Until five years ago, we were all one clan. They were part of the Bosha. Their father, Olen, was our High Elder. But there was a rift and they abandoned their own people. They left us—Chev, his sisters, and about half the clan.

"Before the split, their father and mother were trusted in every way. People went where Olen said to go, whether it was an order to follow the herd, to take kayaks out to fish, or to go on a gathering trip that would take days."

The slope of the trail turns downhill as we navigate a tight bend that reveals the open sea below us. The view from this spot looks over the section of the shore where Lo's clan is camped—the remnant of *your* clan. The people you left behind. I think of the fighting that took place between your clan and mine when you visited us five years ago. If what Lo says is true, that must've been right after you and your family had torn away from your own people.

We continue down the trail and the smoke from the hearthfires of Lo's camp disappears behind a wall of trees. From here, the path descends sharply; it won't be long and this walk will be over.

"So what happened to end that trust?" I ask. I'm not sure if I'm pushing too hard or asking the wrong questions, but I want to keep Lo talking.

"All right." Lo stops beside a fallen tree that looks as if the last bad storm uprooted it. Its trunk crosses the path. Leaves, still green, sprout from branches that fan across the sloping ground like the spread fingers of a hand of the Divine. She sits down and pulls her legs up, perching her chin on her knees. I sit opposite her, in a patch of ferns that edge the path. "Olen began to lose the clan's trust when he turned us away from the ways the Divine had ordained for us as mammoth-hunters—the ways of our ancestor, Bosha. Do you know her story?"

Bosha . . . The ancestor Lo's clan—your clan—is named for. "I'm sorry," I say. "I may have heard it when I was a boy, but I don't remember."

"I'm happy to tell you," Lo says. "It's a story I love to tell.

"Bosha lived a long time ago. She was a great hunter. With her husband she had two children—twins—one boy and one girl. One day, while Bosha was out hunting alone, she brought down a mammoth. The mammoth did not die quickly, though, and while it still had strength, it began to crush her. Knowing that her death would mean hunger and suffering for her family, Bosha pleaded with the mammoth. She didn't beg for her own life, but for the lives of her husband and children. She asked the mammoth to use its dying strength to travel to the door of her family's hut so that, when the mammoth died, they would have food to survive. The Spirit of the mammoth was so impressed by Bosha's love for her family, it honored her request.

"After Bosha's death, her husband grieved her deeply. In memory of her and her great skill as a hunter, he promised the Divine that he and his family would eat only mammoth and other herd animals for the rest of their lives.

"The Divine was moved by the sacrifices of Bosha and

her husband, and she brought a great clan out of their offspring. Since then, the Bosha have always lived off the herds.

"But Olen turned us toward a new way of life. We built kayaks to hunt on the sea and we gathered more greens and berries. Some people murmured that Olen was forgetting the old ways. But there was still balance. We still relied on the herds.

"Then a day came that Olen and his wife announced a gathering trip. They wanted to travel to the other side of a stream where more shrubs and sedges grew, hoping we'd find a variety of berries and greens. The plan was to gather, but also to scout for a new home. The grassland where we camped at that time was heavily grazed by bison and mammoths, and the greens were growing scarce."

She tips her face away from me, pivoting her weight so she is facing the sea breeze. Her gaze skims across the tents that make up her clan's camp before turning to the sky like she's studying the clouds.

"Mya was my best friend." This statement pulls my spinning mind to a sudden stop. "We had grown up together. Our fathers were like brothers. I was like a fourth sister to Mya, Seeri, and Lees. So when this trip was planned—just overnight—as usual, I was included. The six of us went— their mother and father, the girls, and me—and in the beginning, I was excited. I was always happy to do things with that family.

"But the day we were gathering, Mya's father ordered us all to split up. He said we needed to cover as much ground as possible. He wasn't worried about any dangers. Cats, bears—our scouts had not spotted any on this side of the creek since the last full moon. He said we were safe. We were all given a digging stick and a large basket of our own and told not to come back to the place we had set up camp until it was full."

I picture the group of you in my mind. I see your father—an older version of Chev—muscular, sharp-featured, intimidating. I see Lo, Lees, Seeri, but most of all I see you, looking much the way I remember you when we first met five years ago. Your hair was shorter then, with pieces that whipped around your face when the wind blew from behind you.

"I was out gathering, and my basket was not quite full when shadows started to close in and become nightfall. I called out Mya's name, then Seeri's, then one by one the names of each member of their family. Nothing. No reply came. Darkness fell fast and I was lost, alone."

Lo drops her head and rubs her forehead.

"How long—"

"All night," she says, cutting off my question as if the words would hurt to hear. "I spent the night walking and calling out their names. By the time the sun came up, I was half frozen. I curled up in a patch of brambles on the bank of the creek that blocked the wind just a bit. When they found me, I was slipping in and out of dreams. . . ."

"I'm so sorry," I whisper.

"When we got back to camp, her family told my father and mother that I had wandered too far and become lost. They put the blame on me. They said that my carelessness had almost killed me. They wanted me punished."

"But you had been in their care—"

"They have no care. They care for no one but themselves. And many people agreed. They'd seen the way the High Elder and his wife acted. They were becoming too proud to follow the ways of the Divine. Their daughters, too, became proud. They began to treat everyone as if they were beneath them."

I wish I could doubt Lo's story. I wish I could believe that your family had never treated her with such callousness. But I know you. I've seen you do exactly as Lo says—I've seen you treat people as if they were beneath you.

And of course, Lo's story brings to my mind the story you told me yourself, about a girl getting lost—the story you told me the night Lees took off with Roon. "She told me—" I start.

"What did she say?" Lo's head whips around and her eyes drill into mine. "She told you about me?"

"About a girl who became lost. She showed me scars she got when she fell, searching—"

"As if those scars are my fault! Those scars are the work of the Divine, to remind Mya of how she wronged me."

The strength of these last words strikes me. After all, you were only a twelve-year-old girl at the time. But then, I don't have firsthand knowledge of that night.

"So . . . did your clan send them away?" I try to imagine the pain of that day. My father is our clan's High Elder. I will be after him. If we were cast out by our own people—

"Not right away. Everyone was either patient or terrified. Mya's father was erratic. People were afraid of him." Lo hops to her feet, standing above me on the fallen trunk she's been sitting on. "But it was in the winter that followed that autumn that the High Elder died—"

"What happened to him?"

"I think the guilt of the wrong he'd done consumed him. He wasted away," Lo says. I notice a biting satisfaction in her voice but I dismiss it. Lo is too kind to find satisfaction in the death of her friend's father, no matter how much his poor judgment had hurt her. "My father, Vosk, argued that Olen had died by the will of the Divine. He said that he, himself, should be named the new High Elder. But Olen's son, Chev, demanded the role for himself, since he was next in line after his father.

"There was a schism within the clan. At the time of his death, Olen had been preparing the clan for a move to the south. We constructed more kayaks for the move, but also for hunting seals and fishing on the water. My father asserted that Olen had led the clan away from the ways the Divine had ordained for us as mammoth-hunters, and for this the Divine had struck him down.

"The arguments over who the Divine wanted to bless with the right to lead were intense. Many people agreed with my father and promised to acknowledge him as their new High Elder. My father encouraged Chev to step aside and follow him, to help make our clan strong mammoth-hunters again. But Chev insisted he would carry out his father's plan to move the clan south. Some followed Chev, clinging to the memories of his father, the way these trees cling to the side of this eroding rock."

I drop my eyes to the windswept soil, gravelly and dry and so shallow the roots of the trees stand out above the surface like spiders' legs. Lo jumps down from the trunk and a cloud kicks up from her feet—dry flecks of weathered bark. As she drops down onto the ferns beside me and stretches out, a musty scent of decay washes over me. "But memories can't support the needs of a clan. The wise chose my father. The rest packed up and pushed off from shore." Lo turns her face to the sky, sheltering her eyes with her hand. "As much as it hurt to see some of our clan choose to follow them, I didn't condemn those who left—Chev, Mya—all of them have powers of deceit that rival Halam's."

"Halam?"

She squints up at me, her nose wrinkling. "You don't know his story either? Halam was an ancient ancestor who was so charming and clever he befriended the Divine. He asked her one day if she would give him a gift—he wanted the power to change the shapes of things. She granted Halam's request, but she warned him that if he used his power to deceive, he would come to regret it.

"But Halam didn't listen to the warning of the Divine. Instead, he transformed his little girl into the shape of a caribou, and sent her into the herd to deceive the others. He instructed her to speak to the other caribou in their language and convince them to run through a narrow mountain pass where he would be waiting with his spear.

"She did as she was told, but when the caribou came running, Halam realized that he could not recognize his child among the animals. In a hurry for a kill, he threw his spear, but as soon as the animal was struck she returned to the shape of his daughter. She died at his feet.

"There is strong danger in a person who can create such powerful deceit they can no longer distinguish their own lies from the truth. Halam was clever and gifted with the power of trickery. But these gifts led him to ruin, just as they will lead Mya and her family to ruin as well."

Sitting up, Lo turns to me. "Do you see this?" She leans close enough to show me the pendant she wears—a thin strip of leather is tied around her neck so that a round disk, a medallion of carved bone, rests just below her throat. On either side of the medallion, the strap is strung with round, uniformly sized beads. The carving on the disk is made up of four curved lines, like two crescent moons facing each other, or—I see now—two curved tusks. "This is the emblem of our High Elder. It signifies the Spirit of the mammoth that feeds our clan. Mya wore it as the High Elder's oldest daughter. When my father became the High Elder, she still had it tied to her throat as they boarded the kayaks the morning they left. My father stopped her. She was told not to take it with her when she left our lands. It was to be passed to me.

"But do you know what she did? She couldn't bear the thought of giving a symbol of status to me—her lowly friend. So she took it off and in front of my father and everyone else she crushed it with her heel against a rock on the beach. She left the bits and pieces on the ground and climbed into the kayak without looking back. My father had to make me this replica.

"I never thought I would see Mya again until we walked into your camp today. It was like walking up to a ghost."

Lo lies back again, and I stretch out beside her, propping myself on one elbow. For a moment, neither of us moves. Something flashes in Lo's eyes—something like an invitation—and I decide to touch her face. But before I can, she sits up and jumps to her feet, checking the position of the sun. "It's getting late."

As we descend out of the peaks, the air around me warms and I realize that sitting still in the cool air has chilled me. Or maybe it was Lo's story. The thought of her alone all night, lost on the windswept grassland, sends a shiver through me even now. At least the rush of anger that rises in me at the thought of your family's arrogance heats me from the inside out. Your father, you, Chev—it's nearly universal.

Seeri must take after your mother.

I realize suddenly that I don't know a thing about your mother, except that she must be dead. You've never mentioned her even once in front of me. . . .

The path ends on the beach about fifty paces from Lo's camp. A boy and a girl are fishing—Orn and Anki, the brother and sister I'd met yesterday, the same pair that Roon met when he first discovered Lo's camp.

Their eyes skim the trail behind us. "Where's Shava?" asks Orn.

"She stayed behind. There are other visitors in the camp today—Chev and his family."

The boy's eyes briefly widen, but then narrow as his mouth contorts into a scowl. He is stocky and bowlegged, and there's something about his squared stance and clenched jaw that suggests he finds this news of your family irritating. I would guess he's about the same age as you. He would remember your departure five years ago.

"They came to visit us," I say. I drag my eyes away from the boy's face. His grimace stirs something uncomfortable in me. "They arrived just before you first camped on our shore." I almost say more—that since you first arrived, our two clans have forged a friendship—but I know that your family is unpopular with the people you left behind, and I don't want to start anything. Yet I can't look at the boy. The look of haughty disdain on his face at the thought of your family offends me, though I'm not sure why.

"So of course Shava would stay," says Lo. "I doubt she even realizes who Chev and his sisters are. She hadn't yet joined our clan when they left. She and her mother were still living with the Manu until just two years ago. That was when our clan stopped to visit yours, Kol. Do you remember that?"

"I do," I say, "but I don't remember meeting you."

"No." Lo looks out over the water for a moment. She's thinking about that visit, and so am I. "We'd been on a long journey. We'd been searching for mammoths, but hadn't had success. My father took only the elders when he approached your camp."

I remember this visit, of course, and as Lo speaks, all at once I remember the Bosha's High Elder—Lo's father. He'd come into our camp looking thin and tired. All the Bosha elders had looked hungry.

"Your clan fed our elders and sent heaps of mammoth meat out to where the rest of us were camped. My father learned that the girl who cooked the mammoth—Shava—was descended from our clan. He took this as a sign from the Divine.

"He invited Shava and her mother back into the Bosha clan. Shava had prepared the mammoth that sustained us, and he believed she would bring good fortune to our clan." Lo pauses, then hastily adds, "I believe that, too."

"Let's hope you're reading the signs correctly," says Orn. "I'm not sure Shava is very valuable. Or bright."

My hands curl into fists at my side. I may find Shava irritating, but she grew up with me and my brothers. When Pek refused to be betrothed to her, one of his reasons was that she was too much like a sister to him. She may be pushy and tactless at times, but I do not want to stand here and listen to a stranger criticize her.

There is something about Orn—a smug sense of superiority—that I do not like. I turn away from him and Anki. I should say my good-byes to Lo and begin the trek back to my own camp.

That's when I spot the paddler out on the water. We all seem to notice her at the same time.

"It's Shava," says Orn. "I thought you said she stayed behind."

We all wait, watching as Shava, with some difficulty,

steers the double kayak into shore. Lo and I run into the waves to pull her in.

"What's going on?" Lo asks. "We hiked all the way here because you wanted to stay."

"I came to get my mother. After you left, so many people asked for her. She lived with the Manu so long, and they miss her. I know she would love to see them, too. I looked for you so we could take the boat together, but you and Kol were already on your way."

Shava stands with Lo on the opposite side of the boat. As we drag it onto shore, Lo speaks to her, but I can't hear her over the splashing and the sea breeze. I hear only Shava's reply.

"I will. I told you that I will." Then she hurries up onto the sand. Without saying a word to me or anyone else, she disappears up the path that I assume leads to the Bosha's camp.

"Don't let Chev and his clan keep you away," I say, once Shava's gone. I would like to speak to Lo privately, but I'm forced to include Anki and Orn. "I want you all to feel welcome in our camp. Chev is our guest, but so is Shava. So all of you could be." I turn to Lo. She fiddles with the pendant of bone around her throat. When I look at her she lowers her eyes. Maybe I'm wrong. Maybe there is a deeper rift here than could ever be bridged by an invitation to a single feast. "You promised to come tonight," I say, in a quiet voice I hope only she can hear.

"And I will," she says. Her voice is a low murmur, matching mine.

She glances up and meets my gaze. At my back, the sea spray is strong, and the breeze blows cold against Lo's face, reddening her cheeks and pinning loose strands of hair to the damp skin around her eyes. "I'll be there tonight, but for now, I need to go. I made a promise to my father, and I need to see it through."

SEVENTEEN

I hike back to camp alone, thinking of Lo the entire time, except at brief intervals, when the thought of you somehow creeps in, unbidden and unwelcome. Your face appears in my mind's eye—the memory of your expression when you sprang from the woods while chasing the elk, landing right in front of me. I remember the sound of your voice when you first saw my wounded back, the curve of your throat above the white bone pendant that hung around your neck at dinner.

The memory of that pendant takes on new meaning now. Do you, like Lo, wear a replica of the one you destroyed?

Later, I hear the feast getting under way in the center of camp, but I decide to remain in my hut a bit longer. I don't want to run into you. At least not until Lo is here. After all that I learned about you today—about the cruel way you've treated Lo—how you preferred to destroy something that symbolized your status and position rather than turn it over to her—I don't think I could stomach another tense and insincere exchange of pleasantries with you.

My mind floats back to the meal at your camp and the question you asked me—what traits would make a woman a good wife. My answer—*cooperation, patience, lack of arrogance*—I realize now that all these traits belong to Lo, and not a single one to you.

The music starts up. Kesh's flute is clear and strong tonight. I can't help but think that he is showing off a bit. But if Kesh is showing off, maybe that means that guests are arriving from the Bosha clan.

Maybe Lo has arrived.

I pick up my new parka, but I hesitate, remembering how I'd believed it to be a gift from you, only to learn that it was actually your way of returning a gift to me. Still, it's the cleanest and nicest I own. I shrug it on.

Out in the gathering place, people are standing shoulder to shoulder. It's impossible to get a view of the whole crowd. My entire clan is here, plus at least ten people from your clan. Smiling and nodding at a few of your clan's elders who I recognize from my visit but don't know by name, I snake between smaller groups, catching snippets of conversations—*How has the hunting been for you this summer? How do you feel after such a long trip on the water?* Everyone seems to be putting history behind them and making friends. No one would guess that our two clans had come so close to war just five years ago.

Out on the far side of the square, near the path that leads away from camp to the meadow, I find Seeri and Pek. Behind them in the gathering shadows I hear laughter, and squinting I make out the shapes of two figures running, a boy and a girl—my brother Roon and your little sister, Lees. A squeal pierces the air—I can only guess Roon has caught Lees, though her laughter convinces me she wasn't too upset to be caught. "Stay out of trouble," I call into the dark as I turn back toward the crowd. They both fall quiet as I walk away.

For a moment I wonder if they might be kissing, but then decide that they are both too young and childish. Probably whispering secrets or planning a prank.

Toward the center of the square, in a tight little knot, I notice my father and mother, your brother . . .

You.

I should come over. It's only polite.

As I slide through the crowd, I feel your eyes on me. A strange tension stiffens my arms and legs.

It can't be nerves. It's only awkwardness, as I prepare to say as little as possible before turning to look again for Lo. Or maybe I'll be bold enough to ask you if you've seen her.

Yes, that's what I'll say.

Just before I reach your side, though, someone catches

me by the elbow. I spin, expecting Lo. The grin is already on my face when I recognize that it is Shava instead.

"Kol, have you seen Pek? We've been looking for him. You remember my mother?" Shava's mother, Fi, stands beside her. It's been two years, but I recognize her immediately. "She only wanted to say a brief hello to Pek."

My grin spreads into a wide smile. The presence of Shava and her mother confirms that members of the Bosha clan are here.

"It's good to see you," I say, while looking past Fi. "Do you know if Lo is here yet? She said she might bring her father."

"Her father?" Shava's mother's voice is the high-pitched call of a startled bird.

"Lo spoke of her father today." Unlike her mother, Shava speaks in low and controlled tones. "She spoke of the promise she made him."

"Oh, yes. Well, I haven't seen Lo yet tonight."

Their behavior is so odd; I need to send Shava and her mother on their way. "Pek's on the edge of the path," I say.

Let them find him fawning over Seeri. The sooner they learn the truth, the better.

But Shava surprises me. She sweeps an appraising eye in your direction, perhaps making note of the fact that you have been watching us all this time. "You go say hello," she says to Fi. "I saw him just this morning. I would rather stay here and talk to Kol about honey."

Shava's mother leaves, and I find myself uncomfortably pinned between Shava and you. "Did anyone else come from your clan?" I ask Shava.

"I'm not sure others will be coming," she says. Her eyes shift to you, then back to my face. "My clanspeople are not very friendly with the Olen clan. We were once one clan, you know."

"Yes, I do know—"

"You do? Because when I spoke about it to your family—to your father and mother—they had no idea—"

"I didn't learn it from my family."

From the corner of my eye, I see you move in closer. Did you hear me just now, acknowledging that I know you were once one clan? Can you guess it was Lo who told me?

A fire burns in the central hearth and its light sets your skin glowing as you move toward me. I can't resist the urge to turn and look at you.

"You know the history of our clan?" you ask. And I know—I hear it in a small tremor in your voice—you fear what Lo may have told me about you.

But why care what I think of you? How could my opinion matter, except to satisfy your own pride and vanity?

"Some," I say. I turn and look into your face, one side lit by the cool half-light of evening, the other glowing warm from the light of the fire. In your eyes there is a spark of something, like an ember just before it catches the kindling and everything bursts into flame. "Lo told me enough."

"I doubt that," you say. "It's a complicated story."

I notice for the first time that you are dressed in clothing reserved for the highest occasions. I would almost believe you were trying to make a good impression, but who could you be hoping to impress? Instead of your usual ill-fitting parka, you wear a long tunic of sealskin, cut to fit the lines of your body perfectly. I assume this is a new garment, constructed from the pelts brought by Pek. The tunic has a hood that lies open across your back, your long hair spilling into it. Leather ties lace up the neckline at your throat, but you've left it open. Around your neck, glowing like snow in the firelight, is the pendant, so similar to the one Lo showed me today. You notice my gaze and your fingers trace across it. "Do you recognize it?"

"I do. Are they identical?"

"This one is ivory. The one Lo wears is bone."

Of course, I think. Bone is porous, rough, and common. Ivory is lustrous, smooth, and strong.

If Lo is to have a pendant of bone, you must have one of ivory.

A sigh comes from over my shoulder and I only just remember that Shava is still beside me. "Do you think we will go hunting for hives again tomorrow, Kol?"

I hesitate to answer. I would love to go. I would love to go *alone*.

Before I can construct the best reply, Shava takes advantage of my silence. She wants to talk about bees. "Mya, have you ever had the chance to taste Kol's honey?"

Once again, I'm amazed by Shava's boldness.

"I regret that I have not," you answer. "I had the chance once. But I was foolish, and I didn't appreciate the value of the offer that was being made."

My eyes lock onto yours. You stare back at me, and your lips curl just a bit.

"Sometimes I let my pride get in my way. I fail to thank someone who saved my clan from a predator, or saved my sister from drowning in dark, icy water. Or I refuse a gift of honey that was offered in the spirit of friendship."

"That's too bad," Shava says. "I've tasted it myself, so I know what you missed. Such a shame. After all, what would life be without honey?" She giggles.

"Please excuse me," you say. Dropping your eyes, you hurry away, melting into the crowd in the direction of the huts.

"Well, she's quite rude," Shava says.

I watch you as you make your way to the edge of the crowd.

"She clearly doesn't like you very well," Shava adds, and

as she says these words, you flick one quick glance over your shoulder.

And I see it: the ember that had been glowing in your eyes is ablaze.

EIGHTEEN

I watch you until the door of your hut pulls back and then falls shut behind you again. When I shoot a quick glance at Shava, I find her staring at me as if she intends to read my thoughts. "I'd like to find my brother Kesh," I say. I don't really need to see Kesh, but I'm looking for an excuse to get away. I move to step around Shava, but she perks up instantly.

"That sounds wonderful. Let's go."

I want to tell her I have something personal to discuss with Kesh, but her face gives away some hidden awareness of my plan. She smiles, but behind her docile features I see an edge of cunning—a mental rehearsal of her response should I suggest that she stay here. Something in that contrived innocence seems pitiful—I see her suddenly as someone well aware of her status as a person others are frequently trying to avoid. Maybe it's because you've made me feel less than welcome myself at times, but I can't help but sympathize with her a bit. "This way," I say. I turn and head toward the musicians in their place by the entrance to the kitchen. I almost offer my arm to Shava, but think better of it. I'm sure she needs no assistance in keeping up.

Kesh stops playing when he sees me approaching. He clambers to his feet to look over my shoulder. "Shava—I haven't spoken to her since she came back," he says, a bit too loud.

I'd forgotten. Shava and Kesh had once been close. They'd played together as children and had been almost inseparable until she fell for Pek.

"I'm so happy to see you," he says, sliding over to make room for her to sit beside him on the flat stone he occupies near the hearth.

"I'm so happy you still play the flute," Shava answers. "I wish I could play."

"I could show you. . . ."

I've never noticed the shyness in Kesh, but I guess there was never reason for him to act shy. Handing Shava his flute, he shows her how to hold it. I slide away when he begins to show her the ideal way to pucker her lips.

Food eventually is brought out and people crowd in and seat themselves on the ground, which has been strewn with clippings of soft stalks that your clan must have brought from the south. The food is perfect—roasted bison and mussels stacked high on every mat. My mother tries to help with the distribution, but an elder from your clan—a man old enough to be my father's father—gently scolds her and tells her to have a seat. He is clearly in charge of food preparation and takes his responsibility very seriously. "This feast is to honor *your* clan. It is our gift to *you*," he says.

His words remind me of the lessons my father has taught me about generosity and service to others, and how the Divine requires these traits in a clan leader. As I watch, my mother smiles and sits down.

A crew of women and a few men of about my parents' age carry out wave after wave of mats. One man weaves through the clumps of seated figures passing out drinking bowls—not the ornately carved cups of bone we drank from in your camp, but shallow, tightly woven bowls coated with resin. Chev follows behind him pouring mead from a large waterskin into every one.

With all but the servers seated, I'm able to scan the crowd more easily—I see Pek and Seeri, Roon and Lees, my mother and father. But Lo is nowhere to be seen. And, I notice, neither is Seeri's betrothed.

Of course, neither are you.

Second helpings are being brought out when I get to my feet. The food is excellent, but a sense of loneliness overcomes me as I notice that even Kesh is leaning toward Shava as if telling her a secret. This is a familiar feeling to me—this sensation of being more alone the greater the size of the crowd. I felt it the morning I met you—it was the feeling that drove me to the meadow pretending to search for honeybees when I was certain it was too early to find them. I needed to escape some invisible pressure, and I have that very same sensation now.

Getting to my feet slowly, I ease into the shadows on the far side of the kitchen and disappear behind it. Moving along the outside of the ring of huts, I make my way to the door of my family's home fairly confident that no one has seen me.

I exhale a deep breath, the kind of breath that burns my lungs like I've been holding it all day, and duck under the mammoth hide that drapes over the doorway, only to step back quickly when someone inside the hut moves.

I'd expected to find the hut empty. Instead I find you standing next to my bed.

"I'm sorry." That's all you say. You don't move, but stand frozen in an awkward posture, caught between coming and going. In your hand is a small cup made of intricately folded dark green leaves that are unfamiliar to me. "I wanted you to have this," you say. You glance around, looking for a place to set the cup, and I become intensely aware of how cluttered my family's hut is. A set of harpoons Pek and I are carving from a core of ivory lies jumbled at your feet.

You set the cup on one of the pelts that serves as a rug.

"It's a gift." From where I stand, I can see the golden color of the thick liquid inside.

You've snuck into my hut to leave me a cup of honey.

"Honey from your home? From the south?"

Your eyes are on the tiny vessel at your feet as if you hope that it will spontaneously answer my question on your behalf. I feel somehow embarrassed for you, though I'm not sure why. "Well, I'm anxious to try it," I say, hoping to set you at ease a bit by acting—inexplicably—like this gesture of yours is completely normal. "Would you like to share it with me?"

Of course you'll decline. It's obvious you can't wait to escape from my company. You're practically twitching with embarrassment.

Just as I'm shifting to the side of the door to let you pass, you answer, "Yes." Clearly, I can't read you at all.

"Oh, all right."

Faint light bleeds in through just a few open vents in the walls, but I'd almost believe your cheeks color pink as your feet shuffle beneath you.

I offer you a place to sit on the haphazard pile of pelts that collectively form my bed. I seat myself on the bed opposite—Pek's bed.

Suddenly I can't quite think how to share the cup. If I were alone, or even with my family, I would simply dip my fingers in it. But the thought of eating honey with my fingertips in front of you seems far too intimate.

Then you surprise me. You pick up the cup and tilt your head back, tipping it above your mouth until the honey runs down onto your tongue. It drizzles onto your lips but you run a finger across them to catch it before any drips onto your chin. All your self-consciousness melts away as you move your finger from your glistening lips and smile. "Your turn," you say.

I take the cup. Before I can second-guess myself, I follow your example. Honey, warm and sweet, trickles onto my tongue. My eyes find yours, and I catch you staring.

"It's excellent. Different from the honey I gather here. It's a bit lighter in taste. Different flowers . . ." I realize that I am talking quite fast. I replace the cup of honey on the floor between us for fear I might lose my grip and let it spill. "Different flowers give honey a different flavor. There's something smooth and mellow in this honey. It's good. Really very good." I wish I could stop babbling. "Did you gather this yourself?"

Even before the question is out I regret asking it. The answer will be no, of course. And somehow asking the question feels like I'm passing judgment on the answer.

"No, I wouldn't know how. I'd like to learn—"

"I'd be happy to teach you—"

You fall silent. Are you remembering the encounter earlier today, when I found you here in camp after hive hunting with Lo and Shava? "Maybe. I think I'd be interested in learning where honeybees hide this far north—"

Something in the way you pronounce the word *north* makes me flinch. You possess the most confounding ability to say things that are insulting or critical without showing any awareness of how your words might sound.

"You really hate it here in the north, don't you?"

"*Hate* is a strong word."

"A strong word, but no less the right word."

"Perhaps."

Should I offer you a taste of the honey I've collected here? Is there any hope that you might see, as I'd hoped on the night I'd first offered it to you, that not everything in my clan's camp is bitter and cold? It's so tempting to offer it again—to have a second chance at the exchange that set us on the wrong path. But I decide against it. I don't want to bring up that evening right now.

"Can I ask you," I start, my voice low. But then I stop myself. Why do I insist on asking you questions? Part of me suspects the less I know of you, the better.

"Ask me anything," you say, which, I must admit, seems a bit bold coming from a girl who, when I first entered this hut, appeared painfully embarrassed. But that was a Mya I've never seen before, and she has vanished.

She has been replaced by the girl across from me—a girl who sits with a casual ease that is clearly calculated. You sit with your feet tucked up beneath you, forcing your posture just slightly forward, leaning into the space between us. Your hair drapes over each shoulder, framing your face and neck in just the right balance of shadow and light. I can see your eyes but I cannot read them, which only makes me want to see them more.

"Fine." I slide my hands under my thighs to ensure I will resist the temptation to brush your hair from your eyes. "Why did your family come to the north to visit us in the first place? It's clear you hold no interest in my clan, and only five years ago there was enough trouble between our clans to stir whispers of war."

You lean back on one elbow and stretch your legs. Your face slips into shadow—all but one eye, sharp and intense, illuminated by a pale shaft of light streaming through an overhead vent. "It's simple—it's because there are boys here. Isn't it obvious? Chev needs to find a mate for me. After all, Seeri is betrothed, but I am the oldest. Chev is hesitant to allow Seeri to marry before me. I think he's afraid if he doesn't find someone for me soon he'll be stuck taking care of me forever."

"I hardly think you need to be taken care of," I say.

A murmured laugh rises in your chest. Maybe it's because of your supine posture, or maybe because a thickened breath of bitterness mixes with the exhale of levity, but the laugh breaks in your throat.

A stretch of leg, an arch of neck that rolls down your spine to your hips, and all at once you sit up. Your shoulders lift from the bed and your face floats toward me, your hair stirring a scent of smoke into the sweetness rising from the open honey. My heart gallops, but there's something else— a heavy ache, a hole behind my racing heart—a clutching hunger that claws at me, calling to my attention the soft curve of your throat, the warm glow of the skin just below your ear, the tension in your lips as they curl into a cryptic grin. "Another question?" I ask, focusing my attention on the echo of your words repeating in my head—*Chev needs to find a mate for me.* "Why wasn't your brother's friend, your sister Seeri's betrothed—why wasn't he promised to you, since you're the oldest?"

The grin vanishes. Your teeth press into the corner of your bottom lip.

"By the time of Seeri's betrothal, I was already betrothed. I was betrothed so long ago I can't remember a time when I wasn't. The match was forged when I was a little girl and still lived with the Bosha clan."

This answer, so calm and measured from your lips, sends my heart sputtering again.

"Another boy? Did he stay behind when the clans split?" It occurs to me that maybe the boy is still in the Bosha clan. Maybe you hope that you will be reunited.

"No," you say. "He came with us when we left for the

south, but he never saw it. Before we reached the southern shores, he died."

The next few moments seem to stretch out and pass slowly. I feel your words hang in the air like a ghost. *He died.* Of all the things I'd expected you might say—all the reasons I'd thought you might give for not being promised—this was not one of them.

"As for the possibility of being promised to Seeri's betrothed, you met him, right? He isn't the most subtle or humble of men. Not that I'm particularly strong in those traits, myself. Maybe that's why he doesn't like me—"

"Seeri's betrothed doesn't like you?"

You slide back, the presence of the ghost grows heavy like a weight, and I wish I hadn't asked so many questions. Your attention is on the space behind my shoulder, and your expression has turned dark. "I won't lie to you—the possibility of marrying me instead of Seeri was offered to him, but he had no interest in the idea." You drop your eyes to the floor and then quickly raise them to meet mine. If you are harboring any feelings of self-pity, they don't show. "I imagine he had the same reasons you laid out yourself that night in my camp. Your thoughts on the traits that make a woman a good wife? I believe my sister's betrothed would list the same characteristics—patience, a lack of arrogance—and Seeri has those things. And *that*, I assume, explains why he chose her."

I search my memory, trying to recall exactly what I said that night. I know I deliberately chose things I believed you lacked. Why was I so confrontational? Was I hoping to humiliate you, to punish you for rejecting me?

But then I remember—it was you who wanted confrontation. As soon as things began to settle down, you had to ask a question that would ramp things up again. *What traits in a woman make her a good wife?* you asked me. I had tried to smother the confrontation, but you fanned the smoldering embers. You wanted the flames.

It's my turn to slide back, drawing my damp palms across the coarse coat of a giant bearskin, a pelt I considered luxurious before I saw the riches of furs and hides in your own camp. I'm far enough from you now that perspective returns, and as I take you in, I realize the extent to which you have misled me.

For these few moments, sitting here in this close, dim space with you, my senses confused by unfamiliar scents and flavors and the curl of your lips, I almost forgot all that I learned about you today from Lo. I almost forgot the mistreatment she suffered at the hands of your family, at your *own* hands.

Hands that at this moment rest, palms up, in your lap, feigning innocence.

I glance at the ivory pendant around your neck and think of its bone twin around Lo's.

Bone isn't good enough for you anymore. If Lo can have bone, you must have ivory.

"How did he die?" I'm not sure when I decided to ask, but the question has been turning in my head since you first mentioned him. I know it might hurt you to talk about it. Maybe that's why I ask.

"How did who—"

"Your betrothed. How did he die?"

"I'm not sure that's a story you want to hear or one I want to tell. At least not right now."

What's wrong with right now? I don't ask you; I don't have to. You sit just as before: leaning slightly forward, your hair falling over the front of your shoulders. Your gaze flits all around the room, only occasionally sliding to my face and hovering there, your lips parted slightly as if you are anticipating something.

None of this is by chance, I realize. Everything about this moment—the lingering sweetness on my lips, the glistening expectation on yours—it's all been set in place by you. I lean toward you, taking a tentative step into the center of your elaborate snare, then step back just before the trap can spring. "It *is* a story I want to hear," I say. "We're here. . . . Why not tell me now?"

"Fine." Your voice is clipped and sharp. I've finally pushed you hard enough that you're ready to push back. I knew you would. It's in your nature.

You lean away, your hands balled into small tight fists at your sides, each knuckle a bright white spike. You let out an abrupt sigh, bite back an almost-spoken word, and those angry fists push into the bearskin as you jump to your feet.

"Where are you going?"

"Some people can see things with their hearts. Others need to see them with their eyes."

I scramble to my feet. "It would be helpful if you didn't speak in riddles," I say.

"Bring a spear." You step to the door and draw back the drape enough to reveal a piece of the western sky, tinged blood red. The sun hangs so low, it's hidden beyond the distant hills, but this is the time of year when the Divine treads slowly across the sky, and the sun refuses to set. "You are aware that something happened five years ago, and our two clans almost went to war. To you, the events of that day are insubstantial—"

"That's not true—"

"Maybe someone you knew died—"

"Yes," I say, remembering Tram's father dressed for the hunt, lying in his grave.

"But that day does not follow you. For you, it stays in the past. But not for me. That day five years ago never leaves me. Its ghosts are always here." As you speak, your cheeks flush the same intense red as the setting sun. Your eyes widen with excitement. "There's so much you don't understand. In a way, I suppose I envied you your ignorance. But you should know the whole story about that day. Ignorance never protected anyone for long."

What could your betrothed's death have to do with the death of Tram's father, or any of the events of that day? Somehow I fear that once I learn the whole story of what happened between our clans five years ago, nothing will ever be the same.

You duck out through the door and I follow. "Some people need to see things to understand them. So let's go."

NINETEEN

The world outside is dim and muted—the sky a muted blue, the voices floating from the center of camp a muted hum. We manage to slide around to the trail that winds up and away from camp toward the meadow without catching anyone's attention. For a fleeting moment, I think of our families—my father, your sister, my mother—how could they not notice our absence? But then I realize that they probably do. Perhaps they have all noted that we are both absent. Perhaps they assume we are together.

I let you lead me up the trail, climbing the long, gradual rise that rolls from the sea toward the vast expanse of tree-less fields and meadows that stretch north, all the way to the foot of the Great Ice. The northern sky is cloaked in thick gray clouds and I wonder if ahead it might be raining. The scent of a storm swirls in the breeze—a surprisingly warm breeze that alternates with the chilly northern wind I would expect, and I know that rain is out there somewhere.

You stoop to pick a rock from the path, a smooth round stone like an egg the size of your fist. Crouching, you dig out another, and then a third. I stop, watching your fingers claw at the dry, dusty ground, thinking of the coming rain and how it will bring new life to the wildflowers and support to the bees. The spring was wet but this summer has been dry, and we are due for relief. I glance up at the gray sky, darkening as the sun lowers, and I know the Divine will not make us wait much longer.

Our feet move almost silently across the grass as you turn off the path and head into an open space at the edge of an outcropping of rocks, large jagged boulders that push up out of the ground like the back of a stalking cat. Insects keep a thrumming rhythm all around us, but otherwise, the night is still. You sit on the grass about fifty paces from the line of rocks and look up at me. I guess this is our destination.

Folding my legs beneath me, I kneel on the sparse grass and watch as you arrange the stones you carry in front of you.

"Five years ago . . ." You place the three stones in a line. "Five years ago, my clan was on the verge of breaking. There were arguments, disagreements about what path was best for our people. My father, with the breath of his final days, was advocating for a move south. Because of him, the clan constructed fifteen two-person kayaks. In those days, our clan was not familiar with the sea. We relied almost exclusively on the mammoth herds for food. Our use of kayaks was limited, and only two members of the clan were adept at boat-making. The task was slow, but eventually, fifteen boats were complete.

My father had intended to move the clan—over sixty of us in all—in two groups. But when he died . . ." You fall silent, drawing a line in the dirt between clumps of grass with your finger. "In the end, we took thirteen kayaks and moved twenty-five people. The others—my extended family I'd known all my life—we never saw again.

"But the trip was slow; we didn't know the way, and we were not strong paddlers. At the end of every day on the sea, exhausted and hungry, we had to find a safe place to camp. We had to find food to eat. That was why, when we landed on your shore, we were so relieved. That was why my people were so anxious to go on a combined hunt. We needed safety, shelter, and food, and you offered us all these things."

As I listen to your story, a gust of sharp, cool wind flattens the grass and prompts me to tighten the laces at my throat.

"The first night, we all slept under the stars in the center of your camp. In the morning, before first light, the hunting party gathered. They wanted to head out early, knowing the mammoths were gathered here, in this very place. My brother never forgot it—a place where rocks rose up from the ground like the inverted hull of a boat. He recognized the spot as we passed through here with your parents the day we first arrived, hiking out to the meadow to find you.

"He leaned close to me and whispered in my ear. 'The rocks. There.' He didn't say any more. He didn't have to. I'd heard the story so many times. I knew that this was where she fell."

Before I can tell you that you are again speaking in riddles, you lift the stone at the head of the line in your hand.

"This is Chev," you say, leaning forward on your hands and knees and positioning the stone as if it were on a trek toward the rocks. "He was near the front of the group. The mammoths were huddled against those rocks in the morning mist, and he and the others were following your father."

You lift the second stone. "This is a man of your clan. A man known to be an excellent hunter. A man known for excellent senses." You set the stone back in its place, along a straight line leading toward the outcropping. "This is my mother," you say, lifting the last stone in the line. "She had dropped back after the man from your clan had heard something following behind. Dire wolves, he thought. My mother . . ." You trail off, setting the stone at the back of the line. "She hung back, watching, alert for movement stirring in the watery mist that shrouded the tall grass.

"No one knows exactly what happened as the hunters

progressed, but this is what Chev remembers: there was a cry—my mother's voice. A flash of movement, a sudden lunge forward. The man from your clan . . ." You lift the middle stone and let it drop. It falls hard against the stone at the back, the one representing your mother.

Your mother . . .

You reach forward and grab the stone that represents your brother. "Chev reacted to violence with violence." You stand, and with a flick of your wrist, you slam this strange, rigid symbol of your brother to the ground. It crashes against the middle stone and a loud crack shatters the air, sending tremors along my spine.

I shake with the shock of a sleeper suddenly woken from a dream. All at once, each character in the tale has a name. Each stone at your feet has a face. The truth of what happened that day—I see it all, as if the haze of that day has finally burned away.

I look out toward the ridge of protruding rocks, darkening to blue-gray silhouettes against a fading blue-gray sky, and my mother's words echo in my ears: *One of our men . . .* I see him there, just twenty paces ahead of me—Tram's father—his spear flying from his hand at the dire wolf he imagines he sees stirring in the mist . . . *killed one of their women . . .* And there, ten paces behind—your mother. An older version of you, crouching low, black hair falling over her shoulders, stirring the morning fog.

One of their hunters responded by killing the man who threw the spear. The hunter who responded, who killed Tram's father—Chev. My mind conjures the image of him— younger, slighter, but already possessing a heavy, measured gaze—as he turns to the sound of his mother's voice, sees the empty-handed hunter, his pierced mother, and reacts, pulling the obsidian blade from his belt and cutting down the hunter where he stands.

"It was your mother," I say. "I never knew. . . ." Absently, I lift the stone at the back of the line from the ground, enclosing it in my fingers. "You never told me—"

"Well, I've told you now."

You kneel down beside me, taking the mother stone from my hand. Your fingertips brush my palm. Your hair swirls in a circle in front of me, a momentary storm of darkness. "The hunters were spread out. There was confusion as to what had happened. Before your clan could organize, Chev scooped up our mother's body and rushed to camp. He roused us, shouting a hurried confusion of words. I remember that I understood nothing except that I had to get up, had to run for the boats.

"We were almost there—we had almost escaped—but the wife of the man Chev killed was close behind. She had been on the hunt; her spear was in her hand. She caught up to us on the beach and took her shot. She missed my brother but struck the boy beside him, my betrothed. Chev managed to pull him into the kayak before we pushed off, but his wound was bad. I remember the trail of red as his blood ran into the sea. We landed later that day in the place we now camp, but he had already died. Like my mother, he never saw the land where he would be buried.

"He was seventeen."

Without speaking, we both get to our feet and start down the trail. I think of the girl you were, twelve-year-old Mya, and how much you lost that day. Your mother, your betrothed. How different a person you would be if that day had never happened.

Did you love him? I think not, since you never say his name, but then, maybe his name is too precious to say out loud.

Chev's face comes to my mind—his willful brow and unyieldingly stubborn gaze. He led half your clan into the unknown—his own mother, led to her death.

You walk slightly in front of me, the mother stone still in your grasp. We reach the ring of huts and you follow me back to my door.

"He never made it to the south," I say, though I'm not really addressing you. I'm just thinking out loud, letting it all take form and meaning in my mind. We duck into the hut. The space is wrapped in a sheen of amber light as if warmth itself were visible. "He'd sided with Chev—with you and your family. And yet he never made it to see the bountiful south. He could never have known he was going to his death. That if by some chance he'd chosen to stay with the Bosha, if he'd chosen to stay under the leadership of Lo's father—"

"What's that supposed to mean?" The harshness of your voice tears me from my thoughts. I turn to see the same glare of contempt in your eyes that I'd seen on the day of our hunt. "Are you saying that to stay with Lo and her wretched father would have been a better choice—"

"I'm only saying he would have lived. He couldn't have known it then, of course, but his decision to leave with your brother was his undoing—"

"The decision to come ashore at *your camp* was his undoing! It wasn't Chev who killed him. It wasn't Chev who killed our mother—"

Something burns in your eyes, something fierce and frightening, and though it terrifies me, I cannot resist it. I cannot stay safely away.

A quick uptake of breath fills my lungs.

"I'm not making a judgment," I say. "I'm only pointing out the senselessness of it all. None of those deaths— your mother's, Tram's father's, your betrothed's—none of them would have happened, if only your brother and Lo's father—"

"Stop!" You turn in place as if to leave, only to whirl back to face me again. A scent stirs in the air, musky and dark. "I don't know what kind of story Lo's imagination produced for you, but I can assure you that nothing she told you was the truth—"

A flash of heat burns through my chest as the sound of Lo's name rings in my ears. Her name, spat with such venom from your lips, as if it were a common curse.

"Are you saying it's not true that you mistreated her—"

"Mistreated her? Is that what she told you? That I mistreated her—"

"That you all mistreated her. That you, your brother, your father—"

"My father? She spoke against my father, did she?" Your cheeks flush red, whether with shame or anger I can't be certain.

"Do you deny it? Do you deny that her safety was neglected by your father on a gathering trip? Are you saying she lied when she told me that she was lost and spent a night alone, outside on the grassland, while she was supposed to be in the care of your father and mother—"

"I do not deny it. I do not deny those events. Yes, she became lost. Yes, she was with my family. But I am convinced that whatever sad tale of mistreatment she told you is completely and utterly false—"

"Then here's your chance. Free me from my misconceptions. Tell me the truth."

You stare into my face unflinchingly. Without meaning

to, I take a step back. "I will not be made to answer to her lies. She is no longer of any consequence to me." You pause to catch your breath, the words flying out of your mouth like angry bees pouring from a hive. "Maybe Lo is the perfect girl for you. She certainly wouldn't hesitate to accept a gift for fear it was an attempt to buy her affections."

"I have never tried to purchase anyone's affections. Not hers. Not yours." I stoop to pick up the honey in its lovely cup made from a leaf of some distant, exotic tree. I had been so happy to see this gift. It had seemed such a fitting peace offering.

If only it could have been.

"You should take this with you," I say, shoving it into your hand. "I wouldn't want you to be accused of trying to purchase mine."

I get only a glimpse of the western sky—the streaks of red having faded, yielding to the hard dull gray of water in winter—before the door drapes closed behind you.

TWENTY

I return to the feast, but it holds nothing for me.

My brothers Kesh and Roon are busy making fools of themselves, taking turns lifting the heavy stones that encircle the hearth to show off to the girls. Shava and Lees applaud and call out cheers of encouragement. The giddy quality of their voices prickles me and I slow my steps. Even our mother calls for a spear-throwing contest between them, but thankfully the night is growing too dark.

Chev sits near the fire with my parents, my aunts and uncles, and the elders of my clan and yours. A bowl of mead rests within reach of each person. I notice that no one has come from the Bosha except for Shava and her mother—not Lo, not her father, not even Orn or Anki. No one accepted my invitation. Chev stands with a flourish, with the self-importance of someone about to make an announcement of great weight. I ignore him. Chev's proclamations don't interest me.

Instead, I focus my attention on the boys at the edge of the crowd. My eleven-year-old cousins are showing off a handful of spear points they made to a younger boy—Tram. Just seven years old, Tram sits wide-eyed, oblivious to the presence of the man who killed his father. His mother is also dead, having plunged into the cold sea from a kayak in the middle of a moonless night not long after her husband's burial. She left the boy in my family's hut while we all slept, unaware, as she walked down to the shore alone. It was his cries at daybreak that woke us to the horror of the abandoned kayak, floating empty, a dark blue shadow on the dark gray water.

I'm pulled back to the present by the loud cheers of your little sister Lees. Roon has just beaten Kesh in a footrace down to the beach and back, and as my aunt Ama declares him the winner, Lees throws her arms around his neck and kisses him on the cheek.

Poor Roon. He has no idea what kind of pain she will inevitably cause him.

I turn to head back to our hut. I am in no mood for drinking mead and singing songs anymore tonight.

I hear footsteps behind me and spin around, somehow expecting to see you there, but find Shava instead.

"Aren't you staying?"

"I'm tired," I say. "I think I should go in and rest."

"Did Pek go back to your hut?"

What kind of question is this, I wonder. After all, for most of the evening, Shava has been getting reacquainted with Kesh.

"He might have," I lie.

"Well, if you see him, tell him I wish him the best. Now that Seeri's brother has allowed her to break off her betrothal—"

"What? When?"

"His announcement, just before Kesh and Roon raced. Didn't you . . . You saw them race, right? I felt so bad for Kesh. He says Roon cheated when they were on the beach—didn't go all the way to the water, like he was supposed to—"

Behind her, from the layered gloom of evening shadows, Kesh calls her name. She turns and slides away, offering only a vague wave over her shoulder to me.

I head back into my family's hut, and as I pass through the door I'm surprised by a murmur of voices and the rattle of beaded bracelets on a wrist. My lie to Shava wasn't a lie after all. Pek stands in the center of the rug, right where your cup of honey had been. Seeri is with him, and as I step in through the door the two of them spring apart.

"Sorry," I say, but Seeri nearly knocks me over on her way to the door. The mask of happiness on my brother's face shatters as she moves out of his reach.

"No, don't apologize. I . . ." Seeri searches for something

to say, and my heart aches. I hate to be the one coming between them. If what Shava says is true and Seeri will be breaking off her betrothal, the two of them should have a bit of privacy together.

But before I can say another word, Seeri has said a hasty good night and fled.

I fall onto my bed. "I'm so sorry," I say. "I swear, Pek, if I'd known the two of you were in here—"

"Did you hear? He's going to do it. Chev's breaking her betrothal. He said he didn't want it to stand in the way of a possible alliance." Pek picks up one of the ivory harpoons and twirls it. "Father will speak to him for me soon—I'm sure. But Kol, our parents won't let me marry until you are at least betrothed. You know that, don't you?"

I remember what you said earlier—that Seeri would not marry until you were betrothed. "Pek, I will do everything I can."

He's at the door. It's so dark inside the hut now; he is little more than an outline. "I'm going to go find her and head back to the feast. I'd rather sit with Seeri in a big crowd than sit without her in here."

And then he's gone.

Songs and laughter go on long into the night. The hut, though empty, feels crowded with ghosts—your mother, Tram's father, your betrothed. Even Tram's mother lends her presence, stirring a sense of regret, both for the things that have happened and for the things that never will.

Voices still ring out from the feast when I finally fall asleep.

In the morning, I pretend I'm still asleep when I hear my mother rise to start cooking. She moves around noisily behind the hides that divide the hut into a separate sleeping area for her and my father. She groans as she dresses; I can tell that last night's mead is hurting her a bit this morning. It takes her longer than usual—her feet shuffle a bit more slowly—and I hear my father's voice, deep and rough, asking her a question I can't quite make out. It may be a request to be quieter so that he can sleep.

Eventually, the rustling stops, and she finishes her routine and heads out into the early light.

It isn't long, though, before she returns. I hear her speaking my father's name, in a loud whisper designed to wake him but not the rest of us. "Her mother," she says. "She wants to speak with you. You better wake up because I believe it's serious."

My first thought is that she is talking about Seeri—that Seeri is the "she" my mother refers to. But she said her mother wants to speak, and Seeri has only a brother. Whose mother wants to speak to my father?

After an extended exchange, my father finally asks in a voice loud enough to be heard by the entire hut, "Well, what's so important that she has to wake me before dawn?"

"She wants to discuss a betrothal. Not Pek this time, of course, poor girl. She's had her taste of that disappointment, and she sees what's going on with Seeri. It's Kol she wishes to discuss with you."

At these words I sit bolt upright. They can mean only Shava. Shava's mother wishes to discuss the possibility of a betrothal to me.

I'm on my feet and pulling on my pants before my father has a chance to frame an answer. "Excuse me," I say from the side of the hut I share with Pek, Kesh, and Roon—all of whom appear to be sleeping soundly. "May I please add my thoughts to this discussion?"

My mother pulls back the hide between the two rooms and stares at me with a look of disapproval. "You're awake early," she says. "Awake and listening at doors, I see."

This reprimand reminds me of the night I offered you the honey and you accused me of the same thing, even said the same words. "I wasn't listening. It couldn't be helped. It's possible Shava's mother heard you herself. Where did she and Shava sleep last night?"

"The kitchen. There was nowhere else, since I had ten elders from the Olen to find room for. But it's comfortable enough, and warm. I assure you they slept fine—"

"They must have," says my father. "They managed to wake early so they could greet you with this proposition." My father smiles and leans back on his bed with his arms crossed behind his head. I can see the thoughts darting around in his eyes. He's considering the idea.

"Don't bother," I say, and now it's my turn to be heard all the way in the kitchen. "Don't bother considering it, because I will not do it."

My mother turns to me, and her stare carries the weight of a mountain of disapproval. It presses me back into the doorway, but I will not allow her to intimidate me, not on this issue. Not on something as life changing as becoming betrothed.

"Who are you," my mother starts slowly, "to be choosy about a wife? Do you have a line of possible choices leading to this door? If you do, now might be the time to make your father and me aware of them. Because you are the oldest child of the clan's High Elder, Kol. Your brother may marry Seeri and help us form an alliance with the Olen, but it is you who is to inherit your father's position and your child who is to inherit yours. If you never marry—if you never have a child—"

"Then Pek's child will be the next High Elder—"

"That might happen. Or the clan might start to question the will of the Divine. The clan might decide that the Divine has ceased to favor us and has chosen another family to lead. Or worse. The clan could splinter apart. *That* cannot happen, Kol. This clan may move, but it *must not end.*"

"So if my child is to ensure the future of this clan, doesn't it matter who my child's mother might be? You would have me marry Shava? A girl who is so fickle she shifts from devotion to Pek to devotion to me in one afternoon?"

"What makes you think this is about Shava's devotion? Her mother may simply be trying to find her the best match—"

"If her mother is acting on her own, then I pity Shava. But it doesn't matter. Mother, I know Shava is a girl of good intentions. I believe her mother means well, too. But it doesn't matter. Shava is not at all the type of girl that I would hope to marry—"

"When did you and Pek become so incredibly arrogant?" The voice comes from behind me—it's the voice of my brother Kesh, standing beside his bed, pulling a parka over his shoulders. I turn to see him shove the hair from his face and I almost don't recognize him. His eyes, narrow with reproach, preside over features that seem to have aged overnight. His boyish roundness has been replaced by the angular lines of a tightly clenched jaw. "You are both so blinded by arrogance that you have become incapable of judging the value of a girl." These last words he says as he slides his feet into his boots. Without another word, he heads out the door into the brightening day.

I follow him as soon as I can get my own boots on. I run out still pulling on my parka, but summer is upon us, so the morning air has less of an edge to it and the kitchen isn't far. I'm not certain what Kesh intends to do, but I have a suspicion. I'm not sure what I'm thinking—whether I intend to try to stop him or just to be there as his brother.

By the time I reach the doorway of the kitchen, my brother is inside. His unexpected arrival seems to have drawn the attention of not just Shava and her mother, but also the few cooks who rise early to work with my mother in the kitchen. As I burst through the door, I join a group of six or seven people gathered around Kesh. Shava stands dead center, with a face like the sky as the sun comes up.

"Shava," Kesh says. "Before anything more is said between our parents this morning, I have something I want to say myself." My brother, my little brother whose music speaks so eloquently, has never found it easy to put his feelings into words. But he plows forward. "Last night, when you came to sit with me, I felt something change in my life. I felt like something I'd lost had been found—something I'd lost but had never even known I was missing." Kesh takes a quick glance at Shava's flushed face before dropping his eyes back to the floor and continuing. "I'm not sure what you want or what you are hoping for. I'm not sure what kind of man you or your mother would consider a good match for you. But I know that you are the kind of girl I would consider a good match for me." He raises his head and finds Shava's mother. Turning toward her, he continues. "I understand you intend to speak to my parents this morning. I would like to ask if you would be willing to speak to them about me."

Shava's mother smiles, but tears fill her eyes. "I will leave that up to Shava. You will have to ask her."

A rush of wind whistles in the vent like a sigh as Kesh turns back to Shava. "If you are willing," he says, "I would like to marry you."

The room falls silent when Kesh makes this unassuming statement. At first, Shava doesn't respond. She stands studying him, her lips pursed, but she doesn't speak. Then a quiet sob rolls out of her, and my brother Kesh—my sweet, quiet, awkward brother Kesh—steps toward her and takes her by the hand. Her shoulders shake with sobs until he is close enough for her to set her head on his shoulder. She tips her head up toward his ear and murmurs something, but her voice is muffled against his neck.

Finally, Kesh lifts his head and looks at all of us. He smiles, and in his smile I see the brother I know—not the brother who loses his temper and scolds me and Pek on our attitudes toward girls, not the brother who runs out of the hut to stop a betrothal, but the brother who plays the flute and finds it hard to talk in front of anyone not in our immediate family.

"She said yes," he says, and the kitchen erupts in cheers.

And just that fast, my brother Kesh, only fifteen years old, becomes betrothed to be married.

TWENTY-ONE

The morning meal this day is sparsely attended. Feasts and celebrations at this time of year, with daylight stretching long into night and no cold crash of dark to drive people back into the safety of their huts, often run long toward morning. People sleep late to overcome the effects of the revelry and the mead. But my family and Shava's family are seated around the hearth in the gathering place, and a meal of mammoth meat is served. Urar sets to lighting a flame in his oil lamp to draw good fortune to the couple, and my father goes from hut to hut to call the musicians and to personally announce the match.

The musicians, of course, collect quickly, as Kesh is one of their own. They play traditional songs reserved for weddings and betrothals, and more people emerge from their huts. Even an aching head can't stop most people from celebrating the announcement of an impending marriage, especially in a clan that hasn't heard such news in so many years.

By the time the meal is over most of the camp is awake, but neither you nor anyone from your family has appeared. Members of both the Manu and the Olen have offered up gifts to the couple—the old man who prepared the food last night gives them a scraper made from red jasper, and my aunt Ama's family presents them with a fishing net of knotted kelp. All the gifts they receive are personal and painstakingly crafted—an ivory sewing needle, a generous length of twine, a large bison pelt—things that will turn a new hut into a household.

Something hard forms in my throat. I can only suspect that I am jealous. Kesh and Shava, Pek and Seeri. Even Roon clearly has a prospect in your sister Lees.

But today is not about me. Today is about Kesh. I watch him as he sits cross-legged on the ground in the center of the meeting place playing his flute with a force of joy that bends the notes and turns them skyward, as if they belong to the birds or even to the Divine.

My sister-to-be, Shava, sits close beside Kesh. Funny, I think, how a girl can annoy two brothers and enthrall the third. Yet at this moment, Shava's usual anxiety replaced by contentment, I can imagine the sweetness Kesh sees in her. Memories flash, images lighting quickly in my mind's eye, of Kesh and Shava, eight or nine years old, playing on the beach. Before Lil gave him the flute, Shava was his partner in digging up worms. And after, as he learned to play, she was always his first audience when he learned a new song.

Was Kesh in love with Shava even then? Did it break his heart when she fell for Pek? When her family left our clan?

The meal is over but the music plays on. A few of my cousins, too young to remember the last time our clan had a wedding, get up and dance. I move toward the center of the crowd and the sound and movement swirl around me. The world outside this tight circle of family blurs and loses meaning. My mother's sister grabs my hands and spins me around. I close my eyes and try to block out any thoughts beyond this ring of happiness and hope.

For a moment—a brief fleeting moment—it works. But then I open my eyes to right myself as I turn in place, and I notice something move outside the circle of dancers.

A hand pushes back the hide that covers the door to your hut, and a figure steps out into the light.

You.

Chev emerges from the hut behind you and you turn your attention to him, as if the two of you are completely unaware of the celebration going on just feet away. Do you hope to get away to the boats without having to speak to me again—without being noticed?

If this is your hope, it fades a moment later when Shava calls out Chev's name.

Chev stops, his eyes scanning the faces of the people crowding the gathering place. He appears surprised, and well he should. It's almost unheard of for a young girl to so forcefully demand the attention of a High Elder, especially one from another clan. But Shava doesn't seem to care much for the expectations of society.

My mother, who was carrying a skin of water around to thirsty dancers, hurries to the edge of the ring and intercepts your brother. "I'm sorry," she begins. "The girl has just become engaged to our son—"

"Which son?"

"One of the younger ones—Kesh. I believe you met him when we visited your camp. He is only fifteen, so there won't be a wedding until his older brothers are betrothed, of course."

Before my mother can say another word to try to smooth things over, Kesh appears at her side, trailing behind Shava, who walks with a sense of purpose directly to Chev's elbow.

I can't help but move closer myself, my eyes on your eyes, but you never notice. You watch Shava warily, sensing, as I do, that this is no usual greeting.

"Sir," she starts. "I hope you'll excuse me. This may seem like a strange time for me to approach you, but what I have to say cannot wait. I've been watching your door, waiting for you to emerge from your hut all morning. I have something very important to tell you—a warning, in fact, about an attack that is planned against you. An attack that could come at any time."

It seems as if every eye in camp has turned toward Shava—her shocking words release an almost palpable force of tension into the air. My father must feel the pull even from inside the kitchen. He emerges through the door along with several elders from my clan and yours, their focus locked on the tight gathering in front of your hut.

"What's going on here? Shava, give our guests some room." My father's booming voice announces his arrival, and Shava cringes.

"I'm sorry, it's just . . . I just . . . I felt the need to say something, to warn Chev and his whole family about the danger that is coming." Shava's expression clouds with self-doubt. Her gaze shifts over her left shoulder and then her right, until her eyes settle on her mother. We all watch as Fi gets slowly to her feet from the spot where she's been seated all morning beside Kesh and crosses the gathering place with a gravity that makes something spin in the bottom of my stomach.

"Don't worry," says Shava's mother. "You're betrothed to a son of the Manu, and this is your clan now. You owe no further loyalty to Lo."

Lo?

I startle at the mention of her name. What could she have to do with danger and plots to cause harm?

"Shava, if you have something to say, just say it." I'm surprised by the tone of my own voice, but I can feel the sudden weight of your eyes on my face—a weight that fell there the moment Shava's mother mentioned the name of your old enemy. My only thought is that there must be some mistake or even a purposeful deceit. Why else would Shava choose this morning, the morning after you and I argued about Lo, to attach her name to some incredible accusation of a plot against Chev?

"I think we should discuss this inside," you say.

I glance around. People stand in the gathering place—members of your clan and mine—listening intently to the developing tale.

"Yes," Shava says. "Thank you. I think I really would prefer to sit down."

My father leads us into the now-empty kitchen. Shava is offered a place to sit along the wall, and she drops down beside a pile of discarded eggshells. The room is warm. Beads of sweat form on Shava's forehead and temples, creating a frame of moisture around her eyes.

Shava's mother sits beside her, but Chev does not hang back. He enters the room with purpose, followed closely by you. Without hesitation, Chev takes a seat directly in front of Shava. Kesh is last to enter the shade of the room. A patch of sunlight that clings to the top of his head reluctantly falls away as the door drapes shut. Even through the purple shadows of this darkened space, I see the tight pinch of fear across his brow.

Clearly, he knows no more of what Shava is about to say than Chev does.

"Go ahead," Shava's mother prompts. "You no longer need to fear. Your loyalties are with your betrothed's clan now, and Chev is a friend of this clan. He is also the rightful High Elder of the Bosha clan, as your grandmother has told you many times. Tell him what you know."

"I know," Shava starts, but her voice breaks on her words. My mother comes up quietly and hands her a waterskin to drink from.

Shava takes a long, shaky drink with unsteady hands. "I know," she continues, her voice strong and clear this time, "that someone is plotting your murder."

TWENTY-TWO

The room itself seems to suck in a breath.

"And who is plotting to murder me?" Chev rocks forward, moving so close to Shava that only a small sliver of light separates the silhouettes of their shadowed faces.

"Lo—the High Elder of the Bosha clan."

You are the first to react. "Lo?" you ask. "How could it be Lo? Her father is High Elder—"

"Lo's father is dead."

A note fills the air, a chorus of gasps.

"That's not possible," I say. "Just yesterday, she was on her way to see her father. She said she had to help him—"

"Lies," Shava whispers, as if Lo might somehow hear her, or have spies listening in.

Spies . . .

"But why? Why pretend her father is alive if he's dead? What does any of this have to do with murder?" My tone is beyond skeptical—it's accusatory. I lean over the spot where Shava sits. Am I hoping to intimidate her? Behind me, my mother opens a vent in the roof, letting in a shaft of light, but my shadow paints the floor like a stripe of night, keeping Shava cloaked in violet darkness.

"Everything is by design," she answers. "We didn't land on your shore and then discover Chev here. We knew Chev was here, so we came to your shore. Lo wants to manipulate perceptions. She creates elaborate secrets—secrets she claims are to protect the clan. It's a clan secret that her father has died—that *anyone* has died. The truth, she says, would expose our weaknesses."

Shava looks up at Kesh and he smiles and nods. Her eyes move to mine and then quickly dart away. I can feel the suspicion fixed on my face. I do not believe her, and I'm certain it shows.

She looks down and curls inward, but her mother takes her hand.

Clearing her throat, Shava's mother glances from face to face with a sharp light in her eye. When it sweeps over me, from my furrowed brow to my tightly drawn lips, I feel indicted by that light. "My daughter's story is true," she says. "Lo wants to give the impression that those who remained have thrived since Chev left, but that's a lie. They have struggled. Lo blames Chev for taking the best hunters, for taking the Spirits of the game when he left. My family—my grandmother, my mother, me and my daughter—we are all storytellers. We keep the stories of the clan. When we first returned, my mother taught Shava and me all the old stories—stories of abandonment by Chev and his family, about the Spirits following Chev south, Spirits of the herd animals—mammoth and bison. We learned all the stories of struggle, suffering, and death—"

"Lo shares the old stories whenever she can," Shava interrupts. "But her plans for the future . . . Lo won't share those with the elders. Instead, she plots in secret. She quietly converts her followers—her believers—many of whom were so young when Chev left, they hardly remember him. Lo's lies have become their truth. Those who listen to her have been suffering a long time, and hunger has made them vulnerable.

"She works with Orn, who is full of cunning and charisma. He is training to become a healer, and he reads signs from the Divine that support what Lo says. Those who are desperate for something to believe in have put their faith in them.

"She intends to take back the bounty of the clan. She is making a plan to repay death with death."

"But the elders of your own clan," my father starts. "Why haven't you gone to them?"

"I have!" Shava says. "They nod and agree. They say they have counseled her against violence. They underestimate her, and she lulls them into a false sense of control.

"The elders advocate for a change—for a return to the use of kayaks and a camp by the sea. Generations have fulfilled the promise of Bosha's husband to live off the herds, and the elders have come to believe that the Divine has a new plan for us now. They have asked Lo to settle by the water, to construct more kayaks to use for hunting and fishing.

"Lo has happily constructed new kayaks. Kayaks can be used to fish, but they can also be used to spy. Even to attack. But the elders are satisfied that they are getting their way.

"And so Lo has announced a scouting trip, to search for a suitable bay. The elders are to leave today. They will go feeling victorious, believing they have influenced her, and Lo will have them out of her way.

"Eight of the ten will go. Two of them—a cousin of Vosk and her husband—are loyal to Lo. They will stay behind, 'in case they are needed in camp.' With the help of these two elders, Lo has all the support she needs. Ten clan members have vowed to help her, in whatever action she takes.

"She confided all of this to me yesterday, after we learned that Chev and his family were here with your clan. She didn't say what she would do, but she said she would act soon.

"When I went to get my mother, I tried to warn the elders, but Lo had already called a formal meeting of the council, to prepare for their trip. I was terrified to see how quickly she was moving.

"Lo is taking steps. For so long, her plan was nothing but words, but now it is becoming action."

None of this makes sense. I study Shava, huddled on the ground beside her mother. Is all this for attention? Is this a scheme to get Shava noticed? "These are strong accusations—" I say, but my own father cuts me off.

"These are strong accusations indeed," he echoes, but his hand catches hold of my upper arm and draws me back. My shadow slides away, and light cuts across the floor where Shava sits, propped against her mother's shoulder. "Accusations shouldn't be made lightly," my father continues, "but if they're true, Chev has a right to hear them."

Chev gets to his feet, rubs his hands over his face, and sits back down. "You say you are a storyteller," he starts, addressing Shava's mother. "You are Gita's daughter?"

"Yes."

"How many years ago did you leave our clan to marry?"

"Twenty-three years ago."

"Before I was born," says Chev. "That's why I have no memory of you. But your mother, Gita. I grew up listening to her. She is a gifted keeper of stories—"

"She was. She died before the spring came—"

"I am so sorry to hear that." Chev gets to his feet again, looks around as if seeking a place to go, and runs both palms across his head. I notice a frailty in him that I've never seen before. He sits again. "I'm sorry to hear that death came to my old clan, my old family. Can you tell me how many have died?"

"Since you left for the south, ten have died—"

"Ten," you repeat, your voice a hushed whisper. Your hand flies up to your mouth and you drop your eyes.

"We left thirty-seven behind," Chev says.

"And they are twenty-seven now."

Chev slumps forward, his face in his hands. I try to think how many of the Manu have died in five years. Tram's father and mother, a cousin of my father's . . . three.

Ten deaths in five years. It's hard to imagine so many burials.

"You say death also came for Lo's father, Vosk. We may have been enemies at the end, but he was once my father's close friend. Would you tell me the story of how he died?"

Shava's mother nods. "Yes," she says. "I will tell you. Shava will help me. Shava?"

Without further instruction, perhaps acting out a process she has followed with her mother many times before, Shava stands and closes the vents my mother just opened. "You can't depend on outer light to see," Shava says, her hands trembling with nerves, but her voice smooth with an incongruent wisdom. "You must each see the scenes unfold with your inner eyes, illuminated by inner light. Sit. Rest your hands in your lap. Close your eyes."

I glance around. My father sits without hesitating. My mother settles beside him, but it's impossible to tell whether she is showing trust in Shava or her own husband.

Beneath my left foot, a round stone, no more than a pebble, pokes into the thin sole of my summer boots, and I roll it side to side distractedly as I consider Shava's mother, Fi. A stout but solid woman, like the stump of a once-tall tree, her face is lined by a multitude of thin creases that form stars around each eye—the eyes of a woman who has spent long stretches of time squinting in concentration. She was a storyteller for our clan before she and Shava left. I remember many evenings when her words carried me away.

And now she has promised to tell a tale of Lo's clan. Curiosity overcomes hesitancy, and I sit.

I close my eyes. Everyone is seated; everyone is silent. An impatient wind ripples the hide behind my back and rattles in the vent flap, scolding, taunting. The wind moves on, replaced by a deep stillness. Quiet wraps around me like the walls of a cave. Into this space a voice intrudes, the voice of Shava's mother.

It was winter—the kind of cold dark winter that coats everything in the same pale gray—clouds, water, ice, sky. Haze hung like a drape across the heavens, and behind this drape the Divine hid her face, unwilling to give her warmth to the world.

It was during this hard gray time, two years ago, that the Bosha

clan appeared at the far northern edge of the meadow. The last light
of day was burning out when they appeared, and as the sun dropped
hastily behind the ridges of the western hills, their elders descended
the slope toward this camp—dark shadows, purple and blue in the
gathering dusk, like a line of ants marching with an unknown pur-
pose. Kol and Pek, the first to see them, called to their father, who
in turn called his elders.

All the elders gathered in the meeting place to greet the visitors—
each with one hand open and one hand holding a spear.

I remember this visit by the Bosha, of course—Lo and
I talked about it just yesterday—but the voice of the storyteller, the quiet darkness, even the fragments of words
that are carried by the wind into this space from outside
bring the whole experience to life inside me, as if I am facing those elders again. Their gaunt faces lined by hunger,
the sunken eyes of a woman who trembled relentlessly, no
matter how close she sat to the fire in the hearth. Shava
rushing, carrying out mammoth meat that she'd prepared
the day before. I remember the reluctance with which they
had accepted it, and then, once accepted, the ferociousness
with which they'd eaten.

Lo's father, Vosk, told of his clan's travels, of their hike to the
edge of the Great Ice on a long and fruitless search for bison or
mammoth. The elders of both clans sat in the meeting place under a
sky black as soot and talked about hunting and herds and hunger.
Hunger, Vosk believed, was a challenge from the Divine, a test of

patience to pursue the game given to our ancestors for food when the earth was new. He had no faith in a settled life, a camp by the water that took food from both the land and the sea. It showed no faith in the old ways, the sacred ways ordained by the Divine through our ancient ancestor, Bosha. Lo's father, like Lo, watched constantly for signs, for messages from the Divine. Here in our camp, he believed he found one, in the form of my daughter, Shava.

Vosk was rejuvenated by the meat Shava had prepared. It was the first fresh meat any of them had eaten in a long time. He recognized me and realized Shava was a daughter of his own clan. When he learned my husband—our tie to the Manu—had died, he was convinced that it was the Divine's will that we should rejoin them. This meat, brought to him by Shava's hands, was the omen he was looking for.

That night, our family camped with the Bosha clan, and in the morning, we departed. Vosk believed that Spirits of the game—of bison and mammoths—were calling the clan westward.

We ranged farther and farther west in search of the herds. The game was scarce—a few thin caribou sparsely scattered across frozen, unyielding ground—and as we moved away from the sea, we had no fish and few birds to hold us over between kills.

Lo's father was certain that the answer was to move faster across the open land toward the mountains in the far west. He believed that was where the mammoths would be found. Everyone worked to build overland sleds that we could drag to move more quickly. To make the sleds, we sacrificed tent poles and hides, as nights on the plains grew ever longer and ever colder. Every day we covered great stretches of ground, growing weak with exhaustion and hunger. Still, we followed our High Elder. We pushed farther and farther west. Beneath our feet, the rough gray soil became smooth gray ice.

After days spent descending into a broad, unbroken valley that rolled unending to the horizon, the ice broke up. We traveled across islands of smoke-gray ice that floated in a shallow sea, indistinguishable from the bone-gray sky.

We waded with wet and frozen feet, taking turns pulling one another on sleds that floated like small boats. Lo's father carried Lo on his shoulders, insisting we press on, until we came to a place where the ground became nothing more than isolated points of ice—islands the size of footprints surrounded by wide pools and streams of water.

There was nowhere to camp. No dry land would support a tent. Seeing no choice, the elders of the clan announced that we would turn back.

This was a moment of both relief and horror. Who wouldn't want to turn back rather than walk steadfastly into the rising sea? But there was no food behind us, and we knew it. No fish swam in the sterile meltwaters. Unless we came upon some seabirds soon, people would begin to succumb.

Just then, Lo called out. From her perch atop her father's shoulders, she said she could see a mammoth. He was out in the water farther west, and she was determined to make the kill. Before he could stop her, she climbed down from her father's shoulders and, *clutching her spear, she half ran, half swam into the deeper water.*

Of course, her father pursued her. By the time he managed to get to her, she was dropping out of sight beneath the surface, her dark head rising and falling like a bird on the water, floating and diving, floating and diving.

But he saved her. He reached her, carried her back, got her to the safety of a warm pelt in a sled that bobbed upon the sea like a makeshift kayak.

The entire clan strove to restore Lo to health. The effort was so total—so all-consuming—not one of us noticed what was happening to her father. Recovering his daughter had exhausted him. His arms and legs were going rigid with cold. But he said nothing. Maybe he was unable to speak. Maybe he didn't want to distract us from trying to save Lo.

By the time we looked around to tell him how well she was doing, his body had failed him, his legs had given out, and he had slipped away into the cold gray water.

He was gone.

Chev rises from his seat on the floor so abruptly, the spell is broken and my eyes fly open. For a brief moment, the familiar sight of the kitchen surprises me, as I'm thrust from the past back to the present.

Chev paces, circling the room, running his hands over his hair, and speaking in an angry whisper only he can hear. "And yet the rest of you lived," he says, finally. He sets a hand on a post of the hut and draws in a long, slow breath. "You all survived? How did you make the return trip without food—"

"Lo found us food," interjects Shava. "I was sitting in the same floating sled that she had been lifted into, was wrapped in the same pelt. She let out a wail when she learned of her father's death, and she lunged over the side of the boat.

"It was then that she saw it—its head resting just below the surface of the water. A mammoth. The body of a drowned mammoth. Her father must have been standing on it right before his body slid into the sea.

"By dying as he did, he'd led us right to it. And Lo discovered it. She may have crashed into the water after something in her imagination, but the mammoth she found was very real.

"We fashioned cutting knives at the ends of spears to reach down and slice off chunks of meat and ate them raw, right there, floating in the sleds or huddling on the points of ice. Nothing ever tasted so good.

"That meat was our rescue, and the Divine had used Lo as the means of revealing it to us. Ever since that day—ever since that moment—Lo has been the High Elder of the clan."

TWENTY-THREE

"**T**hat's ridiculous," you say, the words snapping from your lips like wet wood popping in the flame. Your brother, who a moment ago was lost in thought, looks up as if he'd forgotten you were in the room.

"Did you not hear the tale that I just heard?" Chev asks. "Of how the Divine used Lo to deliver food to the clan—"

"Of course I did—"

"And your response is to call it ridiculous? Did it not fill you with grief at the thought of our own people suffering? Did it not fill you with remorse—"

"Grief, yes. Of course I feel grief." Your voice breaks under the strain of the words. I think of the ten dead of your former clan, and I cannot doubt the weight of your grief. "But not remorse," you continue. "I cannot feel remorse for something they brought upon themselves. The Bosha rejected you. We are the Olen clan now."

Chev kneels down in front of Shava's mother. "May I ask you? Do you know why your mother, Gita, chose to follow Vosk?"

"She always regretted it," says Shava's mother. "But he was her nephew, my cousin . . . blood. She felt she had no choice."

"You see, Mya? Some of the Bosha had no choice but to follow Vosk. And now they have no choice but to follow your old friend—"

"Don't call her my *old friend*. Friendship requires truth, and there is no truth in her. There never has been. She is poison, Chev! She poisoned our own people against us—"

"I have not forgotten!" Chev's outburst throws a hush over the room, a hush so complete I feel as if the whole world has gone silent. The rattle in the vent stops; the birds outside quiet their songs. "But Mya, you know I could never wish them harm. So how could I ever accept the thought of them forgotten, abandoned by the Divine? How could I accept the thought that the person they trusted to lead them has led them to ruin?"

"But she has indeed led us to ruin," Shava says, her voice calm, as if a gentle manner of telling will lessen the pain the words inflict. "The two years we have lived with the Bosha have been marked by hunger and cold. Some nights were so cold. . . ." Shava holds out her hand. The skin of each fingertip and each knuckle is darker and thicker than the unscarred skin around it—the lingering record of frost-bite. "Hunger, cold, and hate. Hate for Chev for abandoning us—"

"You hear?" you ask. Like your brother, you can no longer sit still. As he paces, you follow behind him. "Do you see now that she continues to steal the honor you deserve? That she persists at turning the hearts of your people against you?"

Shava, too, rises from the floor slowly, and with her the tension in the room rises. Suddenly I remember the reason we all came in here. . . .

So Shava could share a warning.

"She does persist in turning the Bosha against you, and she has succeeded. She has sent scouts to spy on you, and these scouts have brought back stories of your prosperity in the south. They have told of the ornate canoes you use to travel to a land of plentiful game. And Lo has convinced many of the Bosha that it should all belong to them—the boats and the game and the land. Lo has told them that what the Olen possess rightly belongs to them.

"Lo says Chev is a false leader. And she says she will kill him and take his place."

These words of Shava's still hang in the air as you push through the kitchen door and out into the gathering place. Without thinking, I follow right behind you.

"So you believe her?" I call.

Your hasty steps come to a sudden stop. You turn slowly, your eyes wide, your head jutting forward from your shoulders. You take a single step in my direction.

"Don't you?"

In the bright sunlight I study the way the sun glows hot like a burning coal in your black-as-night hair and try to answer this question, for myself as well as for you. Do I believe that Lo—a person I found to be so honest and uncontrived—is plotting to murder your brother? Or do I think that Shava is a girl with a vivid imagination and a hunger for attention?

"I don't know," I finally say.

"Then I suggest you go to your dear Lo," you say. "Go and ask her yourself. By the time you return with her answer, my family will be gone from this camp, on our way to protect our own."

I don't know what I had expected. Would a man linger in a place where he believes he is being hunted? Of course not. But if I leave now to go speak to Lo, what will you think of me? Will you see me as a peacemaker, or as a traitor to your brother?

I remember the gift you brought me last night—the cup of folded leaves and the golden honey inside it. I want to say something, to apologize for the things I said before. I want to tell you that I never meant to offend you, and to say how sorry I am that I never knew the whole story of the death of your mother and how it was caused by a man of my own clan. I think of the pain you must feel every time you are made to come to this camp, the place she died. Even right now, standing across from me in this empty gathering place, your body practically twitches with the desire to get away. I see this, and I want to tell you that I understand it now. I understand why you hate the north so much, why you've never seemed at ease here.

But I hesitate too long, and the chance is gone. You pivot on your heel and turn away.

My formless words dissolve on my lips as I watch you cross the gathering place and disappear into your family's hut.

I don't wait around for you to leave our camp. Instead, I head straight to the water. It isn't long before I'm halfway across the bay on my way to Lo's camp.

When I reach the western shore, the beach is deserted except for a few seabirds that stand like sentries, watching the water from large rocks that frame the bay like massive shoulders. The sea breeze is cold in my face—colder than it's been all summer. Though the sky is cloudless, the wind reveals that a change is on the way. I gather my collar around my neck after dragging my kayak onto the strip of dark gray sand.

I climb the trail to the ring of huts, but I find no one. The entire camp is deserted. From a clearing that overlooks the camp, voices float down, mixed with the structured, deliberate sound of activity. The whole clan must be together, maybe preparing a kill or readying for a celebration.

I remember the scouting trip Shava talked about. If the story is true, perhaps the Bosha's healer is leading a ceremony to bring good fortune to the trip.

I've just found the path up to the clearing when I hear hurried footsteps heading toward me. A moment later a figure appears—Lo.

She stops short when she sees me standing at the base of the path. For a moment, I think I see suspicion on her face. "I saw your kayak coming across the bay. I didn't know to expect you," she says. "Is everything all right at your camp?"

"You didn't come last night," I say. "You said you would come to the feast that Chev was giving for me, but you didn't."

"I'm sorry." Some of the tension drains from Lo's shoulders, and the line that formed between her eyes when she first saw me softens. "I couldn't leave."

And then I remember. Before she says another word, I remember the excuse she had given for returning to her own camp yesterday.

"I had to help my father," she says. She smiles an easy

smile, and my stomach twists. "He's been working on a kayak, and I wanted to help."

Shava's words ring in my ears. *Lo's father is dead.* Shava said these very words. But not just Shava. Her mother told the story of the hunting trip that claimed his life.

"Your father?"

Something in Lo's eyes dims, but she nods.

"The clan's High Elder?"

"Yes. Yes, my father needed my help." Something creeps into her voice—a tight, clipped note of impatience. "Why?"

I glance around at the ring of huts—sparsely covered in skins, support poles leaning—but that doesn't necessarily prove that the clan is struggling. Lo's clan is nomadic; this camp was constructed quickly and was not intended to last.

"What are you looking for?" The tone of Lo's voice tightens further, until the words all but strangle in her throat. She raises a hand as if to shade her eyes from the sun, but where she stands she is sheltered by my shadow.

"Is there someplace we could go to talk?"

"Of course."

Lo leads me to a hut with gaps between the covering hides that let in light and wind. "I'm glad you came to see me," Lo says, once the door has draped closed behind her. "I was hoping to have the chance to spend more time with you."

"So you could tell me more lies?"

She takes a step back, but if she finds my accusation surprising, her face doesn't let it show. "What lies have I ever told you?"

"You told me that you were helping your father yesterday. But that's not possible. Your father is dead."

Maybe I expected her to argue, but I'm thrown off when she smiles. "I never lied. I said I was helping my father. That's true. I'm helping him by leading this clan. I'm helping him by building a kayak. I'm helping him. That's all true. I never said that he was living and breathing beside me while I did it." Lo slinks past me in the tight space, dropping down onto the pile of pelts near the center of the room. "Come sit by me."

"I'm fine here," I say, though the suggestion sends a wave of heat over my skin. Lo stretches back against the warm brown of a bear hide, and I can't help but consider sitting down, stretching out beside her, taking the time to hear her words, letting her explain everything that's been going on.

When she smiles, as she does now, there is a warm invitation in her eyes.

How could this be manipulation, when her eyes glow with the openness of the wide sky that stretches above the meadow on a summer day? It can't hurt just to sit for a moment, to speak to her. To ask a few questions and discover the truth.

I seat myself on the floor beside Lo's left hip. "My

brother and Shava have become betrothed," I say. "She and her mother will be rejoining our clan."

Something flashes across Lo's face—a subtle flinch.

"Because of this, she felt that she could open up to us. She shared some information with us—"

"What kind of information?"

Sitting close to Lo, I see wariness rise in her. The openness in her eyes abruptly clamps shut. "Can you guess what she said—"

"Kol, stop playing with me—"

"She said that you intend to kill Chev."

Lo shakes her head and starts to laugh. Not a hard laugh, but a controlled, deliberate laugh that has a statement wrapped inside it. "If I killed Chev, Mya would simply take his place. If I killed both Chev and Mya, it would be Seeri, and after her, Lees. I would have to kill them all to reunite my clan—"

"Are you saying it's not true?"

This time it's Lo who stands. She steps to the door and holds it open for a moment, looking out as if watching for someone to appear or something to happen. Then she drops the door closed and the room dims again. She stands in the doorway, light bleeding around the hide behind her, turning her into a silhouette, her features hidden in shadow. She moves back to the spot where I am seated and I scramble to my feet.

"Do you not yet realize?" Lo says. Her voice is rich and dark, like the shadow that hides her face. "There is no Olen clan; there is only Bosha. The Olen are a false clan, led by a false leader. Chev refused to submit to my father when the Divine chose him to lead, yet despite this selfishness, they have thrived while we have suffered. Until today.

"Their hunting range is the Bosha's hunting range. Their bay is the Bosha's bay. They have no right to any of it, and the Divine has chosen this day for it to be reclaimed."

I step sideways out of a small beam of light that falls from a gap in the hides above our heads. Finally, Lo's face is lit enough that I can see her features. They are dressed in sharp intensity: the line between her eyes has returned, and her taut lips are as pale and bloodless as bone.

A sound comes from the hill above the camp, a voice calling out—a name perhaps? Or maybe a word.

Another voice answers and then another.

They each call out the same word. With repetition it becomes clear.

Ready.

One after the other, voice after voice repeats: *ready, ready, ready.*

Ready for what?

The answer doesn't take long. A sound starts at the crest of the hill but gets closer, louder, stronger—the rhythm of running feet. Another sound mixes in—something dragging across the ground.

I push past Lo to look out the door, just in time to see at least ten of Lo's clanspeople scrambling down the hill from the clearing, pushing newly built kayaks to the sea.

"It's begun," Lo says.

"What—"

Lo comes up behind me, her fingers wrapping around my wrist. When she answers, her words come from right behind my ear. "They do not have to go far. We know that Chev is in your camp—he and his whole family. The process of reclaiming what is ours has begun."

I turn quickly, and the twisted sneer on Lo's lips is like a confession. "It's too late," she says. "It's too late to save them from their destruction."

TWENTY-FOUR

Her last few words set off a loud ringing in my ears. The room grows dark a moment and then brightens again, lit by an unnatural golden glow independent of the sunlight that bleeds in from outside. Lo's face, illuminated by this eerie gleam, appears so calm, so lovely. She cannot have said the words I thought I heard.

The ringing in my ears begins to fade, and as it does, the sound of kayaks splashing into the sea rises from the beach, mixing with the calls of gulls, circling, shouting out a warning.

"Where are they going?"

"I told you. The tyranny of a false leader, the wedge dividing a clan—they go to remove these things." Lo's voice is oddly changed—controlled, detached, rhythmic, like the voice of Shava's mother—a storyteller's voice. "When their orders have been carried out, the so-called Olen clan will be no more. We will again be one clan, and we will again be strong." There is no conflict in her eyes, no hesitation in her voice.

"Their orders are to remove a false leader?"

"Their orders are to *end* Chev's tyranny—to end the tyranny of his entire family."

"By what means?"

Lo lets out a faint sigh. "I'm sure you already know."

She smiles at me now, and her eyes invite me to smile back. She wants my complicity. Worse, I can see she thinks she will get it.

"You can't do that."

"Of course I can! Death will be repaid with death— it's what they deserve!" And there it is—a sudden flash like lightning splitting the night sky—the hatred Shava described. The hatred I would not believe in. A bright white flash of rage—fleeting—but in its light everything comes into view. With crisp clarity, the true shapes of things are shown.

I don't waste time with a reply—I push past her. I'm out the door before she can react, running as fast as my legs will move. The path to the shore is steep and uneven and my feet slide on loose rocks. More than once they nearly go out from under me, but I keep running and never slow down.

I only dare lift my eyes from the ground right in front of my feet a few times, but even so, it doesn't take long for me to realize my kayak is gone. The spot where I pulled the boat up onto the shore is empty, marked by a telltale rut in the sand leading back to the water's edge.

Of course they would take it. Without it, I have no way to pursue them across the bay.

Out on the water, I see the black silhouettes of Lo's followers as they head east toward the sun, toward the eastern shore, toward my own clan's camp.

The overland route that I hiked with Lo yesterday is to my left. It will take me much longer than the water route, but I have no choice. I scan the edge of the trees that conceal the trail up the mountains. My empty hand twitches— I think of my spear, tucked inside my kayak's hull.

I allow myself one last glance at the silhouettes receding across the bay before sprinting off toward the trees.

Cloudless, the sky is the clear smooth blue that appears only in summer, somehow closer than the remote gray of winter. The sun throws white light all around, but still, the brightness hinders more than helps. Trees cast splotchy shade on the trail, making it difficult to see roots and other hazards as I run. I make it only to the first bend in the path before the toe of my boot catches on a jagged rock jutting out of the dirt. I find myself sprawled out on the ground before I know what happened, the palms of both hands scraped and dirty.

I sit up and allow myself just one moment to examine

my hands, to study the blood soaking into the thin layer of dirt, turning it sticky and black. A moment later I am on my feet, wiping my bloody palms against my pants and running hard again.

I pass the places Lo and I passed yesterday—the fallen tree where Lo sat, the ferns where we stretched out beside each other. My feet move faster and my legs pump harder. The extra effort makes my chest ache, but I welcome the pain.

I try to imagine what will happen when Lo's people find that you and your family have gone. Will they pursue you to the south? Or will they return to Lo and tell her the opportunity was missed?

And what will she do then?

The higher I climb, the crisper the air around me grows, like I'm climbing backward in time, back into the spring, before leaves sprouted and insects hatched. Turning a blind corner around a cluster of dense trunks and naked, twisted branches, I startle as something small races into the low brush—a hare or maybe a fox. My feet lose their rhythm and my left foot stubs against a root.

I catch myself before I fall, but not before my ankle turns. With the next step, pain shoots up into my knee and down into my foot. Now I fall, clutching the ankle as I roll onto my back.

To the count of ten, I tell myself. *You can lie here to the count of ten, but then you have to be up and moving again.* By the count of three, I remind myself to breathe. By six, I unclench my jaw. By nine, I rotate my ankle once in the air. At the count of ten I'm upright, testing my weight on my left foot. Painful, but bearable.

I hobble at first, then shuffle, until finally, nearing the summit, I run. I wince with every step, but still, I run.

As I reach the crest of the hill—the spot that marks the halfway point in the trail—the sight of the sky confuses me. Dark gray clouds move surprisingly quickly across the bright blue sky. They roll and puff like storm clouds, and at first I think I sense it—the fresh cool wetness on the breeze that precedes a storm. But another scent overwhelms the coolness—a stinging sharp scent that burns my throat.

Smoke.

Half running, half sliding on loose gravel underfoot, I speed down the trail that now descends sharply before it makes its first switchback since the summit. From here, I get my first view of my camp. The neat circle of huts, each one glowing with red and orange flames. Each one emitting a plume of black into the sky.

The ring of huts has become a ring of fire.

Wind sweeps across the valley floor and rises up the steep face of the cliff at my feet. It carries with it the heavy, oily scent of burning hides. A strong gust rattles the still-bare branches, speckled with pale green buds, and smoke mixes into my hair. Another blast hits me hard in the face, my eyes stinging and swelling, blurred by thick tears that streak down the sides of my nose. My lips dry and swell like blisters.

A shadow passes over my head—a large bird is circling, a buzzard—and I startle out of a trance I'd fallen into. How long have I been standing in this spot, riveted by the horror of the scene at my feet? I can do no good standing here. I drag my eyes away and force myself to keep moving.

The farther I descend into the valley, the thicker the smoke becomes. Cinders fly by in the breeze—pieces of charred hide and tiny flecks of wood, glowing red-hot as they spin through the air. As I run, a few sear the skin of my face and hands, but I brush them away and keep moving.

I emerge from the trees at the foot of the trail and walk right into a wall of heat. Sweat pools at my neck and runs down my back. The air is so thick I fear it will choke me.

I allow myself to turn my face to the water for three breaths—just three breaths. No more. As I gulp in cool air, I notice that the beach and bay are empty—there's not a single sign of Lo's clanspeople or their boats. I fill my lungs once, twice, three times. Then I turn and run up the path to the camp that from here is visible only as a red glow at the top of the rise.

As I move closer to camp, voices reach my ears—voices vibrating with panic and fear. The roar of flames drowns out words, but I manage to pick out shouts from my father. He is calling for everyone to move away and head for the water.

Yet no one is listening. Alongside each hut, dangerously close to the flames that dance across the surface of the hide coverings, people are moving—digging, scooping up dirt and throwing it at the fire, frantically trying to extinguish the blaze. My uncle Reeth and his family work to save the kitchen. My brothers and mother use broad flat stones from the hearth to fling dirt at our own hut. Even my father, still shouting for people to give up the fight and retreat to the beach, is helping Kara, the widow whose hut stands next to ours.

I have never seen—never even imagined—so much flame. A spark from the hearth sometimes spreads to a pelt, a wall of the kitchen once caught fire, but never have I seen flames like these. My aunt Ama and her sons run by, carrying full waterskins from the beach, but all the water they can carry has little effect. The trip to the beach is too far. By the time they fetch more, the flames have only grown.

All around me, shouts are punctuated by coughs as people choke on the smoke that swirls and circles, coating and covering everything, rising high above our heads. I look up, my eyes drawn to a darkening pillar of smoke that stretches to the sky, when I realize with a start that it isn't a pillar of smoke at all.

It's a storm cloud. A dark storm cloud rolling in quickly from the north.

The scent of an approaching storm . . . I had noticed it on the peak but then had all but forgotten it. If only it were closer. But watching the clouds roll in, I know they won't come in time. At the rate the fire is burning, the camp will be nothing but cinders before the rain reaches it.

A hand grabs my shoulder. I turn to see my brother Roon beside me, his face bright red and his hair soaked with so much sweat it appears he's been swimming. "Help me," he says. He tugs on my parka like a child. "Come with me to the beach."

His eyes are wide. Is he panicking? I want to help him, but my head spins around as I take in the image of my family and friends, each one desperately working. It might all be in vain, but I know I have to help them. "I can't," I say. "You go and rest. I'll be there soon."

"No!" Roon's eyes blink rapidly. He grabs my shoulders with both hands and shouts into my ear, "I have an idea to put out the fire, but I can't do it alone."

I pull back and study his face when cold water drips from his hair onto my hands. Icy rivulets run down his face. His parka is soaked.

What I'd thought was sweat is seawater. He's been in the sea.

"I have an idea!" he says again, gripping my shoulders even tighter.

I nod, and without another word he turns and runs. It's

all I can do to keep up as he races to the water.

There, half submerged and half resting on the gravel beach, is a two-man kayak. When I get close enough I see that it is filled with water.

He's trying to bring all this water—more than a hundred waterskins—to the fire.

"Yes," I say. "This can work." I wrap my hands around the front edge of the boat and pull, but I can't move it. Even when Roon wades into the water and pushes from the back, there's too much weight. "We need to dump some out—"

"We need all of it. Let's drag it—"

"The hull will rip—"

"Fine! Just . . ." He trails off. We're already tipping the boat, turning it ever so slowly, letting just enough water run out that the back end begins to float up and Roon lifts it above the surface.

"Go!" he shouts, and without a moment to draw in a breath, we take off, carrying this huge vessel of water as fast as we can without letting it all splash out along the way.

Once we get back to camp, Roon shouts and waves, trying to get everyone's attention, but no one notices him. Finally, he takes off his already dripping parka, dunks it into the kayak until it is soaked with water, and beats it against the flames racing across the surface of my family's hut. The burning hides beneath Roon's coat hiss and smoke as the fire sputters, sizzles, and finally goes out.

Everyone sees, and everyone follows Roon's lead. My mother grabs a mammoth pelt that hangs from a post beside the kitchen door—a tool she uses for sweeping out dirt and scraps from the floor—and practically throws herself into the opening in the kayak. Pulling the dripping hide from the water, she flings it onto the wall of her sister's hut. When the flames sizzle and smolder, my aunt drops to her knees, tears running down her cheeks. My young cousins—just nine and ten years old—throw down their waterskins and add their own drenched parkas to the mammoth pelt. A few more hurried trips to the kayak and their hut is saved.

All around the camp, voices go up in cheers. Roon, my incredibly brilliant brother, works harder than anyone. Progress is slow and many hides are lost, but if not for Roon, our camp would have ended in ashes. When the last flame is out, he collapses in the center of the meeting place, his face framed by singed hair, his chest, face, and neck flushed with heat. Blisters form on his hands, still dripping with icy water. He presses his palms to his cheeks and his teeth chatter.

"You'll get sick. You need to get warm." Our mother stays shockingly calm while soot and cinders swirl around her like swarming insects. She bends over him and wraps him in a hide that was pulled from his own bed. It smells of smoke but is otherwise undamaged. Stroking his hair, she whispers to him, "Roon. My youngest, my most over-looked. I promise you will never be overlooked again."

"I'm all right," says Roon. "Take care of Pek and Kesh. They need you more."

I raise my eyes to my mother's face, confused. Why do Pek and Kesh need her more than Roon? It's clear from the heavy look in her eyes that there's something I haven't been told.

"What's wrong with Pek and Kesh?"

Our mother slides a hand under Roon's back ever so gently, her fingers barely touching his skin, but still, he flinches. His teeth clamp together as he sucks in a sharp breath.

"Mother, what's wrong—"

"Shh! Don't upset your brother." When she finally gets her arm around his back she manages to lift him to his feet, each small movement accompanied by a gasp. Once he's upright, I notice a cluster of angry red burns, broken and oozing, at his waist.

The sight sends a wave of sickness through me, starting in my stomach and emanating outward.

"Pek and Kesh—are they worse—"

My mother looks at me behind Roon's back, and the message in her hard glare is clear—they are definitely worse. "Urar is with them," she says, shooting a quick glance in the direction of the sea. "Just now he led them and several others to the beach."

As my mother helps Roon hobble into the kitchen, I turn and race to the shore.

As I get closer, sobs and groans reach me and my legs grow strangely heavy. I slow my steps, listening. Has someone died? The last time I heard people cry together like this was at my grandfather's burial, when I was just a little boy.

But as the line of people at the edge of the sand comes into view, I see that no one has died—at least not yet. These aren't cries of mourning; they're cries of pain.

Lying across the rocky soil of the beach are a half-dozen members of my clan: my twin cousins, only eleven years old, two women who are close friends of my mother, and my brothers Kesh and Pek. All of them have at least one limb exposed, some two or three—arms and legs cut free of their garments, lying bare against the dark sand like recently caught fish. But each body part, sticking out at odd angles to be examined by the healer, is mottled by bright red burns. Each face is gray and tight with pain. My aunt and uncle and a third person—the daughter of one of the burned women—help tend to the injured. They hurry back and forth as Urar calls out instructions.

Pek calls to me through clenched teeth. Urar, leaning over Pek's blistered arm, lifts his eyes for only a moment, just long enough to point to an empty bowl and order me to fill it from the sea. I hurry to do as I'm told, returning quickly to Pek's side. "The Bosha clan. They were searching for Chev," Pek says. He pauses, sucking in a quick gasp of breath. "They thought we were hiding him, so they set fire to the huts."

He gasps again, takes two quick breaths. "A boy lit a torch from the hearth. He hesitated at first, only lighting our own family's hut. Then the kitchen. He demanded we offer up Chev and his sisters to save the camp. When he realized they had gone, he set more and more huts on fire, threatening anyone who came close.

"Then, when everything was ablaze, Lo came."

My heart sputters at the sound of her name. Lo? She couldn't have been here. I'd left her in her own camp when I came back.

They must've left her a kayak. She must've followed her people over the bay when I was safely out of the way, running the land route.

"When she learned that Chev wasn't here, she flew into a rage. She went around the camp ignoring the flames, peering into burning huts, screaming Chev's and Mya's names.

"Then, calling for the Divine to curse our clan, she ran to the shore. She called them all to the boats and they left."

"To go south," I say, more to myself than to my brother.

The healer leans over Pek and drips a steady stream of cold water onto his arm from the shell of a long, thin clam. Pek flinches and squeezes my hand. The healer refills the shell and repeats the process farther down his arm. My brother's eyes bulge over sunken cheeks, yet through it all he stares into my eyes.

"Go to them," he grunts. "To Seeri and her family. To Mya." The healer drapes a soaking hide across Pek's burned arm and a high, bright cry bursts through his lips.

I clasp his other arm—the whole and unharmed arm that appears to belong to a different man—and lean down to speak directly into his ear.

"Rest now," I whisper. "And don't worry. I can stop Lo, and I will."

TWENTY-FIVE

All at once the beach goes dark as if the sun has set, though it's not even midday. The storm clouds I'd seen from the ridge—storm clouds that had seemed so far off—have already arrived. With the loss of the sun, the air chills rapidly; the summer morning has been chased away by something that feels more like an autumn afternoon. Wind blows down from the north, sending burned scraps and cinders billowing through the air like snow.

But it's not snow that is coming. It's rain.

I hear it before I feel it—the thrumming of huge drops against the parched ground. The skies above the beach open abruptly, and cold, hard rain falls with the power of a wave on the sea.

Two of the injured are well enough to stand—one of my cousins and one of the women. They climb to their feet and are helped to a sheltering spot among the brush that grows beyond the dune grass. Urar calls out for help in carrying the others to cover.

I try to help, responding to the healer's shouted instructions from behind me, but in front of me, still lying at my feet, Pek screams at me, too. At first I think he's screaming in pain, his open wounds exposed to the cold hard slap of water. But it's not that. He is surely in pain, but he is screaming at me out of anger. Anger at me for not heading south as fast as I can.

"Leave us!" he seethes, his body twisting on the ground. Watching him, every instinct in me screams with a voice as loud as Pek's to stay. "There are plenty who can help us." He stretches and straightens his body, reaching for me, fighting the pain in order to look me in the face. "There is no one else who can warn them."

No one else who can warn them . . . No one else who can warn *you.*

He's right—I know he's right.

I close my eyes tight and think back on everything my clan has suffered at Lo's hands—the fire, the panic, the pain. I imagine the same scene playing out at your camp.

Pek's right—I have to stop it.

It's almost suicide to take a kayak out in a storm this strong—I know it; Pek knows it. But I can't worry about the risks now. I just need to leave quickly.

I nod at Pek, whose hands have wrapped around my

ankles. He releases me. Without another word—without a mention of the dangers I'm running into—I turn and run down the waterfront to the spot where my clan's kayaks are stored. The assault of the pounding rain slows me slightly, as I struggle to keep the inside of the kayak dry while climbing in, pulling the straps over each shoulder, and tying the sash securely around my waist. Once I am in, though, I get away surprisingly easily. No one is watching the sea. No one is looking for me. There is damage to repair and injured to tend to.

I have no time to dwell on the guilt of leaving them. The sea demands all my attention. Waves swell on either side of this tiny kayak—a boat whose size seems to shrink as the power of the storm seems to grow. Paddling is all but futile. The water swirls all around me.

If there is any benefit at all to the power of the waves, it is the speed it gives me. Almost like the current on a river, there is a current on the sea, and for now it takes me in the direction I want to go—out to sea, away from land, south to the rocky point that borders our bay.

Just stay upright, I tell myself. A capsize now could kill me. Managing a roll in waves like these may prove impossible. I've never tried it, and I don't want to try it today.

Water hits me from every angle—from left and right, from above and below. Sheets of rain mingle with rising waves until I feel that I am drowning in a mix of rain and seawater. I taste brine in the sheets of water that streak down my face from my hair. Water is everywhere. I whip my head around sharply, trying to clear my face enough to search the shoreline for landmarks, not daring to take a hand from my paddle for even the time it would take to wipe the hair from my eyes. The paddle may be all but useless, but without it I would have no hope at all.

The shoreline offers me no help either. Where is the point? I seem to have been carried by the waves to another coast entirely, as if the Divine has carried me away and dropped me into a world of water that has no boundaries. I search to my left frantically, seeing nothing but sea to the horizon. My heart burns with panic. *Where is the shore?*

This is my last thought as a wave hits me hard from behind, scooping under me and lifting me high into the air. When the wave drops me, I roll hard to my left and plunge headfirst into the sea.

Under the water or over the water, you have to stay calm. The terror of drowning out here all alone, of my lifeless body strapped into this kayak as it floats out to sea—these thoughts threaten to crowd out all others. But I push them away. I let in the voice of my father instead, teaching me how to right myself in a capsized kayak. *You have to stay calm.*

I remember that the kayak is like a garment I am wearing, not a boat I am sitting in. I move my body and the kayak moves with me. With all the strength in me, I strike at the water with my arms, my cupped hands churning the sea into a cloud of bubbles all around me. *You've capsized so many times before*, I remind myself. *This time is no different*. I shift my legs as far to one side as they will go and twist my hips sharply inside the boat. All at once the edge of the boat flips and my head breaks the surface of the water.

I'm upright. The rain still falls in cold sheets and the waves still slam into me from all sides, but I can breathe.

My paddle has drifted away, but I spot it. It's not far off—carried by the current away to my left.

My left—the direction I *thought* was east—the direction I thought was the shore side of the boat. No wonder I couldn't see the point before I rolled! I wasn't lost; I was looking the wrong way. The boat must have turned full circle; I was so completely confounded by the storm.

I beat against the water with my hands until I finally reach the paddle. I know I'm lucky to have retrieved it, I know I'm lucky to have righted the kayak fairly easily and to have had my sense of direction restored, but I cannot keep a creeping dread from taking hold. I am drenched—the apron of the kayak that wraps around my torso, my parka underneath—every part of me above my waist is soaked through with freezing water. I know what can happen if I get too cold. Disorientation. Confusion. Slowed movement and slowed thoughts. I could even lose consciousness.

The fear taunts me, provokes me to search the shoreline

for a sheltered place where I could pull in and wait out the storm. I imagine quitting—abandoning my purpose for coming out here, giving up on the idea of warning your clan—and just saving my own life by getting warm and dry. I can't believe how strong the pull is.

I paddle until my arms grow stiff. Even then, even after the muscles burn and strain with every move, I paddle still. I rest when I can, but as soon as I stop moving a shot of cold runs through me and my whole body shudders. And so I press on, still scanning the shore for a place to rest, still dreaming of abandoning my goal, yet knowing all along that I cannot stop as long as my mind stays alert. As long as I remember that I am doing this for you.

You.

Water surrounds me, so much that it blends into nothingness. My mind's eye takes over, and I remember the sight of your face the first time I saw you. I remember the power of your features—so determined, so resolute. I hold that image in my mind—the thought of your sharp eyes and soft mouth, a contradiction on the face of a girl who is a study in contradictions. I think I will tell you that when I reach you. Yes, when I finally arrive at your camp, I think, I will tell you that you are a study in contradictions.

The image of your face that first time I saw you slips away, as my mind sifts through all the different memories I have of you. Unbidden, it stalls on the moment after you killed the cat—the moment you looked at me with so much condemnation in your eyes. How you must have hated me—a Manu hunter raising his spear, a perfect echo of the Manu hunter who took your mother's life.

From that moment forward, every time I've seen you, I've noticed something guarded in your eyes, a darkness that wraps around you like a shadow. And now I understand it. . . . I understand that you were guarding your heart, making sure that no member of the Manu ever caused you pain again.

Out here in this kayak, hurrying to your camp, my heart aches at the thought of the day your mother died and your own clan rushed into kayaks and fled our shores. If only I could go back, if only I could stop the hand of Tram's father, if only I could protect your mother and change the violent history between our clans.

But I can't. I can't change the pain you suffered in the past, but I can do everything possible to prevent the pain you might suffer in the future.

And so I press on. My arms ache and my shoulders burn with pain, but I press on. I have no other choice. If I stop, I could die.

If I stop, *you* could die.

The starkness of this truth startles me, illuminates an awareness in me of something I could not—or would not—acknowledge before.

I cannot let you die, because I cannot face a future without you.

Against a background of blurred pain and fear, this truth stands out so plain, and now that I see it, I cannot divert from the path that leads to you.

A steady beat taps against my shoulders, my back, the top of my head. Drops of rain have changed to drops of ice. I remember the summer sun just yesterday, the bees I spotted a few days ago. But winter isn't ready to give in completely, and this ice storm is her way of making that known.

Focus on warmth, I tell myself. I think of the soft glow inside my family's hut, the warm look in your eyes as you offered me a gift of your own honey.

Your honey—I try to remember the texture, the crisp sweetness, the way I could almost taste the heat of the sun in my mouth. My clenched hands ache with cold and blisters burn on my palms, but I push those sensations away and fill my mind with the memory of that taste—the flavor of sunshine and warmth.

As I let this memory spread through me from the inside out, I notice them for the first time. At first I'm not sure, but then I see movement, splashing, the shape of a raised paddle, the outline of a man's arm.

Lo and her people. There they are! Huddled against the shoreline, tucked under overhanging ledges of ice.

I've caught up to them.

Like me, they searched the shore for a spot to rest. Unlike me, they have nothing to propel them forward, no memory of your face to keep them moving through the worst of circumstances.

And they are novice kayakers, their clan having shunned the water in favor of hunting on land for the last five years. Many of them may never have kayaked before. I watched their silhouettes glide under clear skies across our calm bay, as they headed from Lo's camp to mine. The open sea is different, and their newly made kayaks may not be perfectly sound and seaworthy. They may even be taking on water.

Paddling through the worst of this storm is difficult for me, a seasoned kayaker. How much more difficult must it be for the Bosha? No wonder I caught up to them.

And now I will pass them. With the memory of your face held in my mind, drawing me ever forward like a signal guard on a cliff with a torch raised high, I will reach you in time to warn you.

The effort becomes strikingly easy after I pass Lo and her group. Just beyond the icy cliffs where they've stopped the coastline changes—the rocky bluffs and overhangs smooth out and flatten as the shoreline bends east and the southern faces of the mountains begin their descent to lower ground.

Here, the storm abruptly stops. Streaks of sun break through the clouds ahead of me to the south and the wind shifts. Cold gusts still push from behind me, but a warm breeze blows out from shore.

I allow myself the indulgence of looking over my shoulder, but only for a moment. Checking the sky, I see the reason for the rapid change in weather—the storm has become caught behind the mountains. Dark clouds still haunt the sky just north of my tiny boat, but they are caught—temporarily, I'm sure—behind the peaks that form a gate to the south.

I revel in the smallest benefits of the break from the storm—my face dries in the breeze, my hands warm enough to get a more comfortable grip on the paddle. Other things are just as awful as ever—my soaked clothes still cling to my soaked skin—but I focus on the small things.

Now is the time to make progress. I paddle hard, scanning the shore to the east. With the sun's light, I can see well—better than I have all day. I remember these features. They form the shoreline just north of your camp.

I am almost there.

I paddle on. I will myself to move faster, but my arms slow as if I've grown old in one day. I watch the coastline—an inlet, a rocky bluff, another inlet . . . Could it be that I wasn't as close as I'd thought? The sun still breaks through clouds to the south, but the rays are slanting sharply from the west. How long have I been out on the sea? If the sun were to set as the rain caught up with me again, I would be swallowed up by darkness.

Clouds roll over me, shadowing the water and shadowing my thoughts. Ideas toss around in my head like tiny boats on the waves.

I have to get to you—to get out of the water, out of the rain, out of the cold. It seems like it should be easy, but despite the fact that I can understand the goal, I can't think of how to accomplish it.

Paddle, I tell myself. *Paddle.*

I dig deep into the waves, but my muscles won't cooperate. I dig again and again, but with each stroke, the thought of you slips further and further away.

Darkness closes in at the corners of my vision. The dark calls to me, promising warmth. For a moment, I'm tempted. It would be so easy to stop trying.

I close my eyes and darkness falls fast and heavy, cutting me off from the water, the cold, the waves.

I want to welcome the dark. I open my mind to it, to the possibility of letting go of the pain in my shoulders, the shiver in my chest, the numbness in my fingers. I suck in a deep breath of darkness, letting it fill me.

Yes, I will let go. I will slump into darkness's warm embrace. I will open my eyes one last time, take one final look at the cold sun, and let go.

My eyelids flip open, and something at the water's edge catches my attention.

Movement.

Among low cliffs of gray rock something flashes—light slides in front of dark before disappearing into the shadows. An elk, maybe? I know you have herds of elk in your range, and there are few other animals that would graze on such steep footing. I slow my boat and let my gaze sweep over the ledges. I watch but see nothing. . . .

Nothing.

Gray on gray, shadow on shadow.

The sun stabs one final ray through the thickening gloom, and there it is again. The flash of movement. The glint of light.

My eyes shift involuntarily to the same rocky ledge they'd searched just a moment before.

And there you are.

TWENTY-SIX

You wave your arms. . . . I can see that you are calling to me. I bend toward your words, but before your voice reaches me it breaks into little pieces that scatter on the wind.

It doesn't matter. I don't care what you're saying. I only care that I've found you.

Deep within my core, in a part of me that's been numb with cold since I first set out on this trip, my heart begins to race. Panic wills my eyes to stay open. I need to do this last thing . . . *this last thing.* But what is this thing I need to do? My paddle rests across my lap. I know I need to use it, but I'm not certain that I can.

Holding the paddle feels strange, as if I'm holding it in a dream. It is both heavy and weightless at the same time. My fingers tense and release, tense and release.

Maybe, I think, I've found you too late.

My eyelids fall shut. Letting go feels so good. I loosen my grip, let my fingers go limp. It feels so good, so good.

Forgive me. . . . The words echo through my head, hover on my lips, yet I'm not sure who they are meant for.

Just as I let the shaft of the paddle slide from my fingers, a cold drizzle begins to fall. Drops beat against my forehead and trickle down my nose. Unbidden, focus returns to my mind.

No. I don't want to try. I don't want to have to try anymore.

I open my eyes and watch the tiny dents the rain makes in the surface of the sea, each one a stabbing pinprick. They dot the surface on every side of the paddle. I watch it float away, carried by the waves to the edge of my vision. I hate that paddle. My hands ache and my palms burn with the contempt I feel for it. I tip my head, watching it float to the edge of my reach. I hate that paddle. Soon it will be gone, unable to hurt me anymore.

My hands fall loose at my sides and the water stings my palms like I've dropped them into flames. All at once I remember . . . *the flames, the pain they caused.* I remember Pek, straining through the pain, demanding that I come here and warn your clan.

I remember now. I came to warn you.

I hate that paddle, but it's the only hope I have of reaching you. I watch it move upon the waves. It rises and falls, rises and falls, one moment beyond my reach, the next tauntingly close. At the last moment possible, I lunge for it.

My fingers fight to grasp the wood; my shoulders throb with the effort. Seawater splashes up in protest, as if the water has already claimed the paddle and is willing to struggle to keep it. One last fight I need to win. As I pull the paddle in, the vengeful sea throws saltwater in my eyes, leaving the whole world a blur of gray on gray. Dropping the paddle across my lap, I swipe furiously at my eyes, desperate to bring the world back into focus.

I look up. I see enough to know that a straight line separates me from you—a short, straight line.

It's almost over, I tell myself. One way or another, it will all end soon.

The paddle strikes the sea once, twice, three times. *Again, again, again . . .* Each strike sends a shock through my body as if I am striking rock. *Again, again, again . . .*

Perhaps I can push forward four more times, perhaps only three. I'm not sure, but it doesn't matter. I've lost track anyway. How many times has this paddle struck this unyielding surface? *Again, again, again . . .*

Again, again, again . . .

Ten more times . . . eight more times . . . six more times . . . I lose count and start over. Eight? Six? *Again, again . . .* when all at once a wave of pain ripples through my arms and back as this wretched paddle digs into sand.

I look up. The front of the kayak rests on the beach.

And right in front of me, a girl is wading into the sea, reaching for my hand. A girl with hard eyes and a soft mouth.

I don't remember getting out of the boat. I don't remember climbing up the rock. I must have fallen at least once, though, because when I come to myself in this dimly lit cave, my head pounding and my eyes nearly blind, I discover my palms and elbows are sticky with blood.

"Where . . ." It's all I can manage to push through my lips.

"Lie still," you say. Your voice comes from my right and I turn toward it. Between me and the curtain of rain that falls across the mouth of the cave, a shadow moves before a sputtering glow. "I told you to stop trying to talk."

Have I tried to talk before now?

I close my eyes and concentrate. A large pelt is wrapped around me—a pelt of long, thick fur. Mammoth. A warm and soft mammoth pelt is draped around me, covering the entire length of my skin.

The length of my skin . . . My clothes are gone. You've taken my clothes.

Could that have been when I tried to talk?

Where are we? That's all I want to say. I manage to push the word *where* through my lips once more, but the rest of the question is bitten off by uncontrollable chattering. A shudder ripples through my chest and up through my throat, escaping my body as a deep moan.

A warm hand touches my face, triggering another full-body shudder.

"Can you move any closer to the fire? Kol, can you move closer?"

I sweep my eyes around this small space. Is that the fire? A flickering light dances orange and red against a background of gray. It's lovely, but I feel no heat from it at all.

My eyes fall closed again, and shimmering light ripples like water on the backs of my eyelids. The ground beneath me moves as if I'm still on the sea.

I lick my lips. They're cracked and salty. I force my eyes to open but I don't see you. "You were right," I say. I wait but you don't answer, leaving me to wonder if I really said the words out loud. "You have to go—warn your family. Lo's coming for you."

The effort of saying so much exhausts me. I roll onto my side, retracting into the pelt and into myself. The rushing of the rain rings in my ears. I listen hard, trying to hear you.

"Mya?" Beyond the reach of the firelight, I hear something like the soft shuffle of your boots against the rocky floor. Your breath comes in quick, shallow gasps. I remember you standing in the rain, pulling me from the kayak. Your clothes were drenched, and ice water ran down your face. "Mya? Are you cold?"

"Listen to me." These words are just a whisper—your whisper, your words—from the dark somewhere behind me. Your mouth is so close, I feel the vibration of your breath on my ear. "You need to get warm. I'm trying to save you. I need you to understand this, Kol. What I'm doing . . . I'm doing this to save your life."

I try to work through your words, to make sense of what you're saying. But only some words catch in my mind—*warm . . . understand . . . save your life*. As I try to arrange these thoughts into some sense of meaning, the edge of the mammoth pelt lifts from my shoulder and something made of pure heat and life slides in beside me.

It's you.

Your bare skin stretches along the entire length of my back. Somewhere deep inside me, a flame that was fading catches in fresh kindling.

I want to speak—thoughts light up my mind like flashes of lightning in the night sky. I try to form words. "Mya . . ." is all I manage to say.

"It's necessary," you say into my ear. "I can't let you die."

If I could, I might laugh. I didn't know how close I was to death until your warmth pulled me back from the edge. Like a wave, heat washes over me. In my mind's eye I imagine my frozen blood, thawing and cracking like the ice in our bay in the spring. Each spot where your skin touches mine is like a stone dropped into that bay, sending ripples of warmth radiating outward. These ripples expand, reaching my ears, my cheeks, the backs of my closed eyes. After what has felt like hours of constant shivering, my body finally goes still.

Your breath brushes over my neck, and it feels cool.

I no longer see water when I close my eyes. Instead, I see the sun. I feel its embrace.

Sleep pulls hard at me, but I fight it. I have to stay awake. My thoughts are slow and heavy, but I know I have to tell you something of huge importance. Perhaps the most important thing I've ever said. I search for the words.

When I remember this later, I will realize that it didn't make sense. I will turn these memories over in my mind and I will know that I was weak and my thoughts were jumbled and confused.

But at this moment, this one word feels like the answer to every question:

You.

I feel better now that I've said it. I let sleep pull me from your arms.

TWENTY-SEVEN

When I wake again you are dressed and sitting at the opening of the cave, staring out through a sheet of rain and sleet. The world outside is beginning to lighten. Could it be first light already? Could you have sat up through the short, summer night, waiting for morning?

"Lo's clan . . . They're coming. If they didn't turn back—"

"You told me," you say. "I've been watching for them."

I told you? I remember wanting to tell you, but I don't remember saying the words.

Your pack lies beside you, and you pull out a small wrapped package about the size of your fist. "You should eat," you say. "I'll leave this with you—"

"Leave it?"

You turn to face me, your features glowing in the amber light thrown off by the dying coals of the fire.

"I need to go. To warn them—"

"Then I'm going with you."

"You need more rest—"

"If you intended to leave me, why didn't you leave while I was still sleeping, rather than wait for sunrise?" Something inside me wants to believe you waited to be sure I was recovered, but I know better.

"It will be hard enough to travel in this weather in the day," you say. "At night, it would've been impossible. You told me the Bosha were waiting out the storm, so I waited, too. But I was watching. If I'd seen them, I would've left you to warn my clan."

Of course you would have, but that doesn't matter now.

"Well, I'm awake. So I'm going with you."

Instead of traveling back down to my boat, I follow you through a shower of freezing rain, up a narrow footpath that leads to the peak above us. I look down to the surface of the water and some part of me stirs with the memory of scrambling up the rocks in the dark last night. My bruised hands remind me how slippery and treacherous it was. Yet as difficult as that trail was to climb, the trek farther up strikes me as impossible. Only the smallest cutouts in the rock allow me to place my feet safely as we ascend. "This path is man-made," I say.

"My brother found that cave when our clan first settled here. We use it as a lookout, to watch the sea to the north."

"Watching for what?"

"When we first came here, it was you. Well, your clan. We watched for the kayaks of the Manu, not knowing if you would pursue us."

I'm struck by the sudden realization of how improbable it is that you and I should find ourselves here, together on this morning. The past should have ensured that this day would never come. Your mother and your betrothed both died. Your brother killed a man. You and I should have remained enemies for the rest of our lives. Yet here we are, making this climb together.

My foot slips on loose gravel as I take my next step up the steep path and you spin around quickly and grab my arm to stop me from tumbling. Our eyes meet, but you turn your head, dropping your gaze to the rock underfoot.

Why won't you look at me? Are you embarrassed about last night? Or did the mention of the history between our clans stir some resentment toward me?

I don't ask. Today is not a day for talking. With each step, the urgency to reach your family grows. There will be time to talk later. For now, I focus on my footing and ensure you don't have to help me again.

It isn't long before we reach the highest point of the cliff and start to descend. The terrain drops down into a pass between two rocky slopes, both of which are streaked with flows of water, runoff from what has again become torrential rain.

The trail is little more than a ledge of hanging boulders and rocks, suspended from the wall on our left. To the right, a drop-off plunges to a ravine filled with rushing water. It is a long way down—at least the height of three men, standing on each other's shoulders.

The slabs we cross are wet and slick with sleet. Once—then a second time—you stumble, but you right yourself before I have the chance to come to your aid. You plod on, without even a glance back at me.

My stomach tightens. If one of us were to get hurt—if one of us were unable to keep walking—the other would have to leave them here, alone on these cold, wet rocks. We don't discuss the danger, but our progress slows as we take more care to place our feet.

Gradually, the trail descends to the floor of the ravine, until we are walking alongside the rapids. In places, the trail and the river merge, and we have to scramble over boulders surrounded by rushing water.

Finally, the trail winds down to the base of the cliff. It levels and broadens, becoming a corridor that cuts through two wide swaths of trees.

Through the gray rain, I spot a valley that opens at the foot of the path. This is a view I recognize. We hurry now that the ground is flatter. The trees end abruptly, yielding to a clearing. Below us stands a circle of huts—your camp.

In your meeting place, the elders of your clan are gathered

under the roof. They sit in a tight circle, speaking in hushed tones. Are they planning their defense? Morsk is among them, and when he sees me he gets to his feet, but he doesn't speak. Instead, he gives me a long, critical stare, his eyes full of contempt. He watches me as I follow you to Chev's door.

I'm not sure if Morsk is reacting to his broken betrothal to Seeri, or to the threat of an attack on your clan. Maybe, like you, he feels that nothing good has ever come from contact with the Manu.

We find Chev in his hut with Yano and Ela, who stop their chanted prayers when we enter. From the look in Chev's eyes, I'd say he has been awake all night, waiting for you. Those tired eyes shift to me, and for a rare moment I think I can read your brother's expression. His usual stoic facade breaks. He was not expecting me.

"Where did you find him?" he asks you.

"He was out on the water last night, half dead with cold and exhaustion—"

"Last night?"

"At the height of the storm. He came to warn us."

Your brother turns to me and I can see he's sizing me up, weighing all he knows of me to decide if he should trust me.

I'd been your clan's hero once, when I killed the cat. That was not long ago. But since then, I'd defended Lo when it was revealed that she was plotting to kill him. Could he wonder if I might be conspiring with her? If I am here to give you false information?

His attention slides from my face to yours. He doesn't speak, but he is asking you. This will be your decision to make.

No words. Just a nod of your head.

"Well then," your brother says, getting to his feet. "Thank you for bringing a warning. I'm saddened to hear that Shava's story was all true. I had hoped that somehow—"

"I had hoped so, too, but now I know those were false hopes."

I tell Chev everything I've already told you—the number of kayaks I'd seen launch from Lo's camp, the rough weather on the sea, and the place I'd seen their boats sheltering from the storm.

A plan is made. Chev decides that Seeri will take Lees away from camp to protect the both of them. He tries to force you to go as well, but you won't have it. Perhaps he realizes that your skills with a spear are worth having around; perhaps he knows you are too stubborn to ever follow his orders—it doesn't matter. He lets you stay.

Moments later, all the members of the clan have been assembled under the roof in the meeting place. With the roar of rain and the clatter of sleet against the canopy over our heads, a small voice inside me silently thanks Morsk for his handiwork and the brief relief it offers from the storm.

Everyone listens as Chev outlines his plan. Anyone who wishes to help defend the camp is welcome, but no one will be forced. Those who are injured or otherwise unable to fight are encouraged to stay behind and keep the children out of sight. The rest of us will head to the water and climb the low cliffs that overlook the beach where Lo's clan is most likely to land. We will take weapons, but Chev warns against using them. "Only defensively," he says. "These are not strangers. They are our own clan, our own people."

I flinch at Chev's words, remembering Lo's: *A false leader, a wedge . . . they go to remove these things.* They are coming to remove Chev—to kill him—and to kill you and your family, too.

I hope that Chev is right, and bloodshed can be avoided. But if he is wrong, I am not part of Chev's clan. He is not my High Elder, and I am not obligated to follow his rules.

The cliffs rise to both the north and south of the beach. Chev decides to position himself on the cliff to the north, where the view is best, allowing only you and me to accompany him. The rest of your clan who have come to fight—sixteen in all—split into two groups. Half follow Morsk up the cliffs to the south while the others guard the paths that lead up to these two lookout points. If someone tries to get to Chev, they will have to fight just to get to the trail.

We each have a spear, but once in position, on this windy,

rain-drenched ridge, you and I move wordlessly, collecting a stockpile of large rocks. It's slow, hard work, but the effort keeps our blood warm. When we've collected every rock we can lift, we station ourselves at a break in the low brush that lines the ledge. From here, we can watch for boats approaching the beach far below, but we cannot be seen.

For now, the sea is empty. The gray expanse of water rolls outward to the horizon.

We wait. The temperature drops and the wind increases, blowing hard from the north, right into our faces. Tiny shards of sleet prick the skin of my cheeks.

Hunched beside me, you speak for the first time in a long while. "We met on an early summer day. Today it is winter again." Your voice is soft and low. Your brother, crouched just a few paces away, doesn't seem to hear you. These words are for me only. "How is it possible that winter has returned?" you ask.

"Winter hasn't returned. She isn't really back. She's just making a last assault, hoping to hang on."

"And what will happen? Will winter triumph?" You let your eyes leave the sea for just a moment to glance at my face, maybe to gauge my expression.

"Of course not." As I answer, my eyes fix on a tiny shadow on the water near the horizon. "By this time tomorrow, she will realize she has been defeated. Summer will return with all its force and winter will be a memory."

"There!" Chev shouts and points into the distance at the shadow I am watching, now growing and moving in.

They are here.

We remain quiet and hidden as the first of the boats—I count eleven in all—lands on the beach. As the paddlers step out onto solid ground, Chev emerges from hiding and calls out from our vantage point high above them. "What do you want here?"

A stocky, bowlegged boy spins at the sound of Chev's voice. He lifts his face to search for the source of the sound and I recognize him. This is the boy who was on the beach the day I walked Lo home.

This fleeting recognition robs me of my focus, transports me for just an instant from the present to a moment in the past. But an instant is all it takes.

The boy raises his arm and extends it behind him. *This is the boy called Orn. I recognize his stance, his clamped jaw. . . .* These scattered thoughts distract me until a spear flies from an atlatl in his hand.

Its flight is fast and true, and it pierces Chev's parka just below his collarbone. Rainwater tinged red with blood streams down his chest.

Chev lets out a small sound—more gasp than moan—and collapses to his knees at my feet.

On the beach below, Lo's clanspeople scramble for cover as rocks rain down on them from the southern cliff. Like an anthill kicked by the toe of a boot, measured order is replaced by frantic motion. Screams rise—people may be hurt—but I hardly notice. All my attention is focused on Chev.

Crouching beside him, I place one hand on his chest and one on his back, then gently ease his weight backward until he is sitting on the ground. His eyes flash wide, staring blankly over his suddenly pale cheeks. I bend close to him, squinting at the place where the spearhead penetrated the hide of his parka, but with the rain still falling, it's impossible to distinguish how heavily he is bleeding. I don't dare remove the spear. Instead, I press both hands against the wound.

"We need to get him to the healers," I say. Dark red liquid leaks between my fingers before diluting to a pale pink stream that collects in a pool in his lap. "I can't tell how hard he's bleeding. . . ."

I look up to ask you for help getting Chev to his feet, but you are not watching me. You don't appear to be listening to me, either. All your attention is on your spear. You snatch it from the grass at your feet and raise it to your shoulder.

Chev sees you, too. He reaches forward and grabs the hem of your pant leg. "No." Both of us startle at the strength of Chev's voice. Despite the haze that begins to cloud his eyes, his voice is clear. "He's of our clan. He's Dora's son—"

"He just tried to kill you—"

"He tried, but he failed. That doesn't make it right for you to kill him."

Your face hardens. *You will not listen*, I think. *You will not obey your brother.* But then you let the spear slide from your shoulder, roll to the edge of your fingers, drop from your hand. It splashes in a puddle and thick mud splatters my face.

As I drag the back of my hand across my chin, you drop to your knees and reach around your brother's waist. An embrace? Before I can process your actions, you spring to your feet. "Fighters from my clan are posted at the foot of this cliff, guarding the trail that leads up here. I'll send help," you say, "but I have to get down there. I have to help protect my people." Before I can answer, you turn on your heels and fly down the trail to the beach.

"My knife," Chev breathes. "She took it—the blade I keep in my belt."

It's all I can do not to take off after you. These are the people who set fire to my camp, who caused the pain I saw on Pek's face. One of them has already tried to kill Chev. Any of them might try to kill you.

I grab your spear from the mud, wiping it clean in the crook of my elbow so that I can get a firm grip. I realize there's no question—I must follow you. But I can't leave your brother here to bleed to death. And I don't know how long your clanspeople can hold back Lo's followers and keep them from reaching this cliff.

I'll get Chev out of here. I'll get him into the healers' hands, and then I'll be by your side, fighting.

"Can you stand?" My eyes sweep over your brother's face. He rests on the wet ground, leaning back on his elbows, his eyes closed. "Chev?"

I lunge forward, repeating your brother's name, but he gives no response.

This is it, I think. He's slipped away. The worst has happened.

But I'm wrong. The worst hasn't happened. Not yet.

A noise from behind me—a rustling of branches, a foot catching on a stone or root, a missed step.

I turn and look up into the face of the bowlegged boy who threw the spear that hit Chev. He is so young—he cannot be older than Kesh. A trickle of blood runs from a gash above his right eye. One of your clanspeople guarding the trail must have wounded him as he fought his way past.

Orn . . . Dora's son.

This is my last thought—*Dora's son*—when a heavy club swings down and hits me square in the temple, sending me sprawling into the mud.

TWENTY-EIGHT

The blow knocks me onto my stomach, the sudden, icy black taste of mud in my mouth. I orient myself quickly—to my right lies Chev, his eyes wide, his face the pale gray of mist—to my left lies the hasty, random pile of stones you and I gathered. I stretch out my left arm and my fingers coil around the perfect one—a heavy rock three times the size of my fist. I grasp it awkwardly, its sharp edges digging into my palm, as I thrust myself onto my back.

I fling the stone at Orn with all my strength.

The move exhausts me—I'm throwing from my weaker side and my grip, desperate and uncertain, slips on the icy rock. The wind goes out of me as the stone lands hard against his cheek, tearing open a gash, stark and bright, just below his left eye. Startled, he raises both hands to his face, as if to assess what just happened, his features frozen in shock, and as he does he drops both his club and an ax he held in his other hand. He'd been ready to throw the ax, his attention trained on Chev.

A moment, and his horror transforms to rage. This rage lights in his eyes like a living thing, its attention shifted from Chev to me.

He staggers forward, blocking me from the pile of stones. Chev separates me from your dropped spear. With no weapons of my own, I grab Orn's ax from the spot where it fell near my feet. It's heavy, and sleet already coats the handle. I struggle to grasp it, never taking my eyes off this boy—this virtual stranger—through the ice-encrusted hair that hangs in my face.

Gripping the ax between my muddy hands, I gather my strength and straighten to my feet, but he is ready. He throws all his weight against me, arms extended, hitting me with so much force I cannot hold on to the ax. It flies out of my hand as both our bodies hurdle backward toward the ground.

We land hard against an outcropping of rocks that forms the edge of the cliff. Pain sears through me as my head collides with stone.

His weight pins me down. He claws at my neck, but his hands are wet and slick with mud. His fingers slide across the skin of my throat.

I kick him off and crawl away, creeping backward like a spider, never taking my eyes off the boy's face. Even through the haze of pain, cold, ice, and wind, I see his eyes—the eyes of a boy. I reach behind me, feeling for the point where the ground falls away, as he rushes toward me, his hands extended.

He reaches me, presses a knee into my chest, grabs my shoulders, and pulls me up before slamming me back down. My head snaps back, shattering the film of ice that coats the surface of the rocks. A large splinter breaks free and cuts my cheek. My fingers scramble, clutching at the broken ice. Just as he throws his body forward one more time, I swing my hand up and stab him hard in the neck with the shard in my fist.

His eyes widen as blood bursts from his throat. He slows, shifts his balance, giving me just enough time to roll away.

He stumbles forward. Unable to catch himself, he falls against the ice-covered ledge. He flails, claws, and grasps, but he cannot find a handhold. I reach for him, lunge for his waist . . . his leg . . . his boot, but he is moving too fast, his weight finding no resistance on the ice-slick ground.

A blood-red streak paints the edge of the cliff, disappearing beyond the ledge.

He has fallen.

The sudden quiet stuns me. All at once I notice a whisper—sleet rapping against every surface—the only sound that stirs the air. Even the wind has stopped. I listen hard, focus my ears, and below me I pick out the sound of waves. Did the bowlegged boy land in water or on rocks? I can't force myself to look over the ledge to see if he survived. Exhaustion holds me in place. I lie on my back, letting ice collect in my hair, afraid to move, afraid to know if your brother is dead or alive.

But this is not the time to rest, I tell myself. Rest will come, but not now.

I sit up. Your brother still slumps on his side, exactly as he was. With the wind blowing in from the sea, I call his name with all the strength I can summon.

His only answer is a low and ragged cough, but he's alive.

The relief I feel is replaced quickly by dread. I'm running out of time. I need to get him to the healers.

I need to find you.

I'll send help. Those were your words as you jumped up with your brother's knife in hand and disappeared down the trail. But help hasn't come. What kind of fighting is happening on the ground beneath this cliff? And where are you now? If you're hurt, how will I ever forgive myself for not running after you?

A flicker of panic lights in my chest. Like kindling catching the flame, the flicker spreads, until my heart is racing and my breath comes in quick gasps. I have to get moving. I scramble to my feet, exhaustion gone. Standing over Chev, I suppress the horror I feel at his sunken eyes and address the immediate problem—the long shaft extending from his chest. Like the spears of my own clan, this one is carved from a mammoth's thighbone. If I can find a way to break it, Chev can move without having to pull the spearhead from his wound.

The bowlegged boy's ax lies at my feet right where I dropped it. I pick it up, and Chev seems to know what I intend to do. He props himself up and steadies the length of bone against the ground while bracing the end that pierces his body with two bright red fists.

Three swings of the ax and the shaft splinters. Three more and it breaks. Chev sits up, a short piece of bone, maybe the length of a hand, protruding from the spot below his left shoulder. Maybe it's relief—maybe it's fear—but a bit of color returns to his face.

"We need to go," I say, and tucking a hand under each of his arms, I pull him to his feet.

I'm amazed by how well Chev is able to move. He holds the broken stub of the spear in place with one hand while he leans on my shoulder with the other. He has an uneasy energy—his unblinking eyes never leave the path.

Freezing rain stings my face until we move under cover of the trees. This stretch of forest unnerves me—sound, light, air—everything changes. I shoot frequent glances over my shoulder, afraid that in these unfamiliar conditions, someone might surprise me from behind before I hear them.

I have no idea what we will encounter on the trail. Have Chev's people all been massacred? Have Lo's?

More than anything, I think of you. Like ghostly fruit, newly sprouted leaves hang from tree limbs fully encased in ice, and I think of what you said about winter returning. I had told you that winter would not triumph, but summer would return tomorrow. As ice crunches like gravel under my feet, I hope that time does not turn me into a liar.

Everything is strangely still. I had expected the sounds of mayhem—screams and shouts and crashing through the trees. But for most of our journey we hear only our own boots on the ground. Once, I pick out a distant clamor like someone running, but my ears are not accustomed to the tricks trees play with sound and I can't tell which way the steps are traveling. Before I can decipher it, the sound has faded.

The weather confuses my memories of your camp, but I begin to think we're almost to the huts. I hear a voice from up ahead—someone calling out. The trail bends left and I briefly catch sight of the canopy that shades your meeting place through an opening in the trees. The path winds farther left, and I lose sight of it again, but it doesn't matter. I've seen it, and just knowing we are close makes travel easier.

We follow the trail as it bends back to the right, back toward your camp, and my feet become just a bit lighter. The tight bands around my chest loosen just enough to allow me to draw a real breath. The sleet even seems to slow. But then Chev and I round a blind turn, and we both abruptly stop.

A figure draped in pelts stands in the middle of the path.

My eyes sweep his frame, my hands clenched on the two spears I carry—yours and mine—but then I realize that he is just a boy, a boy no older than Roon. Blood soaks into a scrap of hide he holds against one eye. It forms a red trickle down his sleeve, dripping into a crimson puddle, bright against the bits of ice at his feet.

"Nix." Chev breathes the name like a gasp. The boy does not respond, but stares past us, his one open eye filled with shock and fear. Chev's hand drops from my shoulder and he calls out the name again. "Nix!" The cry takes almost all his strength, but whatever is left in him, he uses it to propel himself toward the boy, falling to the ground in front of him. The boy moans, startling as if he's just awoken. He throws his arms around Chev, dropping the bloody compress to the ground.

Noise floats down from farther up the path—the sound of boots pounding on the ground—and I panic. Whoever hurt this boy could be just beyond my view. I have to be ready. I position myself beside Chev and the boy and raise my spear, ready to defend them.

I see him first between the trees—a young man running toward us, alone. He comes into full view a distance away, but not so great a distance that I couldn't land the strike.

He sees us—sees the raised spear—and lifts his own hands, both empty, over his head. His eyes and face are red and streaked with blood and tears. "I'm not a threat," he calls. "It's only me."

He is too far away, too blood-smeared for us to recognize his face, but Chev and I both recognize his voice.

Before your brother can get to his feet the man is on the ground beside him, wrapping him in an embrace.

Up close, his face is unmistakable—this is Yano, the man Chev loves.

The sweetness of their reunion is cut short when Yano's eyes take in the broken spear and the hole in Chev's parka, blood forming a crust so thick it almost appears to be a separate dead thing pinned to his chest. Yano helps him stand and Chev groans—a sound so full of frustrated, impatient pain that even Chev's strength can't hold it down any longer.

"Will he . . . Can you—"

"I think so. Yes." Mercifully, he knows what I want to say, despite the fact that fear clogs my thoughts so thoroughly I cannot speak. With Yano leading, we start down the short distance separating us from the ring of huts—Chev leaning on Yano, Nix leaning on me.

"Have Lo and her people withdrawn?" I ask, unable to lower my guard. I turn my head from side to side and search the underbrush as we move through the trees.

"They fled to the beach, at least," Yano says. "They were injured—our fighters were pushing them back—when word traveled through shouted warnings that one of their boys had fallen from a cliff. You could see the panic spreading. Then Morsk called out that he would destroy their boats if they didn't retreat. I guess the fear of being stranded drove them all back to the shore."

We finally climb the last rise and your camp comes into view. The sight of it shocks me; the meeting place is so transformed. I remember your clan gathered beneath this canopy. The shade it gave seemed to represent the protection and prosperity you had found here in the south.

But unlike that first night I came here, when your meeting place was filled with the sound of conversation, your meeting place tonight is filled with moans and cries. Men and women are stretched out on the ground, bloody and broken. Some look up as we pass. Their pleading eyes terrify me. Others lie completely still. These scare me even more.

Am I to blame for this? I was friendly toward Lo, unable to see through her lies. Did I contribute to this pain?

I notice a woman washing wounds on a young girl's lower arms and hands and I realize she is Yano's sister, Ela. Yano leads your brother to her and she immediately makes a place for him directly beside the girl she is treating. When the young girl recognizes him, she calls out Chev's name, announcing to the whole clan that the High Elder is here and alive. As the whole crowd cheers I recognize a familiar voice—the voice of your sister Seeri. I search the crowd and find her beside your sister Lees. They are both near the center of the space, binding wounds.

Seeri, Lees . . . But you are not here.

There's no reason for you not to be in camp. The fighting is over. As long as you are safe and well, you should be here.

But you are not here.

My ears begin to ring. My vision shrinks down to a small spot directly in front of my feet. Everything else goes dim around me, but I don't care about that. I need only this bit of focused vision to make it through the mayhem under the canopy. Following this bit of light, this spot of ground right in front of me, I find my way to the threshold of your hut.

The drape that forms the door hangs askew, exposing the shambles inside—the hides that form the walls, hides I'd noticed for their intricate patterns, have been torn loose, their surfaces splattered with tiny droplets of blood.

Outside the hut, I find the shaft of a broken spear at the foot of the path that you led me down earlier today—the path up into the pass to the cliffs and the cave. The sleet is still falling hard and the wind is increasing. Without deciding on a course of action or even letting myself think, I begin to climb the trail.

As the path narrows and heads into the trees, something draws my eyes to the ground—something small and white. Why would my attention be pulled to such a thing—something so simple and plain it resembles a pellet of hail? I bend down, picking up the tiny bead.

I find another white bead, and then another. As I gather them together in the palm of my hand, I can't deny what I have found. . . .

Pieces of your ivory pendant lie scattered on the ground.

TWENTY-NINE

I follow the trail back up into the trees, ducking into the shadows, gauging my progress up the slope by the feel of the ground under my feet—first spongy, turning to gravel, turning to rock. Here, the underbrush thins, the soil too grudging and meager to support roots. Finally, I emerge above the trees.

In front of me rises a cliff, and above the cliff, a canyon of stone. Shivers—part fear, part cold—ripple across the skin of my arms and back as I make my way up the cliff and into the canyon. Climbing down this trail this morning was difficult. Climbing up now, even as the sleet finally slows, might be impossible.

Did you really come this way?

I scramble up and over boulders, each one more slick and treacherous than the one before, water racing around the sides. I come to the place where the trail splits, rocks rising to my right, up and out of the ravine, leaving the rapids below to my left. Ascending the rocky ledge, my feet test every surface, searching for the safest footholds.

Halfway to the summit, I reach a huge shelf of stone—a hanging boulder as flat and smooth as my mother's cutting stone. Ice coats the surface. My eyes trace its edges, seeking the safest route. Water runs off the canyon wall, draining into crevices in the trail—small gaps between boulders and knobs of rock—before spilling over the edge and into the ravine far below. My eyes follow the course of the rushing water as it passes beneath this slick shelf of rock.

That's when I spot you.

You lie perfectly still, directly below the place where I stand, on a strip of rock just above the water. Did you fall? Before I can process all the possibilities, I'm lying on my stomach, lowering myself, feetfirst, over the edge. I hang by my hands for just a moment before I drop into the ravine.

Even through my heavy sealskin pants, the cold cuts into me like daggers as I slide into the water. Surfacing, I call your name, but the sound is swallowed up in the roar of the rapids. I scramble to the side of the stream. The wall is too steep to climb out, but the water runs shallow and my feet find the bottom. *Careful, careful.* My legs brace against the force of the current. If I fall—if the water pulls me away—there will be no hope for either of us.

You lie on your side, facing away from me, your legs

underwater from the knees down. Your hips balance on a small ledge that protrudes from the wall of rock just beyond you.

I call your name again, but you give no response.

The dread I've been feeling transforms to gradual acceptance—you are not conscious. You can't be—if you were, you would answer. But you must be alive. . . . You must be. The position of your body—your head out of water—you couldn't have fallen like that. No, you must be alive.

All I need to do is reach you, to find a way to lift you out of the ravine.

I lean heavily into the current, taking slow, steady strides, clutching at the canyon wall. One . . . two . . . three more steps and I am there.

I reach out to lay a hand on your back, but before I touch you, my hand jerks away. A wide stripe of blood paints the back of your parka from collar to hem.

A head injury . . . blood must be running down from some hidden wound.

Careful to hold on to the rock you lie on, I run my eyes over the stain and up the length of your back to a dry, crusty puddle on your collar, protected by your draped hair. I reach out a hand and gently touch you. To my surprise, you startle and turn toward me.

"You're awake." It's obvious, but it's the only thing I can think to say.

"Where is she?"

"Where's who?" I ask, though I'm certain what your answer will be.

"Where's Lo?"

"I don't know," I say, taking care to look behind me without compromising my balance.

"She found me in my hut—I'd gone to get another spear. She found me, and we fought. I cut her—a gash across her forehead. There was so much blood. . . ."

I remember your hut, the bloodstains on the walls.

"I threatened her, warned her to run back to the beach, but she said I would have to kill her—I would have to kill her or die. . . ." Your voice trails off and your eyes fall shut, as if you have dropped back to sleep.

"Mya?" I squeeze your shoulder and your eyes fly open again.

"She followed me," you say. "She chased me into this canyon. We struggled. . . . We struggled and we fell."

Could Lo still be here? To my left and right, to my front and back, I see no one, yet there are plenty of spaces and crevices between rocks for a person to hide. We need to get out of the open. The cave is our best hope, but we're not there yet.

Despite your quick reaction to my touch, you are far from alert. Talking seems to have exhausted you. You scowl and turn away.

"Mya, you can't sleep here. Mya!" I shake your shoulder, not rough but firm, and you spin around, wide-eyed, as if you'd already forgotten I was here. You whirl so quickly I grab you by the waist to keep you from falling from your narrow perch. "Mya!" Your eyes are already closed; your forehead slumps against my shoulder. I take your face between my two palms. Your cheeks feel warm, despite the cold all around us. "Can you stand?" I shout into your face. "We need to get out of here."

"I can't go now. . . . I'm tired," you say, keeping your eyes pressed shut and jerking your head from my hands.

Cold claws at my feet. If we are going to get out of here, I am going to have to get us both out on my own. "I'm sorry, but we have to go now." Without another word, I wrap one arm around your back and scoop up your legs with the other. I lift you slowly, mindful of my footing under the water, rushing and flashing, as if it, too, were full of panic, hurrying out of these hills.

As I straighten, you wrap your arms around my neck to hold on. "Why won't you let me be?" you ask, though you don't put up any fight and even let your head fall against me.

I don't answer you. I doubt you would hear me. Besides, I'm not sure what my answer should be. I didn't come looking for you because I think you need me. You have too much strength for me to think that way. I owe you; that's true. You saved my life more than once already.

At my core, of course, I know my reasons are so much bigger than that.

But now is not the time to wrestle with motives. I shove these thoughts aside so I can focus on my task. Each step is a new test. My feet are numb inside my boots, and rain still falls in my eyes, though the air is warming. The ice that coated the rocks earlier is melting away, and as I climb closer to the summit, the runoff slows. I force myself to step slowly, holding you close against me to keep our weight centered over my feet. At last, the water is so shallow that I am able to step up out of the stream and onto the rocky trail. From here, it's a short distance up to the crest of the cliff and down the sea-facing side to the cave.

This morning I thought this path was the most treacherous I'd ever crossed. I would never have believed I'd cross this same path carrying you.

I try to remember each foothold in my mind's eye—I'd studied them so carefully this morning—this one was a bit deeper than the others, this next one a wider stride to the left. Rocks the size of men encroach so far into the path that they snag on my parka. In front of me there is a nearly straight drop to the sea.

I stop to catch my breath a moment, looking out over the water. Boats move in the distance—the boats of Lo's clan, receding into the north. Could Lo be on one? Could I have passed her on the trail and not seen her?

A loose rock teeters under my left foot and my mind is called back from the boats to the cliff beneath me. My body goes as still as stone, so still each beat of my heart ripples through me like a wave. I pull you closer and breathe . . . breathe . . . breathe . . . Water runs down my face, drips from my chin to my chest, and I wait, measuring the beat of my heart against the beat of the drips. Time stretches, full of nothing but breath and beats and drips, until at last my heart has quieted.

I turn my head slightly left, and my eyes trace the wall of rock down until I spot the thin shadow of a ledge—the lip of the opening of the cave. The path is too narrow for me to turn; I have to descend the rest of the way with my back to the cliff. The rain has slowed to a drizzle but the sky has darkened. I shut out the sounds of the sea beating against the rocks below, the voices of the gulls calling over the beach farther south. I focus all my senses on the next three steps.

Three steps . . .

A gust of wind blows up from below, such a blast your hair flies briefly into my face, pelting me with needles of ice that cling to the strands.

Two steps . . .

I pause, notice a lull in the wind and mutter a hasty, garbled tangle of words I hope the Divine will accept as a prayer, and then shift our weight over my feet. My left foot reaches back, searching blindly, until it finds the ledge.

One step . . .

Ducking my head, shifting all our weight to the left, I stumble backward into the cave. Folding my body in half to avoid the low ceiling, I let myself tumble onto the floor. Still curled in my arms, you land hard against my chest.

If you were asleep before, the force of the fall wakes you. You sit up, startled, and look around, wide-eyed, until I see you recognize where we are. With only a sideways glance at my face you crawl deeper into the safety of the shadows behind me.

The darkness in this cave is so complete I can no longer see you, but I can smell your blood.

"I think your wound has opened up again."

"No, it's fine." Your words echo against the close walls. Even so, your voice sounds small. "I ran my fingers over it. It's dry."

We need light and heat. I pat the ground, feeling for the remnants of the fire we made in here before.

"The wound is under your hair, Mya, and your hair is drenched."

"My hair is *cold*—wet with rain and ice. It would be warm if it were wet with blood." Injured, bleeding, freezing—yet still stubborn.

"I'm going to try to get a fire going," I say.

My hands search the floor, fumbling across silt and

cinders, until they land on a chunk of splintered wood that flakes at the ends as if it's been burned. A short distance away the ground drops down into a shallow hole—the fire pit.

I crawl farther into the dark, one hand extended out in front of me, my knees grinding against knots of broken wood and nubs of rock. At last, my hand lands on what I remember as a deliberate, orderly stack of firewood piled against the far wall.

It's unnerving to be in a place so dark. It's even more unnerving to be here with you.

As I turn pieces of wood in my hands, my eyes begin to adjust to what little light filters in from outside. Black yields to gray as shadows become objects. I separate kindling and tinder. On a flat rock beside the wood I discover the starter kit—a long whittled stick and fireboard. "Give me just a little longer and I'll get you warmed up, all right?"

I wait, but you don't answer.

"Mya?"

"Go ahead and make a fire. I think I'll just sleep a bit."

"No—*no* sleeping. I need you to stay awake. I need company. Someone to talk to."

"What are we going to talk about?"

Rolling the firestick between my fingers, I hesitate. "What do you think we should talk about?"

Maybe I shouldn't have asked this question. There are

countless things that could be said between us, and probably countless more that should be left unsaid.

I grasp the firestick between my palms, one end buried in a notch cut in the fireboard, surrounded by fistfuls of dry grass like clumps of human hair. Rubbing my hands back and forth, I twirl the stick like a drill. My hands pass down the entire length of the stick once, twice, three times. Friction builds, and at last a ribbon of smoke curls around the board.

Distracted by my task, I almost forget the question I asked you. I'm not sure how long you've been silent. "Mya?"

"Fine," you say, the word scratching in your throat like you've swallowed bits of gravel. "I'll try to stay awake, but you need to give me something to stay awake for."

"Meaning?"

"Why don't you tell me a story?"

"I don't know any stories."

An ember catches. An orange glow blooms in the kindling. I lie on my side and blow a steady stream of breath into the grass, coaxing out garlands of smoke.

"Everyone who's ever lived has a story to tell, Kol."

As the fire spreads I sit up, turning your words in my mind. What could I possibly tell you? All my stories have become entwined with yours. "What do you want to hear?" I ask.

"Tell me something *wonderful*—a story that's startling

and marvelous." Despite your grogginess, there's a lilt of expectation in your voice. "Tell me about the most startling and marvelous day of your life. . . ."

I watch the flame grow until the fire spreads from the kindling to the larger branches. Then I let my eyes fall shut. The light of the fire dances on the backs of my eyelids like the sun overhead on a summer day.

"I lie in the grass with my eyes closed," I start, "listening for the whir of honeybee wings. . . ."

THIRTY

I don't know how long I talk, but I tell Mya everything. Every moment since we met in the meadow—she relives it all through my words.

She sits still, her back against the wall. All the while she hardly moves. At times she flinches, pulls her knees a bit closer to her chest. Everything I tell her—our story—she already knows, yet it's all still new, all seen through my eyes.

Pulling her from the water and carrying her, half conscious, to this cave—those are the last things I describe for her. My words trail off. There is nothing more to say.

The rain has finally stopped. Silence surrounds us. For a moment we sit without speaking. Drips fall at intervals across the mouth of the cave, creating a pattern of sound almost musical in its cadence.

All at once, Mya shifts away from the wall as if reacting to a distant voice calling her name, then wobbles and sags forward onto her knees. I lurch toward her and catch her by the elbow, but she draws away. "The fire." The words slip from her lips with a vague agitation so that I immediately turn and check the fire pit.

"It's fine," I say, but she turns away.

"The fire at your camp, the *fire* . . . what Lo's people did . . . I wish . . ." She trails off. "And Chev . . . he's all right? He will survive?"

"Yes—"

"And the others of my clan?"

"Most . . . most appeared to be doing well," I say, not wanting to lie. The truth is, I don't know if any have died. I saw many hurt, but why burden her with that now?

Mya crawls away, moving toward the opening of the cave. Like last time we were here, I am left with only her silhouette. She sits cross-legged, looking out into a mist that rolls up from the sea, a thick warm haze pushing in to replace the fleeing cold.

Something about the hard, dark shape of her against the billowy clouds is so sad that it sends a shiver through me and I crawl up beside her and sit. Looking over, her profile is fixed and unreadable—neither relaxed nor tense, just intent and focused, though nothing, not even the foam on the waves, can be seen through this fog. She must be focused on something else, something unseen.

I lean toward her, sliding my hand across the cold, damp

space between us. The tips of my fingers graze the back of her hand, trace a slow circle on her cool skin, then come to rest, draped across her fingers. I wait, counting my breaths—one, two, three. When I get to five and she hasn't pulled away, I wrap my fingers around hers.

Her face turns toward me, her brow furrowed, her eyes darkened with concern. Strands of damp hair zigzag across her forehead and hang in her eyes, and unbidden, my free hand moves to her face and smooths them back, tucking them behind her ear. I hardly need to move to reach farther around her head, to feel gently for the spot where the dried blood still clings, and to cup my hand at the nape of her neck, rocking toward her and touching my lips to hers.

Mya's lips move under the pressure of mine, bringing a rush of dark warmth to my heart and flashes of yellow, green, and gold, as bright as summer sunshine, to the backs of my eyes. A cool hand presses lightly to my cheek, slides along my jaw, and a blaze of heat runs across my skin as her fingers trace down my throat, skim my collarbone, coming to stop, palm flat, against my chest. I'm lifting my other hand, ready to wind it around her waist, when I feel the pressure from that palm, subtle but firm.

Her head tips back, her hand pushing me away.

She draws away, and I watch her through eyes that ache to return to her the way I imagine a drowning man's eyes ache for the receding surface. But there's no use in trying to coax her back. Her eyes are already focused beyond my shoulder. She stares into the mist, at something inside herself, something only she can see. Whatever it is, she stays silent about it. Her lips are pulled tight, a fine, straight line, with no hint of my kiss left on them.

Finally, as if she's waking from a dream, the darkness ebbs from her eyes. Her gaze meets mine and she gives me a weak smile.

"I'm sorry," she says. "It's not that I don't want you to kiss me. I want you to, and I want to kiss you back. But kissing you just now made me forget everything else. And right now, there's too much I need to remember."

Her eyes burn with an intensity that magnifies her words. I nod and try to return her smile before dropping my eyes and turning away.

And I realize that the one thing I need from Mya—the one thing I've needed from Mya all along—is for her to let go of the past. And I realize that that may be the one thing I cannot ask of her.

Little time passes before we are on our way, hiking the same trail we hiked this morning. It's easier now that the rain has stopped—*easier*, but far from easy. We scramble up the cliff, shrouded in hazy vapor, then ease our way onto the rocky path above the ravine. I thank the Divine that the fog clings to the cliffs on the sea-facing side of the trail. Once we are descending into the valley, the mist is gone, though everywhere, on all sides of the rocks beneath our feet, water streams, rushing from the summit to the ground below.

We travel in silence, too focused on our footing to speak, Mya a few paces ahead of me. At places the water is high, running over our feet, but then we reach the spot where the trail splits, the pathway following along the ledge that hangs above the water-filled ravine. Progress is slow—we move no faster than wet boots can safely move over wet rocks, which is not very fast at all. My attention never leaves the ground. It isn't until Mya stops, holding breathlessly still on the path for just a few moments too long, that I take my eyes off the rocks beneath my own feet long enough to look up at her.

My ears find focus first—the rushing roar of water passing deep within the ravine, the echo of stones worked loose by the flood, plummeting into the torrent below. My gaze settles on her back, focuses on her straight shoulders, her legs, one foot braced behind her.

Beyond her is the broad flat shelf of rock—the very one I stood on when I came this way before—when I looked down and saw her far below.

Across from her, in a pose that mirrors her own, stands Lo.

I can't see Mya's face. I can see only a sliver of Lo's. Neither girl stirs, not a muscle flinches. A cloud slides away from the sun and all at once we are coated in hot, dry light. Finally, Lo speaks. "Mya. I was hoping I would see you again. I was hoping you were still nearby—"

"You will not hurt her—" I start.

"Mya," Lo says again, in a voice that not only shuts mine out but invalidates it, as if she never heard it, as if I'd made no sound at all, so fixed is her attention on Mya. "I have no hope left—whatever I'd hoped to accomplish, I've failed. I will not make it home." She moves, her hands rising from her sides, and Mya takes a wobbly step backward, her foot landing in a thin stream of runoff that pours from the wall and splashes across the trail, spilling over the side and into the rapids below. Mya's shifted stance allows me a view around her, and I see that Lo is only lifting the hem of her parka, revealing something red and dark and wet. The wound is grotesque, and a wave of nausea swamps me. Something inside me shadows over, dimming my vision, shrouding the injury in darkness and hiding it from my sight. Without thinking, I step back.

But Mya doesn't flinch. Instead, she bends her head toward the wound, daring to move closer to Lo, to a place so close she is almost within range of Lo's grasp. A long slow hiss of breath leaks through Mya's lips until, finally, she speaks. "So deep . . ."

"It is." Lo's reply comes out half cough, half laugh. She gives Mya an eerie smile, her jaw clenched. "I fell . . . when *you* fell, when we struggled right here, before. The spearhead—I clutched it in my hands, waved it at you. Then . . ." Lo sags, dropping onto one knee. The hem of her parka falls back into place, leaving just a watery trickle of blood still visible beneath it, running down the side of her pants. "It wedged up under my ribs when I landed on the rocks." She plants her foot and, trembling, rises back to her full height. "I wanted you to know. If my body was found, I didn't want you to think that you had done it. I guess neither of us did it—"

"We both did it," Mya says.

A cluster of fast-moving clouds fly overhead; shadows flit across Lo's face. She shuffles a fraction of a step toward Mya, though it's impossible to tell under these surreal circumstances—circumstances that seem to hold us suspended above the rules of movement and balance—if she intended to move or not.

"It was my own fault."

"No," Mya says. "It was an accident. A fall—"

"Not *this*," Lo breaks in, her voice a wet rasp. "Before . . . *It was my own fault.*" She quiets, bends at the waist, convulses with a syrupy cough, then straightens. "The night I became lost on the gathering trip with your family. I've been angry for years about the suffering I endured that night, but I've known all along—I couldn't even admit it to myself, but now I have to . . . I have to admit it to you. . . . It was my own fault.

"So much of both our lives turned on the events of that night and what's been said of it since then. Now I am going to the Divine, and I don't want to face her with that lie still on my lips."

"It was no one's fault," Mya says, but I hear something in her voice, some hesitation, like a toe catching on a stone. "It just happened. Let's not think of that now—"

"I have to—"

"No. You have to let me try to help you."

My heart slips out of rhythm as I watch Mya slide forward, stretch her foot over the gap that separates them, and reach for Lo. Strength drains from my legs, the rock beneath my own feet sways, as four arms stretch up, Lo shuddering, her hands opening and closing at the ends of her raised arms. Mya slides closer, eases her hands around her shoulders, and enfolds Lo in an embrace.

Time holds still, as if it, too, were wrapped in that embrace. Every rule of nature—of rocks and water—of blood and legs and feet and balance—every rule is held suspended for one long exhale. Until, with a burst of blinding sunlight, the rules are restored. Mya's feet shuffle over a surface slick with trickling blood mixed with water and the recent memory of ice. Lo's eyes widen, and something like a gasp escapes her lips. "Help me."

But it's too late.

They both jerk, snapping to the side, then righting, almost catching themselves upright, but then tilting, slipping, their arms still entwined, both of them moving as one, plunging into the ravine.

My feet are on the rock, and then they are in the air. Cold burns through me, right to my bones, as I plunge into the water.

White foam rolls around my shoulders, crashing over my head. I dive under, into the current, eyes open, and there, carried along like a leaf on the wind, I see them.

Mya's arm is extended, her hand clasped to Lo's belt, tethering them together. They move as one body, feet kicking wildly, transforming the water into a cloud of tiny bubbles that float toward the surface, blocking my view. As bubbles rise, burst, and dissolve away, an agonizing weight presses down on my chest—I need to breathe.

I break the surface and the sun warms my face. My mouth opens and gulps in air. I reorient myself. Downstream I spot Mya, clinging with one arm to a high rock along the side, her fingers bleached white with cold, clawing at the jagged edge. Behind her, the other hand clutches Lo's hood, Lo's face bobbing up and down on the surface of the current—one moment above, one moment below.

Mya coughs, clutches at the rock, and screams.

Her voice, a sharp snap, echoes like a thunderclap through the ravine. Her grip on Lo's hood has given out. Lo floats away from her, disappearing back under the foam.

I fight against every impulse within me, willing my fingers to peel away from the rock.

The current carries me past Mya, the stream rolling downhill. I follow Lo, kicking hard, trying to pull within reach of her. *For Mya*, I tell myself. *For Mya*. Lo tumbles in the churning current, her movements in sync with the water's movements, her blood tinting the stream pink.

Watching her body rise and fall, with no tension or effort left in her limbs, I know that her Spirit has left her. I know that I have failed. She is carried away now on another kind of stream, to rejoin the spirit of the Divine.

Eventually, we reach the place where the ravine widens, the sharply angled cliffs crumbling into a mass of boulders that tumble to the floor of the valley below. The stream splits, and Lo's body catches on a rock. Here the water turns suddenly shallow and the current calm, and I clamber up onto rocks beside her. I bend, wrap an arm around her waist, slippery with blood, and lift her from the water.

I don't hear her approach, but all at once, Mya appears beside me. She crouches, and with fingers white as ice, she turns Lo's head and brushes her hair aside, revealing the bloodless, blue lips and wide, white eyes of a drowned girl.

Beyond us, the water drops over a jumble of sharply

angled rocks, dividing into three wispy waterfalls that spill to the valley floor below, pooling and rippling into creeks that disappear into the distant tree line.

Mya stays silent, but I notice the sound of my own breath. It rushes fast and desperate in and out of my lungs, reminding me I'm alive.

THIRTY-ONE

By the time the sun is fully up the next day, I am already on the sea in my kayak, far north of Mya's camp. I stole out of the hut I slept in, shrouded in the stillness of the pale morning, anxious to leave without being seen—without having to apologize for my hasty departure.

It's not that I wasn't well cared for. Yano and Ela warmed me up and cleaned and treated my wounds, including an ankle I'd sprained on one of my trips into the ravine— now tucked inside the kayak, unnecessarily splinted and wrapped—and a deep cut on my forearm, the cause of which I could no longer remember.

Like many days following a storm, today the sea is still and smooth. As I stab my paddle into the placid water, I remember Yano's grave expression, his usually bright eyes shadowed with concern, as he asked me how it could be that I didn't remember the cause of a wound so deep.

"I fell too many times. Any number of falls could've given me a wound like this."

"It was in the stream," Mya offered. "I saw it. Your arm tore across a jagged rock when you tried to save Lo."

When you tried to save Lo. I remember these words of Mya's so clearly, because they were the last words she said to me. Once we returned to the Olen camp—once our wounds had been bandaged and she had offered this explanation for my cut—Mya withdrew to her hut and stayed there. Ela carried food in, but brought nothing back out. No message for me. No explanation for her silence.

"When you tried to save Lo" is the only explanation I have.

Does Mya blame me for failing to save Lo, for letting Lo die? Is that her reason for avoiding me? Or does she worry what horrors will come back to her, the next time she sees my face? Will she see Lo's lifeless body as I pulled her from the stream?

Whatever her reasons, it was clear she didn't want to see me. So I decided to leave quietly.

The last thing I want right now is a confrontation.

The sun hangs high overhead, dipping only slightly to the west, when I drag my kayak up onto my own clan's beach. My aunt Ama and two of her boys are far out in the bay, fishing. They don't see me, but the sight of them out in their boats comforts me with its normalcy.

Pulling the kayak into the tall grass, I notice the thick, slightly sweet smell of burned fur mixing with the salt in the air. Hides are spread across the beach—hides with charred and singed edges. These must have been pulled down from damaged huts and judged to be salvageable. They are damp, bleeding dark puddles of water into the sand around them. I imagine they were washed in the sea and spread out to dry in the sun.

A tight knot forms in my stomach. I'd hoped that I could come home, really *come home*—that I could silence the echoes of the horrors of the last few days. But as I hike up the trail, I realize my home is no longer the safe refuge I remember.

The huts stand like half-dressed skeletons against the bright blue sky. Some are stripped of hides completely, leaving only the frame of bare mammoth bones hunched over like bending backs. Others have holes ripped open, gaping like fresh wounds—a gap in a wall or a roof torn away. I find my mother and father with several other elders in the gathering place, studying hides scattered on the ground, deciding which should be used and which should be rejected. I notice a pile of sealskin pelts beneath my mother's hands. These are her own, tanned for her as a gift from Pek. Her plan was to stitch them together, to make a luxurious blanket for her bed.

She looks up, her eyes hazy with thought, but when she

sees me the haze clears and she jumps to her feet. Then she's hugging me, kissing my cheek, while at the same time repeating my name over and over, scolding me for leaving without letting anyone know.

"Pek knew," I say.

"Pek doesn't count. You need to tell someone with sense."

My father comes up and lays a hand on my shoulder. Turning toward him, I catch a glimpse of something in his eyes, something I've rarely seen there—the fading shadow of fear. His hand clamps down tight and the shadow fades, so swiftly it's almost easy to believe it was never there at all, but his other hand clasps me on the opposite shoulder and I am sure.

What had they thought when Pek told them I had headed south, alone in a small boat in that storm? All at once it rushes back to me—my confusion on the water, my soaked and freezing clothes, how close I was to death when Mya found me.

Tears spring to my eyes. I draw my father into an awkward embrace to hide my face from him.

"I want to help," I say when I feel collected enough to speak. "With the huts. I want to help—"

"You need to rest," my mother says, not letting me get the words out. "Look at your ankle. This wound on your arm. What happened to you? What happened . . ." She trails off. Is she afraid to know the answer?

"Chev was injured," I say. I know I need to tell them everything, but I also know I don't have the strength or the will to tell them everything now. "He survived. He's healing. But Lo . . ." I look down, draw in a deep breath, then look back at their expectant faces. The words stick in the back of my throat. I have to spit them through my lips. "Lo died. It was an accident. She drowned."

The light in my mother's eyes dims. She shoots a fleeting glance at my father. "And the others? From the Olen?" She doesn't have to ask—I know what's on her mind. Lo's goal was to kill Chev's whole family. She wants to know if she had any success before she died.

"There were many injuries," I say, remembering the horror of the scene under the canopy, "but everyone from the Olen clan survived."

My mother's eyes brighten, and the tension at the corners of her mouth softens. "Pek will be so relieved to know Seeri is all right."

I learn that both Pek and Kesh are in our family's hut. Urar has dressed their wounds with cool wraps and offered up countless prayers and chants, but their burns are extensive and healing will be slow. "Seeing you safe will help their pain," my mother says. Her words send a shiver of dread through me, and I hurry to find them.

When I duck under the charred pelt that forms the door

I find Urar sitting on the floor, chanting softly, his voice barely above a whisper. My brothers Pek and Kesh are both in bed, both apparently sleeping. A tangle of scents hangs in the room—the sweetness of mead mixing with a heavy, darker odor, like mud from the bottom of a pond. "I'm sorry," I say. "I couldn't hear you from outside."

Urar flinches at the intrusion, but then a small sound, not more than a gasp, escapes his lips and he gets to his feet. He holds me at arm's length; his brow, wet with sweat, furrows as he squints through the dim light at the long cut that runs along my forearm. "Rest," he says. "That is first. Later, when you wake, I will treat that with oil and herbs."

"Yes," I say. He hesitates, perhaps waiting for me to follow his direction and lie on my bed, but I stand still, nodding in agreement, not wanting to hobble and let him see that my ankle is splinted. Finally, he nods in reply and squeezes my hands. With a hint of a smile—something quite rare from Urar—he ducks out through the door.

I collapse onto my bed, but it's not the bed I had before the fire. The thick stack of pelts and hides I've always slept between has been thinned considerably, as have the other stacks of pelts that form the beds around the room. Patches of dirt, once hidden completely by soft rugs, peek through the hides that remain on the floor, scattered about in an artful effort to cover as much of the ground as possible.

How many pelts were destroyed in the fire? The hides

and furs that filled this hut were the reward of many lives spent hunting—my life, my parents' lives, my grandparents' lives. How long will it take to rebuild what was destroyed?

Stretching out, I unwrap my ankle and discard the unnecessary splint. Restlessness grips me. I'm up on my feet, pacing, trying to get used to the changes in the hut, to the overwhelming strangeness I feel in this place where I once felt at home.

Home . . . it's a word I don't understand anymore. I don't feel right in this hut. It floods me with longing for a time that will never come back. A time when I still felt trust— trust in neighboring clans, trust even in strangers.

My brothers sleep on, their breaths coming in even rhythms almost in time with each other, filling me with the creeping sense that the air in the room is being devoured. I'm forced to leave this strange hut and head out into the strange sunlight. Nothing feels right. Nothing feels familiar. I can't imagine that it ever will again.

Like the morning of the day I met Mya, I'm driven by a desire to get away, a need to escape the confines of camp and be alone for a while. I think first of the meadow, but then reconsider, knowing the meadow would be the first place Pek or anyone else would look for me. Instead, I decide to head for the trail that leads over the hills to the western side of the bay. I know that near the summit that path divides— a seldom-used, nearly forgotten trail splits off and descends north and east to the far edge of the meadow. It will be a longer trek, giving me more time alone.

I start up the trail from its mouth near the beach. Even the slant of light seems strange. Unfamiliar songs of unfamiliar birds fill the air.

I climb quickly, not pausing until I reach the summit. A breeze stirs the lower branches of the trees with a whisper, like ghosts shuffling by, and I shudder. After a bit of searching, I locate the overgrown path that winds east toward the meadow. At the first switchback, a gap in the trees opens on a wide view to the northwest, and I stop.

Looking out, I can see to the horizon, a line so flat it could be water, though the ground is the golden yellow and green of the grasslands. I look as far out as I can, as if I can look back into the past, back to the day a family left their camp on a gathering trip, and a girl became lost.

My eyes search the land in front of me as if I might see that day—as if that day were a bend in a river that flows from the past to the place I stand right now.

But that day is not a place where the river bends, I realize. It's the place where the river splits. On that day the Divine dropped a stone in the river, diverting it into two streams. One clan continued west. Another clan turned south. Separate courses, both leading toward death.

The death of Mya's father, Mya's mother, Mya's betrothed.

The death of Lo's father.

The death of Lo.

Wind blows across the peak from the bay and the scent of seawater brings me back to the present.

I hurry downhill, and when I reach the meadow—the first place that truly feels like home—I drop down onto my back. Though I felt only restlessness in the hut, now I feel nothing but exhaustion. The hike brought back fatigue to every sore muscle in my body. Warmth surrounds me. A whisper in the grass quiets my thrumming thoughts: *shhhhh . . . shhhhhh.*

Sleep swoops down on me with wide-stretched arms, wrapping me in an embrace, pulling me up, and carrying me away before I have a chance to resist.

I wake with a start, as if summoned by a voice. I sit up, noticing the sun far off in the west. It's almost time for the evening meal.

What questions will I be asked tonight? I expect I will have to tell about the attack on Chev, my fight with the boy, the death of Lo.

How will my mother react when she hears that I may have killed Orn? That I let Lo die?

These questions darken my thoughts as I climb the trail back toward my camp, which suddenly seems so far away. I think of Manu, lost, far from family and clan.

When I reach the summit, my steps quicken. I'm

propelled forward by the knowledge that around the next bend, the trail turns toward home.

I reach the overlook and sweep my gaze over the familiar scene in front of me—the sea to my right, the sloping plains to my left, and the eastern mountains in the far distance. And directly below me, a view of my own clan's camp.

Even run-down and blighted by half-stripped huts, this is the place of the people I love.

But as I look down on the camp, confusion rises in me, and I have to question what I see. How could this be the same camp I stepped away from earlier today?

Every hut is complete; every structure neatly covered in smooth, fine pelts. Sun glints off the roof of the kitchen, newly covered in a dark hide of glossy bearskin. And draped across the doorway of my family's hut hangs something new—pelts stitched to create a sort of banner of contrasting colors, pieced together in an intricate design—a field of dark fur as a background, dotted with lighter pieces to suggest stars in a night sky.

I've seen pelts stitched in patterns like this only once before, in Mya's hut. This, *all this*, I think, my eyes moving from one repaired hut to another, could have come only from the south, from Mya and her people.

I tear my eyes from the view and race farther down the trail, wondering if I will find Mya herself in my camp. But as the trail draws close to the bottom of the hill, I catch a glimpse out over the bay.

Boats.

Three intricately carved canoes float just a short distance from shore. Two rowers sit in each one, as if waiting to push out. And in two of the three canoes, a body lies between the seated oarsmen. The canoe closest to shore bears the body of a young girl, lying as if asleep, covered all over in red ocher—the color of blood, the color of the dead.

This is Lo, making her final journey home.

The second canoe is farther out in the bay. Bright red ocher covers the length of the body that lies in the hull, standing out against the gray water, but it floats too far away for me to see the person's face.

It doesn't matter. I don't need to see his face to know that it's Orn, the boy I let fall from the cliff, the boy Chev called Dora's son. I had been afraid to look down, to know if he had lived or died.

But now I know. Now I know he is dead.

I hear voices coming from the beach, though my view is obscured by the trees. A man speaks in a steady, command-ing voice. Chev. He is answered by the voices of my father and mother. They are thanking him for the gift of the pelts. They wish him blessings as he heads across the bay. "As you return the dead to the Bosha," says my mother, "may the Divine protect you."

Her words ring in my ears as I descend the remainder of

the trail to the beach. I wonder what will happen to Chev when he arrives on the Bosha's shore. What if some of the Bosha still hope to kill him? What if their elders are not able to intervene? Is he brave to come and face them, or is he reckless?

I reach the beach as Chev is saying his final good-bye to my parents. I step clear of the last of the trees and the three of them come into view.

Only then do I see that there are not three people on the beach, but four. Chev is not facing the Bosha alone. He is taking the girl who stands beside him, dressed in an ill-fitting parka.

Mya.

THIRTY-TWO

Mya's eyes meet mine.

When I left her camp early this morning, hadn't I worried that when she next saw me, she would be transported to the moment of Lo's death? Hadn't I worried that I would be, too? But instead of that awful moment by the stream, I'm carried to the ledge outside the mouth of the cave.

I'm transported to the moment we kissed.

I feel her fingers, thin and cool, wrapped in mine. The pressure of her lips. The heat rising in my chest. The trail her fingertips traced along my jaw . . .

"Kol!" my mother shouts, and the spell is broken. I blink and Mya drops her eyes.

Chev steps toward me and acknowledges me with a nod. "I wanted to thank you for everything you did—I may have died if not for you—but when I looked for you today you were already gone."

My mother's eyes slide to my face. I'm sure my parents were not aware that I'd left without saying good-bye. "I wanted to hurry back to let my family know I was all right. And to share with them the other news—that you had all survived, and that Lo . . ."

"Of course," Mya says. "I'm sure your clan was happy to have you back, safe and well."

"Yes." My eyes sweep over the water, taking in the canoes floating a short distance from the edge of the sand. Urgency rises in me. I have to speak up. "They were happy to know that the Bosha had failed in their plans. That despite the fact that each of us—you, Chev, even me—had come so close to death, we had all survived. Yet here you are, preparing to board these boats. By the will of the Divine, the Bosha's attempts to kill both of you failed. Why would you now climb into these canoes and deliver yourselves to their shore?"

"It was not the Bosha who tried to take our lives," says your brother. There is a softness in his words, an uncharacteristic compassion in his tone. "It was Lo and it was Orn. Both of them came to kill, and both of them died. But the others of their clan left—"

"They left to preserve their own lives!" I'm startled by the force of my own voice, by the tremor of anger in my tone. I glance at my father's face, expecting him to raise a hand, signaling me to back down. Instead, he nods, so I continue. "What do you think will happen when Lo's followers learn that Lo and Orn are both dead? Do you think they will put aside their desire to kill you? To kill Mya? And can we trust that the Bosha elders would be able to stop them if they tried?"

Chev does not reply, and at first, I worry that I have overstepped my bounds. But then I see that he is watching something, and all five of us turn toward movement out on the bay.

A kayak. A long, two-person kayak carrying a lone paddler.

One of Lo's people is approaching our shore.

Time slows down as we stand, as rigid as a row of spears stuck in the sand, watching the kayak draw closer. As the face of the paddler comes into view, I can see that our visitor is a woman. With the long, deliberate strokes of someone who is seldom on the sea, she steers her kayak toward the waiting canoes. She is trying to pull close, craning her neck, stretching to peer over the sides of the boats. Once she is close enough to see into them, close enough to recognize the faces of the dead they carry, she lets out a cry that shatters the silence above the bay.

Not a cry of anger, but of loss.

"Dora," Chev says under his breath. "It's Dora."

He strides out into the water without hesitating, wading

right up to the side of the small boat. He throws his arms around the woman. Still strapped into the kayak, she falls against him and sobs into his chest.

This is Dora, the mother of Orn. The mother of the boy I killed.

It isn't long before Mya has waded out beside her brother. The rowers, too, turn their attention to the kayak, to the woman who they would all have known until five years ago. From where I stand on the sand, the distance is too great to hear the conversation, but it appears that Dora protests the care being offered to her. I watch as she pulls away from Chev's embrace, unties the sash of the kayak, and climbs out of the boat. She reaches into the opening at the front of the kayak—the empty seat for a second paddler—and withdraws what appears to be a pile of sealskin pelts. As the three of them wade into shore, I get a better view of her. An older woman with a small, pointy face and long white hair pulled back in a traditional braid, Dora accepts Mya's extended hand as she carries the pelts up the steep slope at the water's edge.

My mother hurries over, taking half of the pelts and handing them to me. Mya takes the rest of the pile from Dora's hands.

"No, I can carry them," Dora starts, but then she steps back as if seeing Mya for the first time. "Can you really be

Mya?" she says. "How old are you now?"

"Seventeen," says Mya.

"Just twelve years old when you left. My Anki was eleven, and Orn was only ten." Her voice breaks on these last words, and she drags the backs of her hands across her eyes before taking the pelts my mother gave me out of my hands. "I'm fine. I can carry those," she says. "I brought them as a gift, as a symbol of our sorrow and regret for the harm the Manu suffered at the hands of the Bosha." She pauses and takes a deep breath, as if drawing in strength to say what she came to say. "We learned about a fire—the elders, I mean—we had been away from camp, but when we returned we learned a fire had been set by my son, Orn. We pulled apart our kayaks. These are the pelts they were made of. I know these can't make up for what was lost, but I hope you will accept—"

"Of course we will. Thank you," my mother says. She takes the pelts back from Dora and drops them in my arms again. They bristle against the wound that runs across my forearm—the wound I got trying to save Lo—and I wince, more from the memory than from the pain.

"And injuries?" Dora's voice is a tentative whisper, as if she has to ask but fears the answer. "Were there injuries from the fire?"

"There were . . ."

Dora takes a step back. For a moment I think she might

fall, but my mother catches her under the arm. I can't help but wonder how she was chosen for this task. Did she insist she be the one to come, since her own son set the fire? "Could I meet those who were hurt? I need to apologize on behalf of the clan, and on behalf of my family. I know it won't help them, but I need to—"

"You can meet my sons," my mother says. "This is my oldest, Kol. Two of his brothers were injured. Kol, would you lead Dora to our hut so she can speak to Pek and Kesh?"

And so I find myself leading Dora up to the gathering place, a tumult of emotions churning inside my chest. How do I reconcile my anger toward the Bosha with the guilt I feel for the death of this woman's son? As we begin to climb the path, my mother lingers behind us. Over my shoulder, I hear her ask the rowers still perched in the canoes if they would like to come with us into camp. "Thank you," answers the tall, broad-shouldered woman who sits at the front of the canoe that holds Lo's body. "But we will stay here and guard the boats and the Spirits they carry." My mother, a gracious hostess under even the worst of circumstances, promises to bring back something for them to eat.

The evening meal is being prepared in the kitchen. Ahead of us, I see Roon duck under the door, a basket of greens in one arm and a load of firewood under the other. Tram and my youngest cousin are playing, running in circles around us as we walk, but Dora seems blind to it. She plods along, her eyes on the ground in front of her.

We head for my family's hut, and when we step through the door we find Pek and Kesh in bed, just as I left them, but now they are both awake and sitting up. Urar is there, too, mixing something dark and wet in a bowl made of a hollowed-out driftwood log. Shava sits beside Kesh, holding his hand.

As he did when I surprised him earlier, Urar startles as we all enter, but the sight of Dora, a complete stranger, brings him to his feet. "Urar," I say, "this is Dora, an elder of the Bosha clan. She brought these sealskins as an offering of regret for the fire. She also asked if she could meet those who were injured."

The hut is dimly lit—only a single flap is open to let in light—so Urar comes close to Dora and runs his gaze over her features. His is a healer's gaze. My father and mother, Mya and me—we all stand aside and wait. I can see the discernment in Urar's eyes, as if he is listening to the Divine, letting her direct his judgment. His eyes stay narrowed as he walks a slow circle around Dora, taking her in, but then they widen and fill with a warm glow. His verdict reached, he gives Dora a small nod.

"This is Pek," says Urar, motioning.

Dora takes the pile of pelts from Mya's arms and approaches Pek's bedside. "May these comfort you," she says. He sits up in bed and nods, and she drapes a pelt across his legs and tucks a few behind his back.

"And this is Kesh," says Urar. Dora turns toward Kesh and her eyes fall on Shava, folded on the floor beside him.

"Hello, Dora," says Shava, getting to her feet.

"Shava . . . I'd heard you and your mother were staying with the Manu. My daughter Anki told me you were visiting with your old friends."

"Yes. In fact, I've become betrothed to Kesh."

I can't quite tell if Dora and Shava are truly happy to see each other. Their greeting was certainly not warm, but I'm not sure if they are wary of one another, or if the horror of the circumstances is just too great to allow for pleasantries.

"And you are Kesh?" Dora asks. "I'm so sorry for your suffering." Like with Pek, she drapes a pelt across his legs. She wraps a second around his shoulders, though it is certainly not cold in this hut, especially crowded with people.

From outside the hut, the steady beat of a drum begins. The musicians are gathering.

"Are you hungry?" my mother asks. "You're welcome to be our guest at the evening meal."

The hut falls silent. It's as if everyone is holding their breath, waiting for Dora's reply. Do they hope she will decline? Would it be too much to ask for the injured to share a meal with a Bosha elder while the scent of smoke still lingers in the air?

"Thank you," Dora says. "You are so kind to offer, but I need to return to camp. I just wanted to deliver these pelts, and to offer the apologies of the Bosha elders. We didn't know. . . . That doesn't excuse what happened, I know, but the elders . . . We didn't know what Lo and Orn . . . She was trusted—the High Elder. And Orn was my son. My own son . . ." She trails off. Her eyes move to my mother's face before she wobbles a bit on her feet again. This time, my father is the one to reach out and catch her.

"Please sit," he says.

"I couldn't." But even as she protests she wobbles again, and my father, his hand under her elbow, leads her to a rug beside Pek's bed. She sits, and as she does, she continues to speak, though her voice is quiet, as if she is speaking to no one in particular. "Lo was such a lost girl. She made terrible mistakes; she and my son led many people the wrong way."

My father gestures for all of us to sit. Sweeping my eyes over the bare patches of dirt I'd noticed this morning, I scatter the pelts I'm still holding on the floor. Dust swirls in the shaft of light that falls through the partly opened vent overhead. All at once the room grows stiflingly hot. Sweat beads spring up on my lip and the back of my neck.

"When the elders returned before first light this morn- ing, we found the entire clan awake. Even the small chil- dren, who of course had stayed behind, were out of their beds, helping clean wounds. The whole camp was in chaos—everything smelled of smoke and blood. I found my daughter Anki. She had stayed behind with the children. I asked about her brother. Where was Orn? It was then that they told us all that had happened.

"They told us about the fire, about what Orn had done here in your camp. They told us about the attack on the Olen's camp in the south.

"And they told me my son had died.

"No one knew for certain what had happened to Lo, though they suspected that she . . . But it wasn't until I came here . . . It wasn't until I saw her in the boat . . ."

She quiets. Her hand goes to her mouth, and I know she is remembering not just the sight of Lo's body, but of her son's, too.

"They were so close—Lo and Orn—almost like twins. They would think and act as one." Her face contorts into something between a grimace and a shattered smile. "They were dangerous together, because they each fed the worst within the other. Yet something about them drew people to them. They ignited hope. They read signs about a prosperous future that the Divine was planning for us. Many people found them impossible to resist—"

"I'm sorry. I have to ask . . ." I can feel my mother's glare. Does she find it rude that I've interrupted? That I intend to question Dora? My mother may feel that way, but then, *she wasn't there*. She didn't chop through the shaft of a spear protruding from Chev's chest. "Why didn't anyone stop them? Couldn't you—couldn't *someone*—stop them?"

Dora tilts her face toward me, her eyes meeting mine. I see now that she is not as old as I had thought, just very weary and worn.

"They planned it well. For so long, the elders had tried to convince Lo that we should settle on the water—that we should stop following herds as her father had always done.

"Finally, she began to yield. She focused on building new kayaks. She announced she was sending the elders on a scouting expedition. She was very cunning. We went away so pleased that morning, heading west along the coast in search of a suitable bay, convinced she would soon agree with our own plans for the clan. While all along, they were preparing something different . . . something much darker . . ."

My mother leans forward, placing herself between me and Dora. She's noticed, as I have, Dora's voice growing thinner as she speaks, fading into a whisper. "Why don't you let me bring you something to eat? I could bring it in here—"

"I'm not saying we were innocent," Dora says, completely ignoring my mother, her eyes wide and unblinking. "We know the weight of our guilt. We know there will have to be consequences for what happened. Lo and Orn didn't act alone.

"But in the end, it happened as they say—*you die the way*

you live. They lived for vengeance. And for vengeance they died.

"Out of all of them, everyone else came back alive. Only those two—only Lo and Orn—lost their lives."

She drops her eyes. Turning away, she picks up Pek's hand, as if he were her own son.

As if he were Orn.

Later, I stand in the shallow water, holding the kayak steady as Dora gets in, ready to return to the western shore. The kayak bobs, thumping against my leg, as Dora moves slowly and methodically, tying the belt around her waist. Chev and Mya are there, climbing into the only canoe with room to sit.

When I wade out of the water and back onto the sand, my parents are talking about the burials. They will be tomorrow, when the sun is at its highest point in the sky.

The rowers wait until Dora is out in front of them. Then they dig hard with their oars. I watch them recede across the bay, remembering how I'd watched the Bosha cross the bay in the same way. When they are so far away that they are no longer distinct individuals, but mere dark shapes blending into one another, I think I see Mya look back, but I cannot know for sure.

THIRTY-THREE

I am alone in my family's hut, dressing to do something I do not want to do.

My mother stands at the door. She tells me everyone else is leaving. It's time to go. I tell her not to wait. I'll come on my own. Soon, I promise.

"I won't leave without you," she calls through the door.

I step outside, barefoot, still tying my pants at the waist. "Just go," I say. "I promise I won't be long."

My mother raises her hand to shield her eyes from the sun as she looks at me, and the lines at the corners of her lips deepen. She will wait. My mother has had to wait for so many things. For the bay to thaw. For the herds to return. For the first kill of the spring.

For the Divine to provide wives for her sons.

I should not test her patience now. I drop my head and step back into the hut. I have no choice. This task will not go away. I lace up my boots, pull the elk-hide tunic over my head, and join my mother outside, where the sun is reluctantly climbing out of the eastern sky.

A two-man kayak waits for us on the beach. The rest of our party is far out on the bay. The wind is in our faces, slowing us, and by the time we land on the western shore, the sun is directly overhead.

It's time.

A girl approaches, helping my mother alight from the boat. She is familiar to me; I've seen her in this very spot. The day I hiked the overland trail with Lo, she met us right here on the beach.

This is Anki, the sister of Orn.

She glances over at me, and I can't quite read the emotion on her face. Does she know that I am her brother's killer? She can't possibly. If she did, I doubt she would look at me at all.

"Mya was asking for you," she says. "She was on the beach earlier, looking for you."

I hear voices. Up ahead, on a ridge above the Bosha's camp, a crowd is gathered around two open graves.

Chev stands at the head of the circle of mourners. I try to imagine the conflict he must feel today—reunited with his old clan, but at such a great cost. Beside him stands a man dressed in black bearskin—the Bosha's healer. He begins a chant, asking the Divine to pull back the hides that drape the doors of her land, to open wide the entrance to receive Lo and Orn.

Something inside me flinches. I swallow, and hot anger burns down my throat.

As the chanting continues, two drummers beat a rhythm that rolls out from this ledge, vibrating out over the sea. From behind me, a dancer emerges. He wears a broad mask made of twigs and vines, bent and twisted into the face of a mammoth.

A wide mammoth hide is spread at the bottom of each grave, and in the center of each one rests one of the dead. Orn is dressed in a hunting parka, a spear clutched in his hand. I can't help but notice the details of this spear—a thick bone staff hafted with sinew to a black flint point. It is identical to the one that broke off in Chev's chest.

Lo is also dressed in hunting clothes, but her hands are empty. Around her neck, she wears the bone pendant, the symbol of her status in the clan.

Up close, I can see how thoroughly both bodies have been rubbed with red ocher—face, hair, clothing—it coats them like the blood that coats a baby as it emerges from the womb.

The dancer completes circle upon circle upon circle around the graves, as the sun slides slowly into the west. All the while I feel Mya's presence. I want to look up, but I can't. Sweat trickles down my back, yet I shiver with cold.

Beneath my feet, I notice the shifting of my shadow, bending toward the east, toward home. Still, the drums play on
and on, the music rising, carrying the Spirits up, bearing
them to the Land Above the Sky.

Finally, the last note is struck. I turn quickly, striding
off into the meadow to the east, not wanting to speak to
anyone.

Voices die away, until only the sounds of the meadow
remain—the thrumming of insects, the whisper of the
wind. I lie down, surrounded by tall grass and clusters of
tiny blue flowers.

I try to listen for bees. Eventually, I hear footsteps. Someone lies down beside me. I don't have to look. I've been in
the dark with her enough to know her by the cadence of her
walk, the sound of her exhaled breath. . . .

She slides her hand over and wraps my fingers in hers. I
don't pull away. Warmth floods through me, like it did that
first time in the cave, the night she saved my life.

We lie still for a long time. "You were right," Mya says
after a protracted silence. "Summer has returned. This parka
is too heavy for this day."

"It's also too big for you," I say. "Why do you wear it?"

"It belonged to my mother."

And just like that, one of the many mysteries of Mya is
solved.

We fall silent again, content to listen. Eventually, I hear

it—the whir of wings. She does too. We both sit up. Without a word or even a glance, we focus on the bee. We both climb to our feet and follow him.

He joins another, then another. They move with purpose, following their secret pathways over a sea of blue and violet blooms. After following them for so long I'm convinced we've gotten confused and will never find the hive, we discover it in a grove of withered spruce, tucked beneath a ledge beside the sea.

I slide down onto the ground in the scant shade of the trees, staring out over the water. Mya sits facing me, her back to the sea. Before I can shift my gaze, she lifts her hand to my face.

I turn to her, and I'm startled to see her cheeks damp with tears. I wipe them away, and she kisses me.

This kiss is different from our first. Mya's lips are warm and urgent, sending heat like white light through the very core of me, chasing away all my darkness.

Slowly, we stretch out our bodies, easing onto the ground. I pull her close to my chest, encircling her in my arms. At first she doesn't move, but then silent sobs come, her damp, hot face buried against my neck. When her body finally stills, I kiss her again—the slowest kiss I can stand.

I pull back and look into her eyes. The sun forms a tiny fire in each, a signal fire, a light far away, but bright enough to guide me into the future.

I cannot go into the past. I cannot stop change. Change is coming. But lying here beside Mya, I realize, for the first time since we carried Lo's lifeless body down the cliff, that the future may hold some good.

My eyes drop to the pendant around Mya's neck, the pendant of ivory, the twin to the pendant of bone still wrapped around Lo's neck in her grave.

Absently, my finger touches the flat disk at the center, carved with the image of two mammoth tusks. "You fixed it," I say. "I found pieces of it scattered at the foot of the trail where you and Lo—"

"This was my mother's," Mya says. "Hers was ivory; mine was bone. When we moved—when she died—hers became mine."

This simple story indicts me. I unfairly judged Mya, assuming she wanted ivory since Lo had a pendant of bone.

"It hurt me to do it, but I broke it on purpose and left it there. It was a clue for you. I knew you would find it, and you would know where to look for me."

"You knew—" I pull my hand back, tucking it under my head so I can steady my gaze. "How did you know I would look for you?"

"Because . . ." She rolls onto her back and her eyes fall shut. "Because I trust you."

I trust you. A breeze stirs the leaves above our heads, and cut-out shapes of light and shadow move across us like ripples on water. *I trust you. . . .* The words echo, fade, and return to echo again through my mind. Since the morning of that first hunt, I have longed to hear those words.

Mya kisses me again, and her hand slides up under my tunic and glides over my chest. Her skin is warm. The sun disappears behind a cloud, and shade encloses us like the walls of a hut.

"Mya."

Her other hand finds my wrist. She guides my hand up under the hem of her own parka until it's resting against the warm skin of her back.

She kisses me again, and half sighs, half whispers my name. "Kol."

That's when I know. I know we will survive. I know that we will move and there will be fierce, hard, startling changes.

I will feel lost.

But I won't be lost. We will be together. And together, we'll find ourselves again.

I let both hands glide across the soft skin of Mya's back, and I know. *I know.* Wherever Mya is—a cave or a hut or a boat out on the sea—wherever she is, I'll be with her, and I'll be home.

ACKNOWLEDGMENTS

The characters and events of *Ivory and Bone* would still be stuck in my head and heart if it weren't for the efforts of so many wonderful people who helped bring them to life on these pages.

I want to thank Alexandra Cooper, who understood this story from the beginning. I owe you so much for shining the light of your editorial talents on an early version of this manuscript, and helping me see the better book within it. Thank you for asking all the right questions, and for working alongside me as we uncovered the essence of Kol's story. Your input has been invaluable.

Of course, Alexandra would never have read this book if Josh Adams had not read it first. Josh, I am quite sure that no other literary agent could have done what you did for this book and for me as an author. I cannot thank you enough for sharing the power of your vision. You have set me and my stories on the best possible path, and I am so fortunate to have benefited from your talents.

Along with Alexandra Cooper and Josh Adams, I want to thank all the people who worked with them to bring this book into the world. At HarperCollins: thank you to Rosemary Brosnan, Alyssa Miele, Erin Fitzsimmons, Jessica Berg, Olivia Russo, Patty Rosati, and Kim Vande-Water. At Adams Literary: thank you to Tracey Adams and Samantha Bagood. To everyone else whose work has contributed to this book, thank you. I am indebted to each of you for your enthusiasm and efforts. Thanks also to Sean Freeman for your contributions to my beautiful cover.

So many other writers have helped me along the way, but I must thank Amie Kaufman first among them. It would take twenty pages to properly acknowledge the difference your help and friendship have made in my life. Thank you for your constant encouragement, for taking the time to read, and for sharing your talent with me at the time I needed it most.

Kat Zhang, you have been with me almost from the beginning of my writing journey. You are so talented and supportive, and I am so proud to call you my friend. Thank you for reading and giving me your thoughts, and for the text messages, progress check-ins, and emails that assured me I was not toiling alone. I couldn't have made it through without you.

Thank you, of course, to all the Pub(lishing) Crawl contributors and readers. Your enthusiasm is simply more than I could ever have expected or imagined, and it has made a huge difference in my life.

Thank you to all the scientists whose research and writing fed my imagination, and helped me understand the world of my characters and the lives they lived.

The goal of writing this book could never have been accomplished without the support of my friends and family. Naming all the friends who have laughed, cried, and laughed again with me along the way would be impossible, but please know that I appreciate all of you so much. To my sister, father, and stepmother, I can't thank you enough for your inexhaustible faith in me and your constant encouragement. I also must mention the unconditional love and support I received from a special cat and dog, Sylvester and Memphis, who kept my lap and feet warm. Thank you for instinctively understanding that the best writing is done while peering around a furry head and between taking breaks to throw a ball.

Thank you to my son, Dylan. You are simply the purest light in my life. You never give up, and your example makes it impossible for me to give up. Your talent has always been an inspiration to me, and you never fail to make me laugh. Your sincere concern for me and my art is one of the truest gifts anyone could ever give me.

Thank you to my husband, Gary. I never knew an artist until I knew you. You live a life devoted to the art of your music, and being a part of that life has taught me how to live a life devoted to my writing. How could that gift ever be measured? You came into my life (or, rather, I dragged you into it), and you filled it with music, laughter, and love. I have the life I have because I have you.

I couldn't thank all the people who have blessed my life without thanking God for bringing them to me. God has worked so many miracles in my life. This book is not the least of those miracles, but it's not the greatest, either. I believe that God is Love, and all the people listed here prove that to me every day.

Thank you all so much.